The Elephant Tooth of '95

A Story of Family, Romance, and New Beginnings

Rana *Baydoun*

Praise for *The Elephant Tooth of '95* by Rana Baydoun

"In equal parts humorous and poignant, The Elephant Tooth of '95 by Rana Baydoun is a wonderful novel whose original plot is buoyed by delightful cultural details. It is a story that inspires strength and hope even during hardship."

– Edith Wairimu for Reader's Favorite

"The Elephant Tooth of '95 is a feel-good read. This would appeal to anyone who enjoys personal accounts of everyday experiences, especially those colored by distinctive cultural and historical settings. A good beach read."

– Online Book Club

"A romantic comedy book and self-discovery book that reads like a movie. Eternal bonds of love and friendship are built with resilience in a country inflicted by war and gender bias. One of the best-recommended love story books."

– H.J. Chammas, Award-Winning Bestselling Author

"An inspiring book for young women to find their way and that taking a chance is a good thing to do to grow as a person."

– J.M. for Online Book Club

"A very inspirational book showing how one can strive in bad situations."

– Dagni Botes for Online Book Club

"A young woman trying to navigate a modernizing world, while still holding on to traditional values. A light summer read."

"It portrays the Lebanese Culture and how they had to overcome the effects of war and move on with their life fighting against all odds. The music sets the mood for every chapter hence enjoying the novel more. Moreover, Rana uses humor throughout the book which had me giggling throughout."

- Kerren Hapuch

"Surprisingly creative. This book had its moments and it was charming."

- Mira Moloney

"Mesmerizing and heart-warming. The story follows a young woman making her way into adulthood, balancing her desire to become a modern woman while respecting her family's traditionalist views. Witty and relatable from start to finish, this novel takes you through the highs and lows of the life of a resilient heroine while she attempts to make her way in the world."

- Shelby Bradford

"Is marriage the basic purpose of a woman's life? Is a woman allowed to fall in love while struggling against social norms? A strong woman fights her way against all odds to survive against religious discrimination and poverty."

- Ammarah Azhar Khan

"I would recommend this book to anyone who enjoys coming-of-age stories, learning about diverse cultures and traditions, and anyone who enjoys romance novels."

- Helena Fern

"The author paints a realistic view of love; thus, it is not always great and good but sometimes fails and one must start over again."

- Joyce Zimba

"The novel has the following dedication: To every woman who chooses to write her own story. I concur with it and would further recommend this book to anyone who needs a bit of inspiration or hope in their life or simply wants something light to read to feel good."

- Plamena Pavlova

"If you like small towns, women trying to figure their lives out, and family drama this is the book for you!"

- Warisha Tabassum

"This book is more than a young adult and her experiences, it touches on life and serious events that happened in the past that molds people's way of life and their mentality"

- Lucreatia Alexander

Paperback ISBN – 978-9948-25-641-0
Hardcover ISBN – 979-8832-08-854-9

Acknowledgments

I wrote this book for my children.
Being brought up in a mixed family, half Lebanese, half German, my children always ask me questions such as, "What was it like to grow up in Beirut during wartime? How did you spend your evenings with power cuts?"

"I loved it!" I always answer. My childhood was super fun, full of love and warmth, and enriched by music from around the globe. I enjoyed every moment of growing despite all the challenges we faced.

This book is my present to them, hoping to remind them that "Even during the toughest times in life, there's always room for laughter."

My journey to finalize this book was bittersweet. It was a draining and demanding task that challenged me at different levels. I certainly couldn't have made it without the support and encouragement of so many people who are important to me.

The first and biggest "thank you" goes to my supportive and out-of-this-world husband, who must have read and reread this book at least 20 times. A huge "thank you" goes to my amazing daughter Yasmina, who clearly explained that although she absolutely loves my book, Harry Potter is still her favorite.

To my sweethearts Marya and Marco, "I can't wait till you are old enough to read it."

To my sister Reem, "For bursting out loud at my jokes − over and over again."

To dear Aya Solh for her repetitive question, "When will you finish the book? I wanna read it!"

A wholehearted "thank you" goes to Fida Hamdan, Al Hamdan, Kamal Kalot, Fouad and Rasha Charara, Miriam Ismail, Karma Solh, Walid Chaaban, Mounir Chalhoub, Yasser, Abd El Kader, and Rayan Kouatly.

To my lifelong friends, Bahaa Tabsh, Rania Fahel, Baraem (Pam) Ismail, Hana Sabra, Josette Khoury, Joumana Ezzedine, Marwa Beydoun, Rima Makky, Youmna Abdo, Rola Haffar, Celine Gruere, Linda Rustom, Silvina Junker, and Nassima Amin, "Having you in my life is a treasure."

To Habib Chammas, the best-selling author of "The Employee Millionaire," "Your kindness is pure gold. You made publishing this book possible."

Lots of appreciation and "Danke" go to my uber-welcoming and loving German family. I am incredibly grateful to Martina, my favorite sister-in-law and my fantastic editor, "All your sleepless nights were definitely worth it."

I also would like to especially thank my eclectic work colleagues for spicing up my life with flavor!

Finally, I am forever grateful to my loud and loving Lebanese family: my parents, uncles (Ammi Nana), aunties, and cousins & Co, for their unconditional love and support.

To every woman who chooses to
write her own story

Table of Contents

To listen to the songs listed above, please click this link:

https://spoti.fi/3vHOoVf

Chapter One - I'm Too Sexy

Mood Music:
"I'm Too Sexy" by Right Said Fred

"The journey of a thousand miles
begins with one step."
– Lao Tzu.

I climbed out of my bed and looked through the window. It was a spring Monday in Beirut, one of those mixed-weather days that always confused me. "Is it warm enough to be in a t-shirt, or will I get cold?" The air was warm and stagnant. Smog filled up the sky. I put on a denim shirt and a pair of black jeans and got ready to start my day. "Bye, Mom." I kissed her and grabbed my purse. She stood facing me as I waited for the elevator, circling my silhouette with her hand, "May God let you sparkle like a diamond in the eyes of your enemies as well as your beloved ones." She always did that whenever one of us was about to go out.

I drove along Manara Corniche, heading towards the American University of Beirut (AUB), and took a right turn just before its sea gate. I parked my car next to a smelly garbage container in a hidden alley that I knew well. I tried to park at that spot whenever possible. Having to drive a car with a design dating back to the Flintstones era was not easy. Students' judgments were sometimes harsh, and their cynical labels were stamped on other students' foreheads for years to come. Of course, I wanted to avoid that, as I was only 19 and people's opinions mattered. To be honest, it was not only my car's design that was outdated but its technical efficiency as well. It broke down countless times and refused to start, especially on cold mornings. As a result, I was a regular customer of Moe's Garage, the only auto repair shop on my street.

Moe, the owner, was my sister's classmate back in primary school, but practically speaking, he was more like a distant cousin. Every day after school, his father used to drop off a bunch of kids: my sister and me, Moe, and his two sisters, at their home, where all afternoon we played pretend war games. Moe was a smart kid but decided to manage his dad's garage instead of going to college. My mom, a strong education advocate, tried hard to change his mind, but in vain. In the end, my family benefited from his decision. We had a reliable mechanic whose shop was a minute away from home, and we didn't even have to make an appointment for car check-ups.

Whenever my car refused to start, I walked to his garage, gave him the keys, and asked him to let me know when it would be fixed; then, I went home to watch TV. Well, it wasn't that simple. Before I could even relax, Moe had to open my car's hood, which was not easy at all. It was mission impossible even for me. My car was intelligently designed in such a way that only a few people could decipher its locks. The man who sold it to my dad, a salesman in a nearby fabric shop, was one of them. Whenever my car needed to be fixed, Moe sent one of his teenage interns to the fabric shop asking for help, "Mr. Shafik, it's your old Renault 16 again. Can you open the hood, please?"

Typically, while I was waiting for the previous owner to arrive, many nosy pedestrians (specifically males) offered conflicting advice on what to do. One man would say, "You'd better change the engine, my dear, before your car breaks down in the middle of the road." Another passerby would interrupt him, "What are you saying, man?! It's obviously the battery that needs changing."

Whatever it was, my car was a hopeless case. I still remember that rainy afternoon when I glimpsed my friend Nadia running towards me, covering her head with her microbiology book, shouting, "What's happening today? It hasn't stopped raining for a second since morning! Can you drop me off at home, please?"

I beckoned her over and jumped into my car to escape the water pouring down from everywhere. The waves were splashing the vehicles parked along the corniche, and the streets almost drowned with water. Nadia climbed in, complaining, "They mentioned in the news that a storm is coming, but I didn't imagine it to be this strong!" She rubbed her hands together, trying to feel warm. Automatically, I turned the heater on, assuring her, "It'll warm up now." What happened next was totally unexpected.

The moment the heater was on, the car's dashboard erupted and showered my friend all over with water as if somebody threw a full cold-water bucket on her. And no, it had nothing to do with the ice bucket challenge. The challenge wasn't even invented back in 1991. Nadia and I ended up soaking wet, laughing our heads off. While driving, wiping my face, and drying my hair with Kleenex, I promised myself to buy a decent car once I graduate and start working. This brings me back to the beginning of my story: The reason why I was going to the American University of Beirut in the first place: to find a job.

I locked my car and strolled along the long seaside corniche, enjoying Beirut's warmth. I took a deep breath and smelled its unique Mediterranean scent. A tacky young man sitting on a stone bench smiled flirtatiously, "Hey, ya Amar (beautiful), would you join me for a cup of coffee?" I ignored him and continued walking. I was used to that kind of annoying attitude. Whenever I strolled along the corniche, I received comments ranging from poetic compliments to X-rated street slang. I was not Ms. Lebanon, but it happened simply because I was a girl. In our Lebanese culture, macho guys hanging out on Beyrouti streets share the common fallacy that flirting with girls is their innate legal right. It doesn't matter to them if they are totally inappropriate or indecent, as long as they are enjoying it.

I leaned on the rusty fence of the corniche sidewalk, contemplating. The clear water helped me to reflect on my life. I graduated with a BSc in Nutrition and Food Technology a month ago, but to my greatest disappointment, NGOs didn't shower me with job offers as I had hoped. As sad as it was, I had to face the fact that I was neither going to be a member of one of the anti-famine delegations in Africa nor was I going to be relocated by the FAO to Santiago or Milan. Ironically, that was the reason I chose my major in the first place.

"Where can I find a job?" That was the only question buzzing around my head. Of course, I was well-trained to run a dietetic clinic. But nope! Not a good idea. I couldn't pretend to follow a healthy lifestyle because I didn't. My primary sources of nutrients were chocolate and pastries filled with chocolate. It would have been a bad choice for my future clients to follow suit. I was blessed to have a slim body no matter what I ate, but not all body types reacted positively to such a sugar/caffeine-congested diet. Naturally, I also considered other options, including working in the research and development of a food factory lab, but I quickly abandoned that idea. Lab work was not the best career option for me. Like any other science student worldwide, I had had my share of lab accidents. There were three memorable accidents, to be precise.

The first one was at a chemistry lab, where I dropped concentrated acid on the floor and ruined the expensive leather boots of one of the girls in my class. But that was a minor incident – well, for me, not for her. Then there was the zoology lab incident, where a few glass tubes slipped out of my hand and broke. No one got hurt, so there is no need to talk about it. The third one was a life-changing experience. It was the first time ever that our Food Technology and Nutrition (FTN) Department witnessed such a catastrophe.

While watching what was going on, Dr. Amin, our chairman, continuously brushed his mustache with his fingers, but he said nothing. Lola, our lab supervisor, finally broke the silence, "Is this my cooking pot that I see through the smoke?" I looked at her with a guilty look, "I'm so sorry, so sorry." She covered her mouth with her hand and gasped loudly. As far as I could see, her pot had turned partially black and bottomless.

Why did I choose her metal cooking pot, of all things, instead of using one of the lab beakers for my experiment? I had a valid reason. Lola considered our lab her own kitchen and kept her personal cooking stuff next to the beakers in our lab cabinets. So, technically speaking, it was her fault, not mine. I glanced at her and saw tears in the corner of her eyes. That cooking pot must have meant a great deal to her, or it might well have been the horrible smoke around us that caused her tears. In any case, it was too late to save her cooking pot or all those chemicals from burning and exploding.

"I don't quite understand how this could happen. We have excellent safety procedures and instruction manuals. Didn't you follow the manual meticulously?" Dr. Amin asked with his British accent. He had lived most of his life in London.

"Of course I did!" I took a deep breath and explained to him what had happened. "First, I added NaOH to the water that was in the beaker. Then I placed the beaker in Lola's cooking pot, which I initially filled up with ice, you know, to cool the temperature down."

I avoided eye contact with Lola as I spoke. "But I don't know what happened! While I was stirring the beaker with a glass rod, the beaker broke, and out of the blue, the heat was coming out nonstop. I didn't know what to do. Basically, that's when I called for your help. I was terrified that the chemical reaction might reach the other substances in the lab." I spoke hastily and dramatically, expecting Dr. Amin to calm me down and tell me something like "It's ok." or "Don't worry!" but instead, he kept quiet.

Amid that chaos, a group of students rushed into the lab to check what was happening. My experiment was the breaking news all over our campus. An incident like this was rare and an excellent topic for gossip. "Is there going to be another explosion? The fumes coming out are trop coloré (colorful)," a girl asked in an English/French mix.

One of the guys standing beside her held her hand tightly, assuring her, "Don't worry, babe, I'm here."

"I have to ask you to leave now," Dr. Amin said, escorting the students out.

Later that week, Dr. Amin called me to his office and said, "My dear Noor, I understand that it was never your intention to blow up the lab or endanger any of your fellow students. But I truly believe it would be better for your academic future to join the non-thesis program, thereby releasing you from all this horrible lab work that you don't quite like." I didn't argue with him. He had a valid point; I hated lab work. I knew it, and he knew it. Surely, he also had to consider the future of AUB's lab facilities and the insurance premium they had to pay.

Shifting to the non-thesis program was stress-relieving for both my fellow students and me. According to the university policy, I had to take a few extra courses to compensate for not submitting a thesis, which I considered a piece of cake compared to lab work.

I watched a small bird standing on the fence next to me as it flapped its wings and flew away. It reminded me to stop daydreaming, move my butt and start doing what I was supposed to do: find a job. Surprisingly, our FTN department's bulletin board was empty except for one elegantly handwritten ad hung right in the center. I read it carefully:

DanielCo, a well-known family company, requires a sales rep for food ingredients in the chemical division. Fax your CV to Mr. Nader on 01-453251 or by mail to POB 1616 Sin el Fil, Lebanon.

"No lab work?! That's perfect!" My eyes widened in disbelief. I faxed my CV the same day, and within two days, DanielCo invited me for my first-ever job interview.

Chapter Two - The Chauffeur

Mood Music:
"The Chauffeur" by Duran Duran

As a result of the Lebanese civil war, Beirut, the capital city, was divided into two parts in 1975: the East (mainly Christians) and the West (mostly Muslims). Since I lived in West Beirut with my family, I didn't get the chance to meet many people from the East.

By the end of 1990, the war was over, and the demarcation line between the East and the West was dismantled. Consequently, the American University of Beirut decided to shut down its off-campus program on the eastern side, resulting in the transfer of all its OCP students to the main campus in Western Beirut. It was an unforgettable scene for many older students like me, who stood mesmerized watching the newcomers roaming around our campus.

They were walking with heads up high in the sky, dressed up stylishly. To me, they were a different breed, as if they came from another planet. It wasn't only their clothes that stood out. They behaved differently and talked differently as well. They greeted each other as if they were French, struggling to speak Lebanese, "Bonjour, kifak, ça va (*Good morning, how are you, fine)?*" They were open with public affection. Girls kissing their male friends or hugging them to say hello suddenly became a common greeting ritual on campus.

It wasn't long before my first contact with the "aliens" was established. I knew our campus well, so I helped one of the newcomers to find her dorm. She headed to the same dorms where my Mom had resided as a student back in the 1950s. We talked timidly at first, then we blabbed and laughed, and it didn't take long for us to become good friends. We were no exception. Eventually, AUB students blended nicely together, so it became difficult for me to differentiate an Ahmed from a Pierre. And it wasn't that important anymore.

****

Although, in 1990, the Lebanese civil war finally ended and the demarcation line ceased to exist, somehow, the borders remained strong in many people's minds. I moved around in a well-defined area previously known as "West Beirut." I never dared to cross the former borderline next to the National Museum, nor did I imagine setting foot beyond the Sodeco area.

At that time, my lack of knowledge of eastern addresses became a problem. I had no idea where the company DanielCo was located, which turned out to be my first interview obstacle. According to the ad, it was located in an area called Sin el Fil, which literally translates as "the Elephant's Tooth." How did the Lebanese come up with such an exotic name? We didn't have elephants in Lebanon. We didn't even have a zoo!

Road maps, GPS, and Google maps were non-existent then, and my parents were as clueless as I was. Luckily, my car's previous owner, Mr. Shafik, knew the eastern part well. "It's quite close to this very street," he told my dad when we visited his shop. "I'll take Noor there for her interview and wait down in the car until she is done," he suggested.

"That's so kind of you," my dad replied. "But I'd never accept that. You're a busy man. We'd be grateful if you showed her the way, perhaps over the weekend?" On the big day, I walked reluctantly towards the company's main gate, dressed in a navy-colored suit and red top. "Not bad, not bad at all!" I murmured as I entered one of the three elegantly designed office buildings belonging to the Daniel family. The buildings were guarded by many security guards, clearly hiding their guns inside their pants.

"Good morning. My name is Noor Beyrouti. I have an appointment with Mr. Nader." I smiled at the middle-aged man in the reception area. His eyes were glued to the surveillance camera screens in front of him. Slowly, he lifted his head, saying, "Yes, of course, please have a seat." He pointed to the left. The stunning waiting area was not like any other waiting area I'd seen before. It was more spacious and brighter, and the ceiling was higher than average. An enormous mosaic art piece, typically found in Greek churches, hung on the wall behind the main leather couch.

Gently, I walked on the shiny beige marble tiles, listening to the sound of my footsteps. I scanned the place thoroughly. What struck me most weren't the numerous art pieces on the walls or the red Persian carpets scattered here and there, but rather the quietness of the place. Despite the continuous flow of elegantly dressed people going in and out of the building, it had a serene ambiance, a unique one that you could only find in a museum or an art exhibition.

I didn't have to wait for long. A young lady in a mini skirt approached me, "Demoiselle Beyrouti? Please come with me." She escorted me to the elevator, indicating, "Il est au cinquième étage."

Huh?! What did she say? My French was a minus, limited to "Je t'aime (*I love you*)" and "au revoir (*see you*)" from French songs. The tightly dressed young woman must have read my face. She opened the elevator door and pressed number 5.

*****

Mr. Nader was young, too young to be a department manager. He was elegant but in a cool way, looking like one of the fake managers in Hollywood movies. He welcomed me in French, "Bonjour mademoiselle Beyrouti. Please have a seat."

"Bonjour," I replied, "Ummm, I have to confess my French is at a basic level."

"Pas de problème! English is our business language here, so don't worry," he said in a strong American accent. "Would you like something to drink?"

"May I have a fresh green apple juice with no ice, please?"

He paused. "I'm afraid we're limited on options here. I can offer either coffee or tea if you'd like."

"Then just water, please," I replied, fixing my bag on the coffee table, making sure that it did not fall off.

He ordered two glasses of water and an espresso. Mr. Nader cleared his throat and quickly went through my CV. "Let's start then. You have a BSc from AUB." He looked at me in surprise. "But you're only 19 years old? How did you manage to graduate at such a young age?"

"Well," I tried not to seem arrogant, "I was doing so well at school that I skipped two grades in primary."

He nodded and continued reading. "You've already started doing your MSc degree, good, good, and what about your work experience? Nothing is mentioned here." He flipped through my CV backward. A man brought in our water, thus interrupting our conversation.

"Merci," Mr. Nader said and took a sip of his freshly prepared espresso.

"To answer your question, I'm afraid I don't have any work experience yet." My heart started beating fast. "Sometimes, I help my sister at her consultancy office, doing basic stuff such as answering the phone, sending faxes, or buying sandwiches for her."

I asked him if I should add that as my work experience, but he shook his head. I was getting worried and couldn't hide my feelings any longer. He must have felt my anxiety because his voice became more solemn. "Listen, Noor. It's not a big deal. Daniel Company is one of the country's oldest enterprises, and we do have excellent training programs."

He looked straight into my eyes and asked, "Where do you see yourself in five years?"

I loved his question. It brought back many childhood memories. "I'm hoping to pursue my education and do my Ph.D. in the U.S."

I came up with this plan a long time ago when I invented a miraculous bubble gum facial remover, using ingredients I had found at home, including shampoo, olive oil, and soap.

It was a solution that removed bubble gum residues off the face after the gum popped on it, leaving the skin clean and soft. It was a miracle in a bottle. At least that was what the other kids thought. I considered myself a genius – I had to be called Dr. Noor at some point in my life.

Mr. Nader rested his elbows on his desk, staring at me. "Mlle Beyrouti, do I understand you correctly? Are you planning on leaving us before you've even joined?" Oops, I didn't see that coming.

Suddenly, something happened to me that had never happened before. My mouth went dry, my heart started beating like a drum in my chest, and my ears, well, I couldn't hear anything anymore. I turned around to grasp what was going on. I went completely deaf. I drank my water until the last drop, but my mouth was still dry. I watched Mr. Nader's lips moving, but no sound came out of his mouth. I pressed my ears several times to unblock them, but that didn't help either.

I panicked, with millions of questions flashing through my mind, "What was happening to me? Was I dying? Was this the end?" I was about to get out of my chair and run away, but instead, I forced myself to sit still. My eyes were roaming around the room, searching for salvation. Then it hit me. I was not dying! Of course not. The office must have been a pressure chamber, which was why I couldn't hear anymore. It was a trick interview question to check how alert I was.

"Mlle Beyrouti … Mlle Beyrouti?" His voice made me realize that I was able to hear again.

"Finally, they must have stopped the pressure." I was relieved. The interview's pace got faster afterward, da daa da, da daa doumm, and one thing led to another. Mr. Nader asked me if I would quit my job once I got married. Of course, I would. He didn't ask me any further questions.

I watched him silently for a few minutes as he drew endless vicious circles on the paper in front of him. Then he stood up abruptly, saying, "Thank you, Mlle Beyrouti, let me walk you out."

*****

"Hi, Mom." I leaned down and gave her a big kiss on her skinny cheek. She had a cup of dark Turkish coffee, served in a Bulgarian pottery mug. She barely noticed that I was there, all caught up in her routine of comparing the Holy Quran to the Bible. Her daily mission was to find the common points rather than the differences. She took notes and explained her findings to friends and family regularly. "God is for all, and his message is the same for all," she used to preach.

Mom was unique, strong, and rebellious, like a character from a Woody Allen movie. She sat confidently, wearing loose black pants and my dad's check shirt. Being "a la mode" was not her top priority – saving the world was more like it. However, she could have been a fashion icon if she had wanted to. She had what it takes, the taste and the looks. She was a tall, pretty, blondish, athletic woman with piercing black eyes. She looked a lot like Julie Andrews but behaved like Che Guevara.

"Ouuff, it's too foggy in here. Mom, how many cigarettes have you smoked?" I waved my hand, trying to get rid of the smoke in front of my face. "Don't start on me now! We live in a free country. I smoke as much as I want to," she answered in her loud, hoarse voice. Until the age of eight, I was one of those "lucky" kids to have their mom as their school principal. She was strict and intimidating. At the age of nineteen, nothing much had changed. My mom was still strict and intimidating. But somehow, her lectures grew on me to the point where I started enjoying them. I began to understand how she functioned and why it was more important for her to feed the street cats rather than have coffee with random neighbors. She was eccentric and different from any other Lebanese woman I had met.

When she graduated from high school, her dad, an influential judge at that time, didn't allow her to go to college. As was the tradition in the 1950s, he wanted her to get married. But Mom refused and insisted on continuing her education. She used her savings to enroll in a British university through a distance learning program. Eventually, my grandfather was forced to give in, and he enrolled her at AUB.

I peeked at her, dragging on her cigarette while I sneaked into the kitchen to have lunch. Our white kitchen used to be the most beautiful and elegant in our building, but that was some years ago. Unfortunately, several bombs and shells had fallen on our building, changing its style to vintage shabby.

"Hello," Dad announced in his deep voice. He kissed Mom and went to change clothes. Mom and Dad fell in love at AUB back in the 1950s and married directly after graduation. Naturally, their marriage had ups and downs, and they definitely passed the "for richer or poorer" test.

Dad used to be the managing director of a well-established educational institution, but he resigned eventually due to ideological conflicts with the chairman. I will never forget that day when Mom gave us the news at school pick-up. She whispered discreetly, "Your Dad is changing jobs, but don't worry. Everything will be ok." Riwa, who was ten years old then, predicted correctly that Dad would join a local newspaper. She connected the dots when she overheard him confirming an appointment with that newspaper's owner. As for me, maybe because I was only eight years old, I hoped that he would own a chocolate shop.

It wasn't an easy time for us kids. Our lives were turned upside down. Our lives revolved around that educational institution that managed 100 schools around the country, including my school. My mom, the principal at that time, had to resign as well.

Dad gave up his brand-new Mercedes and Escort Patrol and bought a small green 504 Peugeot. We had to let the bodyguard go but kept the driver. Many of our family "friends" miraculously disappeared. We led an entirely new lifestyle: no more trips to Europe and no more VIP classical music concert tickets, which, for me as a kid, was the only good thing that came out of my dad's career change.

Dad walked into the kitchen, followed by Mom. He lifted me and turned me around, laughing. "How did you do in the interview? Did you astonish them?"

"Put me down, Dad … Mr. Nader seemed to like me," I said, giggling. Dad put me down finally.

"Describe this man. Was he decent?" Mom asked, frowning deeply. "I'll enquire about his upbringing."

"No, really, Mom," I said, "There's no need. He seemed like a perfect gentleman. Besides, it's an important company. They would only hire decent people, right?"

"Of course, my darling," Dad added.

But Mom interrupted, staring at me, "Don't tell me such nonsense! Vicious men are everywhere: doctors, lawyers, police officers, you name it. You need to watch out. You're still young and innocent. Never forget that a girl's honor …"

"… is like glass; you can glue it together once broken, but you will always see the scars!" I continued her favorite saying.

*****

Chapter Three - Who the F*** Is Alice?

Mood Music:
*"Who the F*** Is Alice?" by Smokie*

"Noor, please send these faxes to these numbers here. And remember, you need to place the paper like this," my sister told me, pretending to send a fax. "Otherwise, my clients will receive a blank page." She grinned.

"Riwa, I know how to send a fax! You've already explained it to me several times since that incident, plus it happened only one time, and I managed to deliver the fax personally."

"It was an urgent fax," Riwa sighed. Unfortunately, she could only afford to hire someone like me for her errands, someone who got paid with KitKats and Oreos. "I'm in a hurry, so please focus. Here's your to-do list for today." She handed me a paper with about ten jobs and rushed to the washroom for a final makeup retouch. I followed her, going through her list one by one.

"Ummmm, delivering catalogs, making phone calls, taking appointments, no problem. Aha! Here comes the interesting part, buying lunch: one fajita sandwich from Bliss House. I'll make that two. Thank you!"

"Just finish your list first, ok?" Riwa said.

"Ok," I rolled my eyes, "But don't be late for lunch."

Two years after graduating with an MBA degree, Riwa, my elder and only sister had opened a consultancy firm in a cozy office next to the seaside corniche. Although her office was in a district once famous for the oldest profession in the world, it didn't bother her. Only on those evenings when we stayed in her office extremely late we heard women fighting or X-rated swearing at passers-by from their windows.

I was dying to get to the sandwich job, so I focused and was done with my to-do list at precisely one o'clock. Riwa was famous for being notoriously late, so I was not worried about her when she was still not there by two o'clock. I was more concerned that the sandwiches would get cold and soggy. The tempting fajita smell became irresistible, so I grabbed a sandwich and continued reading "Port of Call," a novel by Amin Maalouf. Slowly, I drifted away with the events of the story.

A few chapters later, the phone rang. "Noor, it's me." Riwa's voice sounded different. "I need you to come to the emergency room of the American hospital right away. Hurry up. It's urgent." Her voice was alarming.

"What happened? Are you okay?" My heart was beating fast.

"Yes, don't worry," Riwa answered. "I'm fine, just come right now. I need your help."

Luckily, the American hospital was close to Riwa's office. I went straight to the emergency room, a place I knew well due to my numerous visits. To my surprise, it was crowded with young men, women, and children. "Why are there so many patients today? Was there a car bomb somewhere?" I asked a security guard at the entrance.

"No, not today. Not yet, in any case, but it's a Friday afternoon. It's practically the weekend. It's always busy on weekends."

One of the nurses led me to Riwa. I moved the curtain slightly and entered her room. She was lying on a small white bed, looking as white as her bedsheet. Her naturally red lips were pale in color, and she looked completely drained. "What happened? Why are you here?" I freaked out. Unlike me, Riwa was hardly ever admitted to the hospital.

"I almost fainted at my client's office. The doctor said I might have anemia. Good, you're here. I'm going to the lab for some tests. Please wait for me here." Riwa explained.

"Sure, I'll be here, don't worry," I assured her.

Riwa left me alone in the small emergency cubicle. It was too noisy outside and too busy. I hated emergency rooms on weekends. The whole atmosphere was disturbing, children crying, men shouting, and women arguing. I laid down on her bed, closed my ears, and started humming:

Autumn Leaves:
The falling leaves drift by the window
The autumn leaves of red and gold
I see your lips, the summer kisses
The sun-burned hands I used to hold

My relaxation didn't last for long. Without even knocking, a middle-aged, fake-blond nurse barged into the room and announced in a cold voice, "I need to take some blood. Please stay still."

I looked at her hands. She held a syringe in one and empty blood tubes in the other hand. As she came closer, I sensed the smell of cigarettes that lingered on her uniform. When I grasped what was going on, I immediately sat up straight on the bed, muttering, "Oh, no! There's a mistake here. I'm not Riwa. I'm her sister. Riwa went to the lab."

The nurse raised her eyebrows. "Yes, of course!" She put her arm on my shoulders to make me lie down. "Don't be scared now. Let me fill up this tube with your blood."

"No way!" I jumped off the bed.

"You just have to wait for my sister! She'll be here any minute now." It was like I hadn't said anything. The nurse insisted, "Sweetie, don't worry, I won't hurt you. I'll be very quick."

"Ok, listen, I'll go find Riwa for you," I said. But she stood tall, blocking the door.

"No!" her grimace changed, and I saw her yellow teeth as her voice got louder, "You're not going anywhere. Alice, Alice, come here immediately. I need help."

My eyes became like saucers, and I started shouting, "Who's Alice?" Another nurse stormed into the room. Was this for real? It was hard to believe what was happening.

I was not sure if it was my shouting or mere luck that Riwa arrived at that very moment, "What's going on?" Poor Riwa, although she was barely able to talk, she managed to clear up the misunderstanding.

Finally, after sorting out who was Noor and who was Riwa, the nurse looked at us in disbelief, "Wow, you look same-same!"

We got the results later that afternoon. Riwa was anemic to the point that she needed a blood transfusion. The medical staff was surprised that she could still stand up in her condition. Mom was furious and blamed it all on Riwa's unhealthy eating habits. "I keep telling you to have a variety of food. Have a salad. Some fruit. The key to a healthy diet is to have some variety." Mom was right once again.

When the news spread, our uncles, aunties, cousins, and neighbors rushed to the hospital, volunteering to donate blood. The most suitable donor was a black belt three Dan, a karate instructor, and my uncle's friend.

There must be a study proving that a blood donor's traits could be passed on to the blood recipient. Otherwise, how would Riwa, out of the blue, lose interest in gymnastics and start learning karate and Japanese?

*****

It was kind of expected that I would get invited for a second interview at the Daniel Company. My second interview was scheduled with the big boss, Mr. Daniel himself.

"Mr. Daniel is on the phone. Please have a seat." I was escorted to his uber-chic office by his assistant. I sat down on one of the two swivel leather armchairs, facing him without making any noise.

"Hello," I whispered in order not to disturb him. Mr. Daniel was in his mid-50s, with dark brown hair, with blue eyes standing out of his round reddish face. His spacious office was elegant and artistically filled with sculptures, antiques, expensive decorations, and lots of plants. Several silver frames with pictures of him together with celebrities and politicians were perfectly positioned on the bookshelves behind him as if to tell his guests, "This is my social circle!"

Being an interior design lover, it was the perfect opportunity to check out a real-life beautifully designed office, a masterpiece, to say the least. His black leather couches must have cost a fortune. And not to mention his dark wooden desk. I had no idea what kind of wood it was, but it was like those desks shown in society magazines. I glanced at the gypsum beams on the white ceiling and the marble flooring reflecting the sunlight. I couldn't find a single flaw. The finishing was made to perfection. An expert must have designed his office.

"Auf wieder sehn, Herr Muller," Mr. Daniel ended his conversation, scribbling a few words on a paper in front of him. Then he stood up and put his firm hand forward to shake my hand. Amazing! He didn't forget about Lebanese courtesy despite his long business conversation.

I was halfway to standing up, saying, "Good morning Mr. Daniel." But before reaching a full standing position, I toppled over and fell back on my chair, which automatically zoomed off backward at top speed to the other side of the room. My face froze under such speed.

Thankfully, my chair was slowed down by the Persian carpet, and it stopped just before I crashed into an engraved crystal vase. Mr. Daniel was shocked! So was I, but I didn't say a word, not even to apologize. Instead, I went about pushing my chair back to its initial position. Of course, I could only do that after freeing its wheels from the carpet fringes first.

Once back at my initial position, I waited for Mr. Daniel to say something. He took a long stare at me, smiled, and with a pinch of cynicism, commented, "That was quite a start! Are you ready now?"

I nodded.

The rest of the interview went smoothly without any other misfortunes. Mr. Daniel asked me general questions about my upbringing and my family. He also checked if I was a member of any terrorist organization or militia. Of course not! What kind of interview question was that?! Before ending the interview, he briefed me about DanielCo. I instantly fell in love with it – its prestigious history, the fact that it represented major medical, computer, and luxury brands, and that it owned its makeup factory. Working for the Daniel family became my dream.

The cherry on top was, of course, Mr. Daniel himself. He was a gentleman in every way. He was successful, prominent, and a man of vision. I had been searching for a personal mentor all my life, and here he was, standing in front of me.

*****

Chapter Four - Melissa

Mood Music:
"Melissa" by Julien Clerc

Rrrrrrinnng, the sound of our black rotary telephone woke me up. I heard Mom answering the phone, and a few seconds later, my bedroom door was wide open. "Nooooor, Noor wake up; there's a Mr. Nader for you on the phone," my Mom announced quickly and then rushed back to the kitchen to continue cooking stuffed zucchini with rice and meat. I got up from my bed, still half asleep.

I didn't study architecture, but I thought it was common sense not to stretch a residential apartment along the full length of a street, except if the initial intention was to build an indoor jogging course. Why was our apartment 25 meters long and designed like a hotel with rooms lined up one after the other?

No need to nag. I knew that to do the talk; I needed to do the walk. I passed by my parents' room, then the bathroom, followed by my sister's room. My steps got faster as I walked along our long corridor, passing the kitchen quickly. Finally, I sprinted through the dining room to reach our TV room and the phone.

I leaned on the wall and paused for a second to catch my breath. "Hello, Mr. Nader." "Good morning, Noor, ça va? I want to let you know that we have decided to hire you. So, welcome to our team!" His voice didn't show any excitement, unlike mine. It was the best news ever since Dad bought a power generator for our home to solve the repetitive power cut problem. Mr. Nader informed me that I could start in two weeks, on April 1st.

"Yey! My first job! My dream job!" I shouted out loud while doing my dance of joy, a dance that Riwa and I had created to the famous song of Julien Clerc: Oh Melissa Lisa Melissa, oh Melissa oh, oh. I clapped, then put my hands behind my ears and shook my hips to the beat, shake it, shake it.

*****

Like every Sunday, my Dad left the house very early and brought us a typical Lebanese breakfast: either Manakeesh, Kunafa, or Balila. It was a "cooking-free day" present to Mom.

After breakfast, Dad drove us to Sawfar, a beautiful Lebanese village where we had spent our summers as kids. My grandfather's house was getting older, but it kept the charm it had always had. To get to my grandparents' house, Dad took Sawfar's main road, then took the right turn next to Donna Maria's castle, the most beautiful castle I've ever seen. Any Disney princess would have loved having it for a home. Even Elsa and Anna could have easily fixed their sisterhood issues over a cup of hot cocoa at a snow picnic in its garden. Sadly, no one lived in the enchanted, deserted castle except for the watchman and his family. My cousins and I were always kind to them, so on several occasions, they let us wander around the rooms that had hosted parties for celebrities and other famous, rich people at one point in time. It was a delight to see the beauty of the castle's interior with our own eyes.

I felt privileged to have spent my childhood summer holidays at my grandfather's house. It was located in the most luxurious area of Sawfar, in-between my dream castle and some politicians' villas and mansions. Our family's place, however, was of a different caliber. It could be described neither as a villa nor as a castle. Not even close. Somehow it looked like a stone cottage ready for renovation. As for us, the seventy-plus family members, we just loved it.

We arrived a bit before lunch. The flowery garden was already crowded with uncles, cousins, and people I had no idea who they were. It was like a beehive, with people serving coffee, cracking walnuts, or having side talks over a cigarette. After kissing and hugging each cousin, uncle, and aunt, I went to do what I loved to do there: drinking freezing water directly from Ein el Mai (water spring). Then I climbed trees, picked flowers, and ran after butterflies.

The first time I visited my grandparents' house after several years of war was an eye-opener. The whole place was much smaller than I remembered it: My auntie's room, where we used to play football as kids, had barely enough space for two beds and a closet, and the stone wall which I used to climb with difficulty as if it was the Empire State Building, was only a few rows of stones high.

My secret hideaway was a set of stairs at the end of the garden that was well concealed by untrimmed plants, exactly at the boundary of the French ambassador's summer house. Naturally, Riwa and my cousins knew where to find me and directly interrupted my daydreaming session. "Look, we got figs, lots of them. We picked them from the tree next to the kitchen." Riwa put the basket in between all of us.

Hassan, my younger cousin, said, "Do you remember how we used to swim in the pool over there and how our auntie Lamia refused to put on her swimsuit? She always insisted on jumping in the water in her dress." Pointing at the pool, I smirked, "She was right! This isn't exactly a pool! It's just a small water irrigation tank." We all chuckled. Our hands were already sticky from the yummy red figs we were having.

Riwa, dressed in her mountain outfit, a checked blue shirt, and jeans, said, "The worst thing that I've ever witnessed here was when Khodor fell in the huge irrigation tank at the ambassador's house." Hassan and I cracked up laughing.

One of my younger cousins, Sofia, interrupted, "Wait, what happened? Was I also there?"

Hassan explained, "No, you and your siblings weren't even born then. Riwa, Noor, I, and a few other kids from the neighborhood were playing in this garden. As usual, we decided to have an adventure, so we sneaked into the ambassador's garden without letting anyone see us, especially not their grumpy watchman." Hassan couldn't go on with the story as he started laughing.

Riwa continued, "We sneaked into the ambassador's garden through an opening, here in this fence." We all turned to where she was pointing, but the fence had been repaired. "We went directly to his garden and made a big mess by moving things around. We threw garden tools and buckets into his pool, turning it muddy. We did this to annoy his grumpy watchman, who used to yell at us whenever we were noisy. Finally, we went to the deep water tank, which the watchman used to water the trees behind the ambassador's villa, and climbed the tank's stone wall. There were around ten of us. The wall was about 2 meters high, but only a quarter of the tank was filled with water. We challenged each other to run on the edge of the tank without falling in.

Splash! Khodor, one of the kids, fell into the water, which was green and full of insects and disgusting in every way. Khodor tried to get out by jumping into the water, but he couldn't reach the top of the wall. Instead of helping him, we were laughing our heads off. Finally, one of the boys grabbed himself and let down a rope for him, but it didn't help. Whenever we tried to pull him out, we started laughing, dropped the rope, and Khodor fell into the water again. Finally, the watchman heard our hysterical laughter and came to check what was going on. When we saw him approaching, we got so scared as if we saw a ghost, jumped off the wall, and ran like crazy to our grandfather's house, except for Khodor, who was still stuck inside the tank."

My sister peeled a fig, smiling. "This is so yummy. Ummm, where was I? Ah, yes, the watchman got Khodor out of the tank with a ladder. As for us, we got a lecture from Teita, my grandmother. The following day, the ambassador's guards fixed the fence in-between the two gardens, preventing us from sneaking in there anymore."

"You forgot the most important part," I complained. "When Khodor returned to the house, he was soaking wet, dripping water all over the place. He took a hot shower, but since he had no extra clothes, Teita gave him my uncle's grey sports shorts. And, don't ask me why she also gave him my very own velvety purple top to wear. Why would she do that? I was half his size, both in length and width. Poor guy, how he struggled to squeeze himself into my top, but in the end, he made it." I grinned. "And that, my dear cousins, was the first time I ever saw a guy in a crop top."

It was a wonderful afternoon with positive vibes, beautiful weather, and a loving family. I should have been having a great time, but something was aching from within. My mood was slowly shifting from overly happy to unbearably melancholic. I couldn't figure out what it was at first, but when I glimpsed the fig tree standing all alone by itself, it all came back to me. I understood where these sad feelings came from. "To be honest with you guys, Khodor ruining my favorite top was not the worst thing that happened to me here. It was one of my good memories.

There's a memory back from 1982 that I can't seem to forget. It's from the time of the Israeli invasion of Beirut. At that time, two of my uncles – your fathers –, two aunties, Riwa and I, and other relatives stayed in our Teita's small house to escape the war in Beirut. Each family settled in one bedroom, and we all had to share one washroom. One day in the afternoon, directly after lunch, I heard screaming and shouting from outside. There was a lot of commotion, so I ran out to the garden. It was an excellent excuse to escape my forced afternoon nap.

The first thing I saw was your dad, Hassan. He was arguing with several armed men; all dressed in camouflage uniforms. Everyone was shouting. Uncle Jamil was, ummm, how can I describe him? He was way more than furious, about to explode at any second. I stood next to the door, watching what was going on. My Teita sat still in her white dress, saying nothing, while your mom was sobbing, begging your Dad to let go. She was scared that if he continued fighting with them, they would shoot him. I was too little, so I didn't understand what was happening. A few moments later, when the shouting stopped, Teita took my hand and led the other kids and me to one of the bedrooms. She told us to pack our bags because we had to leave. A Syrian army troop confiscated my grandfather's house and threw us all out. To our dismay, they specifically chose Teita's house because it was on top of the mountain with an excellent view of Israeli bases. Uncle Jamil couldn't change their minds. No one could. Within an hour, we were all in our cars, loaded with as much as we could squeeze inside: clothes, mattresses, towels, and food."

Sofia looked at us with big green eyes, "It must have been scary. What did you do then?"

Riwa replied, "Each of our uncles fled with their families somewhere – to other Lebanese villages or Syria, ironically. Our mom and dad were already in Beirut and refused to leave as they were involved in community work. They sent us with Auntie Lamia to Switzerland, and we stayed at Uncle Ibrahim's house until the war was over."

I continued telling my story, "I never laid my eyes on the place again until years later when the Syrian army deserted it. I was shocked: The house was stripped to the bones. The windows, doors, furniture, blankets, and even our bicycles were gone. All the trees in the garden had been cut down and used as firewood during winter. All except for this one fig tree, she's a survivor." The silence followed was only broken by the sounds of ladybugs moving in the grass and birds singing in the trees around us.

"It's getting chilly," Riwa said, and we followed her back to the house. Unlike all our previous trips back from Sawfar, I was not singing out loud in the car as I normally did, and Dad didn't have to turn on the radio to shut me up discreetly. I remained silent. On the winding road to Beirut, I was overwhelmed by a mixture of love, laughter, and peace. A feeling that words couldn't describe. It was a feeling of genuine belonging to an old family mountain house, its people, and its surrounding piece of land.

Chapter Five - Train of Thought

Mood Music:
"Train of Thought" by AHA

Working at DanielCo was not as exciting as I thought it would be. All I did was read and read and read. Mr. Nader called it my "induction phase." I called it my "going crazy phase." There was a huge amount of material covering not only food topics but also detergents, foam, and paints. I had to know what substances such as lauryl sodium sulfate, polyurethane, and methyl paraben were used for. It was incredibly boring.

Long attention spans were never one of my strengths. I needed a break. I needed to talk to someone, anyone. Everyone at work seemed very busy or out of the office, so I called Riwa at her office. "Hi, Riwa. Can you talk?"

Riwa was working on a presentation, and she was running late. "Why are you calling me now? You know I'm busy. I have a meeting in two hours. Do you need help with something?" she asked in a grumpy voice.

"No," I lowered my voice, "but I'm bored. I don't know what to do. Our manager keeps on telling me to read and read, but I'm done reading. I want to do something else."

Riwa sighed impatiently. "Seriously?! I don't have time for this nonsense now. Bye."

"What should I do now?" I murmured to myself as I stood next to the window looking at the world outside.

Ruba, Mr. Nader's assistant, a bright young hyper woman, was responsible for explaining to me how things got done in the chemical division. She must have been a few years older than me by her looks. She seemed well-informed about business in the chemical division. On my first working day, I noticed that my new colleagues were roaming around her like moths around a flame. She answered any of their questions automatically.

Ruba was extremely busy. I doubted she would have time at all, but she just winked at me, saying, "When the guys are out, we'll talk."

It was like magic. At 9:00 am, everyone left within seconds, and the office was empty except for the two of us. The phone barely rang, and all I could hear was the A/C fan. After Ruba had prepared coffee for both of us, she leaned back in her chair. "Finally! I can only work when the guys are out."

I nodded understandingly.

She handed me a piece of paper and a pen. "I'll explain to you in detail all the administration work you need to know, and Mr. Nader will handle the sales part. First, I have some important tips for you. I've been working here for three years, and I can assure you from experience that it'll make your life much easier if you follow those few rules." I listened eagerly.

"As you know, this company is owned by the Daniel family. We report to Mr. Daniel, the eldest brother, which means we strictly follow his orders. Mr. Daniel is meticulous about everything here. He wants things to be done in a specific way. Let's start with the most important rule: how to answer the phone. Always say your name first."

She grabbed the receiver to demonstrate. "I answer the phone saying 'Ruba alo?' Never forget to say your name first."

I nodded again.

"Great, let's move on to other points then."

*****

During my first week, Ruba also introduced me to our colleagues: the finance division team, the team responsible for the warehouses, the truck drivers, several senior managers, and of course "le chef" of our canteen, Aziz, who, in addition to sandwiches and coffee sold an exquisite chocolate selection. All the people I met were friendly and funny. Everyone asked me a lot of questions, such as which university I went to, what West Beirut was like if I had a boyfriend or not (I didn't), or how many chocolates I expected to buy daily (Aziz insisted on knowing after realizing I was a chocolate addict).

At lunchtime, I always joined Ruba in the canteen. She brought her home-cooked food in a Tupperware container while I bought sandwiches from Aziz. I liked eating there. It was an inviting place full of vivid young people talking, laughing, and smoking.

During one of those lunch gatherings, a young man in a blue shirt and loose jeans walked toward me, saying hi with a broad smile. "So you're the new girl in the chemical division. My name is Rawad, and I'm heading the team of the medical division." "Oh, yes! I've heard about you. But I'm not so new anymore. I've been working here for more than a month now."

Rawad was an engineer who was also an AUB alumnus, a few years older than me, and supposedly the right hand of Mr. Daniel. It turned out that he also lived in Beirut's western part, not far from my parents' home. He gave me a few tips on which road to take during morning rush hours.

The more we talked, the more he opened up about work at DanielCo. He told me that the biggest challenge he had faced at work was when one of his international guests had been abducted by a local militia. The news had gone viral in the international media. "I just dropped him at the hotel for him to freshen up before our next business meeting, but he never came out of his room again. No one could help. It became an international issue."

Another story he told me made perfect sense. Now I understood the reason behind Mr. Daniel's terrorism-related question he had asked me during my interview. Rawad explained, "One of my team members, George, was a militia member before joining DanielCo. During one of our daily business meetings, he bragged about bombing a specific building during wartime. To our biggest surprise, Stephan, another team member, got hysterical, indicating that the building which George had blown up belonged to his (Stephan's) family. As a result, George and Stephan stopped talking to each other, and our department's team spirit changed for good."

*****

I divided up my time between work and my AUB master's classes. Sometimes my courses were in the morning, but Mr. Nader didn't mind, as long as I made up for that time. After completing my induction phase, I joined my colleagues on their customer visits for "on-the-job training." In the beginning, I was kind of shy. Being the only girl on the sales team and the youngest by far didn't help. But all the guys were polite and supportive. With time I stopped feeling intimidated and eventually reached the point where I genuinely enjoyed their company. Ultimately, I became so comfortable around them that they stopped announcing whenever they were about to tell a dirty joke, and I stopped leaving the office in order not to hear it.

Wael, a Chris Isaak look-alike, came into the office strutting like a rooster. He had a private meeting with Mr. Daniel, a privilege only granted to those "special people" whom Mr. Daniel trusted. The rest of our team met our big boss once a week in the afternoon when he was usually tired and grumpy. Mr. Daniel was not always grumpy. He was merely philosophical and enjoyed confusing us, like when he insisted on using the word "paradox" in every fax, letter, and conversation. Most of the time, it was completely out of context, but he used it nevertheless. Just as we, his staff, got optimistic that the paradox phase was about to end, we received invitations to attend a presentation on "What is a paradox? And what does it mean to us?" by Mr. Daniel himself.

In another philosophically related matter, he took me entirely off guard during my first division's meeting by asking me, "Mlle Beyrouti, tell me, what would be a better choice in your opinion – looking in a mirror or through a window?"

What was I supposed to say? I was clueless. There was no need for such an embarrassing situation at the beginning of my career. I looked at my colleagues, searching for help, but obviously, I was on my own, so I tried, "A mirror?" Mr. Daniel nodded, smiling. "Yes, exactly! We should always look at ourselves, at perfection."

Coming back to Wael, who was also an AUB graduate like me. I followed him with my eyes as he walked toward my desk. He handed me a small note, saying, "juice compound market study."

"What's that?" I asked.

"Mr. Daniel wants you to prepare a market study on juice concentrates in the Lebanese market ASAP."

"Oh, thanks," I felt so special, "I'll start right away." I turned the paper and wrote down a few points. I waved the post-it note at Wael, who was about to sit down at his desk. "I'm done. I'm going to his office right now."

I heard Wael's quick steps behind me, and before I knew it, he put his hand on the lift door, preventing me from opening it.

"Wait, wait! Noor, where do you think you're going?"

"To Mr. Daniel, to show him my work." I thought Wael would be impressed by my speed, but he wasn't.

He raised his eyebrows. "Let's talk for a moment," he said, gesturing with his hand for me to follow him. I sat in front of his desk, feeling stupid even before he opened his mouth. "Tell me, Noor, didn't you take a marketing class at AUB?"

"Nope. It was an elective. Why?" I replied.

"I see." He thought for a few seconds. "Ok, so let me explain to you what a market study is. It is a thorough report of several pages prepared after a lot of market research. You must gather information about your market size, major brands, and target clients. Remember, you can't submit it handwritten. It needs to be typed. It should be something similar to this one."

He grabbed an elegantly typed market study about the paint industry in Lebanon from his desk drawer and handed it to me. "Here, take a look at this, and try to prepare something in the same manner." As I was about to return to my desk, he stopped me, "One more thing Noor, you can't just walk into Mr. Daniel's office. You need to make an appointment with his assistant."

*****

Chapter Six - Hello

Mood Music:
"Hello"
by Lionel Richie

I flipped through Wael's report. It looked good. It looked very good, professionally written, well organized, and straight to the point.

It was tough for me to prepare a market study of a similar caliber, especially if I considered the fact that I had never done any market study before. During my studies, Riwa prepared all my business reports on any topic: including statistics and management. She thought it was much easier than correcting my reports. She even volunteered to fix the parts written by my classmate Vivian. Riwa believed that we both had no clue how to write reports. When Riwa read Vivian's opening sentence to our paper "Our target: The nutrition department of the American Hospital," she asked us cynically, "Are you planning a terrorist attack against the hospital?"

Riwa and I accepted that I was not born for writing reports, as much as she was never going to be Ms. Tidy. We sort of helped each other out, I cleaned up her room, did her filing, and in return, she wrote my reports. But that was as a university student. As a working woman, however, I could not rely on Riwa anymore. I had to prepare the market study Mr. Daniel asked me to do. I needed chocolate.

The following day at 8:20 am, I was still not at work. My car didn't start. It was too early, so Moe's garage was not open yet. I had to take a "Serveese," a shared taxi, our typical means of transportation. Back then, all the Serveese cars were old Mercedes cars. They drove on predetermined main roads and charged a fixed rate depending on the location.

My simple request to go to work in Sin el Fil, thus crossing the virtual eastern/western Beirut border, drove several of the taxi drivers crazy:

"Sin el Fil? Are you kidding me?!" or "Imagine that! She wants to go to Sin el Fil early in the morning!" they blabbed out loud to themselves.

Finally, one Serveese accepted to take me to work, but only on the condition that I would pay five times the standard price. I agreed.

I wasn't a big fan of Serveese for the following reasons:
1- Passengers discussed politics and daily problems, which was draining.
2- Serveese drivers honked repetitively at potential customers standing by the road. The noise was disturbing to my ears and caused me nausea.
3- I had already had a few incidences where the passenger sitting next to me tried to harass me.

The taxi driver who agreed to take me was an older man, friendly but quite loud. He had an innate urge to talk. He started by asking the one question everyone in Lebanon would have asked, "What's your family name?" Then he went on asking typical questions such as, "Are you engaged? Married?" But since I was single, he couldn't continue further in that direction. He honked.

Finally, he asked me, "Ammo (meaning uncle), why do you want to go to Sin el Fil?"

"For work," I said.

In Lebanon, a young person would call the older person uncle (Ammo) or taunt (auntie), and the older person would also strangely call the younger person the same, i.e., uncle or taunt. For example, I addressed my cousin Hassan's mom as "Uncle's wife," and she would also call me "Uncle's wife" – a bizarre system!

The taxi driver explained that there hadn't been any East or West Beirut in the good old times before the war. "You know it's the political game, the conspiracy of the big countries." He honked. "The Americans, Saudis, the Syrians, and even the French. They're all jealous of Beirut. They want their cities to be as beautiful as our capital." He honked again.

"Why would anyone be jealous?" I asked. "We have regular power cuts, a high inflation rate, unemployment, insufficient social security, and ..."

He interrupted me firmly, "It's not our fault. It's the big countries' fault."

I decided to be quiet.

In Lebanon, we tend to blame most of our problems on others. There is always some kind of conspiracy theory going on. If we don't know who to blame, we blame the Italians. No kidding. A typical Lebanese saying is: It's the Italians' fault!

The monologue continued all the way until we arrived at the office.

I greeted Toni, our new colleague who had joined earlier that month. He winked at me as he was talking on the phone. I took a seat, hanging my purse on my chair. I watched him as he made business appointments. He was a funny, quite good-looking guy; tall, dark blond, and extremely generous. He had already bought me lunch on several occasions and never allowed me to pay. "Out of the question," he used to say. He was wearing a jeans shirt and a pair of jeans pants that fit his body perfectly well.

Toni had an athletic figure, which was obvious. When one of our colleagues asked him about his sports routine, he told him that he did weight training regularly and went swimming every weekend. He also loved jogging along the seaside, and whenever the sea was rough, he went surfing with his friends.

I smiled when I saw him coming to my desk, asking, "You were quite late today, is everything ok?" I told him about my car and how it wouldn't start.

"I can take you to your client appointments if you'd like." It was so sweet of him to offer his help, but I had to stay at the office to prepare for my market study. He also proposed to drop me home later, but I also refused because it didn't make any sense for him to go to West Beirut when he lived on the eastern side. I decided to ask Rawad later to drop me at home… it was on his way.

*****

Chapter Seven - Rock Me Amadeus

Mood Music:
"Rock Me Amadeus" by Falco

I read my market study at least 100 times. It was professional in every way and included tons of important information. My report didn't come out haphazardly. It was the result of one whole week of hard work, gathering information, calling on clients and governmental entities, and getting our suppliers' input.

For my report's style, I chose a minimalistic approach, a straight-to-the-point format. There was no need to waste time with details or paragraphs. I decided to remain top-line and leave it mainly with only titles.

The first page of my market study featured the following:

Juice Market Study
The Lebanese juice market consists of:
   A- Juice products
   B- Drink products
       The juice products are either:
       a- Packed in tetra packs or
       b- Packed in bottles
           The tetra packs could either be:
           i-   1000 ml tetra packs or
           ii-   250 ml tetra packs

Although I felt that I did a good job, I decided to double-check with Riwa. She was the expert, after all. I left my market study on her desk and waited for her in the TV room to discuss the matter further.

Dad was just discussing an important topic with Mom. He was holding his pipe in his hand as he always did when contemplating. I overheard part of the conversation, so I understood why their tone was so serious.

Many years before, as we were all fast asleep, a loud and familiar sound woke us up. It was a bomb. Being brought up during the war, it was easy for me to distinguish the sound of a bomb from a mortar shell or an RPG grenade. While kids in Europe learned about recycling and creative thinking, I, like any other Lebanese of my generation, learned about safety precaution measures and calculating if a place was safe or not in a mortar shell attack. But it was not all bad. In the shelter, I learned how to knit, do cross stitching, and play cards. The kids bonded together. When it wasn't that dangerous, we all played war games in the stairwell of our building. We had toy guns, pistols, and plastic knives. I had my very own M16 toy rifle.

The bomb must have been placed in the vicinity of our building. Our TV room was full of smoke, the smell of gunpowder, and the window glass shattered on our apartment floor. It was weird because there wasn't any particular battle going on during that month. We watched from our balcony, as all our neighbors did. It was obvious that the bomb had exploded in the building across the street. From the shouting of people who rushed to the scene and our neighbors' discussions from one balcony to another, we knew that it was a one-time thing; no new battle had erupted or anything of that sort. That was a relief. I helped my mom clean up the shattered glass and then went back to sleep as we had school the next day. In my family, there was no excuse dramatic enough to skip school, not even a bomb.

Dad stood next to Mom, pointing with his pipe at the building across the road. There was lots of banging and workers roaming around in the destroyed apartment.

"Finally, it seems they're going to fix it," Dad said confidently.

Mum shrugged, "After all those years. I wonder who bombed the apartment in the first place."

Dad shook his head, "I don't know, but I'm sure the police know."

Two theories were circulating in our neighborhood regarding that incident.

Theory no 1: The landlord bombed the apartment after his tenants had gone out. They paid little rent as per their old tenancy contract, and it would have taken him years to win a lawsuit to throw them out. So, he blew up the apartment. No casualties were reported.

Theory no 2: It was all about the assassination of an undercover politician.

*****

Riwa came back right at dinner time. I updated her on the latest news about the bombed apartment and the ongoing construction and asked her if she could have a look at my market study. I had barely opened my book to read when she stormed into my room, yelling, "What is this? This is absolute rubbish. Don't call it a market study. Just don't …"

I tried to interrupt her, "But the information …"

She didn't even let me finish my sentence. "Yes, all the information is there, but tell me, how on earth did you come up with such a format? I've never in my life seen anything even similar to this."

"I thought it was simple and easy to read," I tried to justify my idea, but Riwa interrupted me by asking, "Remind me, didn't you take a marketing course at AUB?"

Why was everyone asking me the same question lately? If it was such an impressive course, how come no one recommended it when I was still a student? "Nope," I replied. "Can you fix it, please?" I looked at her with sad eyes.

"Give it to me. I thought we were over this phase of me writing your reports?" She grabbed it, still blabbing when storming back to her room.

I called after her, "Don't rewrite it, just fix it." But we both knew that was impossible. In a few hours, I was going to receive a brand-new report – a masterpiece in Riwa's style.

I was right. When I woke up the next morning, a new and upgraded market study had already been placed neatly on my desk.

*****

When I reached the office, the first thing I did was call Mr. Daniel's assistant, asking her for an appointment with the big boss. She answered directly, "Bien sûr, come down before his next meeting starts."

I went down to the first floor and sat on a beautiful armchair in the waiting area. I had been to Mr. Daniel's office a few times before. The first time was during my job interview, and after that, during our weekly division meetings. I enjoyed meeting him. I felt important. I also liked to look at the two framed pictures of German houses hung on a wall next to his assistant's office. I took the opportunity to read their captions: "Fachwerkhaus – Rothenburg" and "Alte Bauernhäuser – Schwarzwald". I had no idea what that meant, but the houses looked beautiful. It was my dream to visit Germany one day.

Mr. Daniel's assistant stared at me awkwardly, so I returned to my seat. Mozart's best-loved Symphony No. 40 played in the background, but it got disrupted by some loud noise. I could not identify it at first, but gradually it became clearer: It was Mr. Daniel lecturing someone. Actually, that would be downplaying it. He was yelling at someone. I could not understand what he was saying, but clearly, he was about to explode. It didn't take long for his office door to open, and an older lady paused next to the door.

It was none other than the company's cleaning lady, Mme. Haddad. Mr. Daniel was still yelling, "Mme Haddad, I'm warning you for the last time: I never ever want to see a fly in this building. I mean neither black nor blue, neither big nor small. Do you understand me? Flies are forbidden here, they're not allowed in my company, and if I catch sight of a fly, just one fly around here, I will hold you personally responsible." Mme Haddad just stood there, nodding repetitively. He banged on his desk, "Listen carefully. For every fly that I see in MY company, I will deduct 20 dollars from your salary." I gasped, wondering if that was even legal.

Mme Haddad left his office, apologizing. As she walked past, she winked at me, saying, "May God help you. He's in a terribly difficult mood today." I bit my lips. I was doomed.

"Bonjour, Mr. Daniel." I knocked at his office door, smiling. I had mixed feelings. On the one hand, my heart was shivering with fear, but on the other hand, I was glad to show my mentor the report that Riwa and I had prepared.

"Bonjour Mlle Beyrouti, please have a seat." He took a medicinal alcohol bottle from his desk drawer and cleaned his hands. I was used to that by then. He glimpsed at a few papers on his desk before he finally looked at me and asked calmly, "Have you been enjoying your work here?"

"Yes, for sure. It's been great! Everybody is nice to me, and I'm learning a lot." I handed him my report, clarifying, "Mr. Daniel, this is the juice market study you requested."

He looked straight into my eyes, and his first question was, "Is this a positive report? I assume you already know that I don't accept negative reports."

I nodded, "Yes, I've already been warned. I assure you this is a very positive report." I smiled.

He read carefully, nodding now and then. "Mmmm, yes, très bien (*Very good*)." Then suddenly, he frowned, stopped reading, and looked at me with an offended look. "Excuse me! What did you write here? Did you write, and I quote, "highly requested in the market"?!

I answered with confidence, "Yes, I did. I refer specifically to the pineapple juice concentrate we source from the Philippines. It's highly requested in the Lebanese market."

"And you dare to repeat it?" he asked me.

I was puzzled. "I have statistics to back it all up."

"Mlle Beyrouti, Mlle Beyrouti!" He was shaking his head in disbelief. "No, no, you don't get it. You can't use the word "highly." YOU, Mlle Beyrouti, are not allowed to use the word "highly." "Highly" is a much bigger word than you. It's a bigger word than all of my company, bigger even than Lebanon."

He looked at the ceiling, searching for a word. "Only NASA can use it."

"NASA????" I shrieked and burst out laughing.

I laughed and laughed until tears came out of my eyes. I just couldn't contain my laughter. I couldn't believe that he limited the use of the word "highly" to NASA. When I finally managed to stop laughing, I got a tissue from the silver tissue box in front of me and wiped off my smudgy eyeliner. I glimpsed at Mr. Daniel with watery eyes, fighting the urge to laugh even more.

I wondered what he was going to do with me. I was fully aware of what he was capable of. After all, I had just witnessed how he had shredded poor Mme Haddad only because of an insect, a fly. But my heart was leaping for some reason. I was happy. I felt he enjoyed the conversation as much as I did, and at a certain level, we were bonding.

I didn't dare to look him straight in the eyes. I was afraid I would start laughing again. I heard him saying casually, "Yes, please do laugh, Mlle Beyrouti, laugh as much as you want. It's a funny story, after all."

There was a hint of a smile in-between his words. Before I left his office, Mr. Daniel said, "Keep up the good work, Noor."

*****

Chapter Eight - Kalashnikov

Mood Music:
"Kalashnikov" by Goran Bregović

Growing up in Lebanon was fun, adventurous, and creative. It was also challenging and spontaneous. I had a lot of free time at home due to no school days. During most of those free days, we had power cuts, which meant no TV. I, like all the other children, had to be creative. I read a lot, made crafts, built stuff out of cardboard boxes, and did scientific experiments. I didn't do any extra curriculum activities. I learned mostly by myself or by trial and error. For example, I learned how to swim when I went to the beach with our neighbors. The girls, who knew how to swim well, asked me to join them, and I did. I almost drowned, but a lifeguard saved me. I kept jumping in the water, and the lifeguard saved me each time I jumped until, ultimately, I stopped drowning.

We grew up in a loving and protective family, but we were also exposed to other kinds of emotions. In Lebanon, there's some child-unfriendly terminology that must have affected me in some way:

1- A famous lullaby that my Mom sang to me at bedtime starts off quite nicely: "May God grant my baby health. May my baby fall asleep." This is followed by an interesting line: "We will slaughter a pigeon for my baby." Seriously? Did anyone consider my potential nightmares?

2- A typical Lebanese mom pampers her child by calling him or her Habibi (my love), which makes sense, but when a Mom wants to pamper her child extra, she would go up a notch and say "tooberni inshallah," which literally means "may you bury me." No comment.

As a kid in Lebanon, being faced with grownup topics, such as power cuts, buying tap water, and the scarcity of flour and sugar was completely normal. Another topic I was also well familiar with was weapons. Hunting is an essential topic in Lebanon. It is mentioned in the news and discussed at parties and in coffee shops, especially during peak season. Lebanese men have always bragged about their hunting skills, how they can withstand harsh weather conditions, just waiting for the right moment, and then – bang!

I always thought killing birds was brutal, mainly when Dad brought back tiny little birds from his hunting trips so Mom could fry them and serve them with olive oil, lemon juice, and garlic. I still remember Dad walking into our home, dressed in a green military-like uniform with a cap covering his partially bald head and feeling so proud of his success. "It was a good catch today," he would tell Mom. I always looked the other way to avoid seeing those poor bloody creatures dangling from green bird hangers around his waist. They barely had any flesh on them.

I couldn't complain much though. It was my Dad's passion and favorite hobby, which he was pretty good at too. He spent a lot of time and money on his hobby. He must have traveled to neighboring Syria a zillion times to go bird hunting. One day, he took it even up a notch by joining some of his friends on a hunting trip to Hungary. He was not the only one with this passion. I was surrounded by hunters among our family, neighbors, and friends.

I was also surrounded by non-hunters who were in love with their guns just for the sake of it. Our neighbor, for example, was an army general who was not specifically keen on hunting but had a selection of at least 20 different weapons, including rifles, grenades, and a Kalashnikov. His wife hid those weapons inside sofas in their mountain house.

Those men were neither outlaws nor terrorists, but Lebanese men have a unique relationship with their weapons. They cherish them, take them out, give them nicknames, and pamper them as if they were their lovers. Funnily enough, those same men who have no problem spending hours and hours cleaning and oiling their weapons would not spare a moment to help their wives in washing the dishes. "That's not a man's job," they would say.

Collecting weapons as a hobby is not exclusive to Lebanese men. Some women share the same interest. My mom, for example, was known to be a strong anti-war and peace advocate, but she still had her collection of vintage weapons and ammunition. One part of her collection she had inherited from her family, and the other, more contemporary part, she had carefully gathered and selected during our civil war. My mom exhibited her World War II yellow copper and brass casting shells next to our wide book selection. Mom also chose to carefully display the smaller bullets, of which many had not even exploded, on a silver plate in our salon. It was my scary job to dust them every weekend.

Mom also owned an exceptional assortment of engraved swords, which had belonged to my great-grandfather, and brass battle axes, which I have no clue where they came from. Those were hung on the walls of our TV room, right next to our original classical paintings.

Riwa and I spent all morning dusting our weapons collection. Once we were finally done with all our cleaning activities, we decided to go for lunch and have some fun. I suggested a new place for a change. "Somewhere affordable, I hope. I'm having a cash flow problem these days. My clients are not paying on time," Riwa explained.

I was also having a cash problem. It was the end of the month, and my minimum wage salary was about to vanish.

"Don't worry. I know exactly where to go. This restaurant offers the best food you can imagine and costs almost nothing. It's right by the sea, and its clientele includes doctors and other intellectual crowds."

Riwa raised her eyebrows, "Good food, tasty, and only educated people go there. Where do you want to go exactly?"

"To the restaurant in the American University Hospital. I was there last week with one of my friends, Vivian, you know her from when we wrote our reports together. And let me tell you, I was astonished. We paid almost nothing."

Riwa frowned, "Are you sure? That's hard to believe."

"Of course, I'm sure," I insisted. "Do you want to go or not?"

Riwa sighed, "Ok, fine, let's go. It's good to have a change."

As we entered my car, Riwa double-checked, "Are you sure we don't need any extra money? It's about one hour before the banks close today. We can still pass by my bank on our way and get some extra cash."

"No need," I replied.

We arrived at the AUH, a place we knew well due to our many emergency visits, mainly because of my food allergies. I nudged Riwa as we entered the enormous white restaurant. "Remember when you once called the emergency room and told them you had a patient who was turning Chinese after eating Chinese food?!"

Riwa burst out laughing, "Yes, and they ordered me to bring you in immediately."

It was lunchtime. The AUH cafeteria was busy and noisy. Doctors and nurses in their white uniforms were chatting and laughing while a few ladies were cleaning the tables and stacking metal trays on top of each other. I turned around and noticed a few empty tables in the corner. "We're lucky. There's still an empty table for us. But we first have to get our food from there. Follow me."

The queue line moved slowly past the appetizers, salads, bread, hummus, savory pastries, daily dishes, and the BBQ section.

I smiled. "See, I told you it's an amazing selection. Look at the desserts! They're tempting, aren't they?"

Riwa nodded.

Each of us took a metal tray and selected a few dishes. I chose salad, pasta with white cream, rice, chicken, cheese spring roll, spinach pastry, a breadbasket, a few desserts, and juice. Riwa filled up her tray too. As we were standing, waiting for the queue line to move, I tried to sound as casual as possible and raised my voice so people in the queue line could hear our discussion. "Riwa, you didn't tell me; how was your last conference, the one in Washington DC?"

Riwa's eyes went round, and she whispered, "Stop it, don't invent stuff. It's not funny." But I continued in a playful tone, "I heard it was quite impressive, and Professor Peter insisted that it was a futuristic event, a huge success!"

Riwa pinched me, "I told you to stop it."

I smiled and whispered, "Ok, ok, I'll behave." Riwa was my favorite and only teasing victim. She got embarrassed quickly, and her cheeks turned red. But later on, she would laugh about it.

"It's our turn!" I exclaimed, moving both trays to the man behind the cash register.

Casually smoking a cigarette, the cashier typed in our food one by one. I looked at the total. It was getting higher and higher. The prices were almost three times higher than what I remembered. "Excuse me?" I cleared my throat.

"I was here last week with my friend, Vivian, do you know her? She is the dietician with the long curly hair?"

He stared at me, trying to grasp what I wanted to say. I continued, "And at that time, the prices were much lower than today. Why?"

He continued typing in the prices. "We haven't changed the prices if that's what you're asking, but you mentioned your friend works here! In that case, she has a staff discount."

I swallowed, looking at the total on the screen. We were in big trouble. At that time, credit and debit cards didn't exist, at least not in Lebanon. So what we carried as cash was the only money we had with us.

I didn't dare look at Riwa. I bit my lip, glimpsing at the long queue line waiting behind us. I dropped all my money on the counter and asked Riwa how much she had. She counted her money one by one, emptying her purse and pockets.

"Ok, now give me all that, please." I sounded like I had an impeccable plan. I took part of her money and topped it up with mine, saying to the cashier, "There you go! This is for the food on my tray. Thank you, Riwa. I will wait for you at the table over there."

I watched Riwa's face turn tomato red as she was removing dishes from her tray. "I'll remove the BBQ and pasta and keep the salad and the soup. Would that work?" Riwa asked the cashier.

"No, it would still not be enough," he answered.

"Umm, ok, how about I remove the BBQ, the salad, and the soup and keep the pasta dish and the breadbasket?

The cashier used his calculator as it was quicker and looked into Riwa's big, black eyes. "You know what? It's ok. Keep those things and give me all the money you have. You need to move on now. The queue line is getting longer."

"Youuuu! You have no idea what I will do to you at home." Riwa's veins were about to burst.

"You convinced me it was an affordable restaurant. You didn't let me go to the bank to get some extra cash. You embarrassed me and ripped me off, taking my money!" Her voice became louder, and people around us started staring at us.

I interrupted her, hiding my face with a piece of bread, "Shhhh, don't make a big fuss here. You're right. The restaurant isn't affordable, but rather on the expensive side. And yes, I took your money. I'm not proud of it, but what did you want me to do? It was too embarrassing, especially around all these doctors."

Riwa was still grumpy.

"Ok, look, I'll make it up to you. I promise. How about I run all your work and domestic errands this week totally for free?"

Chapter Nine - All I Have to Do Is Dream

Mood Music:
"All I Have to Do Is Dream"
by The Everly Brothers

Several months had passed since I joined Daniel Co's sales team, and I loved it. I met a lot of interesting people, made new friends, and learned a lot of interesting things. It was fun. But there was a teensy-weensy problem: I didn't sell anything. Although my product portfolio was generous, including around fifty items such as fruit juice concentrates, juice premixes, and flavors and colors, I had no idea how to initiate or close a sales deal. In my defense, I never got the official sales training I had been promised.

I made an appointment with a candy factory called Bon Bon and Co to show them our flavor collection. The factory was unheard-of, but somehow I came across its contact details in an old document filed in one of the cabinets. I thought I should give it a try. Bon Bon and Co were located in a small village in the mountains. I bought a few chocolate bars and mango juice from Aziz for the road. The drive was about 30 minutes, and I estimated another 30 minutes to account for the time I might get lost.

The curvy, narrow road slanted upwards, passing through several small villages. The further I went up, the colder it got until I reached an area where mountain fog hid the trees lining the pavement and the nearby houses. The location was beautiful.

The road sign on the right read "Balloune." Perfect! I asked a man standing next to a grocery shop for directions, and he was of great help. He explained how to get there in a typical Lebanese way: "Once you see the first marboro sign (a Marlboro sign), continue straight. Take a right turn at the second marboro sign. After a few kilometers, the factory will be to your left side." I thanked him and followed his accurate directions. Within minutes I was in front of the factory gate.

At first glance, I was impressed that the factory looked similar to any other Lebanese mountain house with its stoned walls and a red-bricked, sloped roof. If it were not for its big red sign, I would never have guessed that someone produced candy there. I had never had a business meeting in such a beautiful place before. It was a fundamental change to the cold and modern buildings I was used to.

At his office, Mr. George, the owner, greeted me kindly. He was in his late 50s, well dressed, and friendly, "Bonjour Mlle, please have a seat." I was praying in my heart that our meeting would be a fruitful one. I had to close a deal by hook or by crook. I just had to.

After the routine introductory procedure, I explained the flavor samples I placed neatly on his coffee table. I clarified that the flavors were produced in Italy and were of excellent quality and tailor-made for the type of candy he produced. I stressed the fact that the colors remained stable even at high cooking temperatures. Then I offered him pre-prepared candy samples. "Mr. George, please try them. The strawberry and orange ones are my absolute favorites."

Despite my enthusiasm, Mr. George did not seem to care at all. I couldn't understand what was going on in his mind because of his oversized thick eyeglasses covering half of his face. I waited a while to give him time to contemplate, but when he didn't reach out for the samples or say a word, I felt I was losing him.

I became pushier, "You see, Mr. George, I do understand that you're used to a different brand, but this Italian company is an award-winning producer, and their prices are much lower than what you're getting right now."

I was talking eagerly, expecting him to collaborate, but again he said nothing. He just gave me a poker face. What did I do wrong? Was my presentation that bad? Why didn't he say anything?

I got restless in my seat, shaking my foot. I also got angry, as I didn't like his attitude. "Mr. George, please tell me, are you interested or not? I'm waiting for your reply."

The silence of his office was only interrupted by distant car horns on the roads nearby. Then it struck me! There was something wrong with Mr. George. He wasn't moving at all. He was frozen in one position, his head tilted downwards and his arm hugging his belly.

"Oh my God, was he dead? How would I know for sure?"

I looked around, trying to get help, but no one was around. I approached him. Was it appropriate to check his pulse? I refrained from trying because, anyways, I didn't know how to read someone's pulse. Of course, I had learned it in Physiology 201, but who could remember such information in extreme panic?

The only thing I remembered was that during that course, one of my classmates was asked to take off his shirt, uncovering his athletic physique to demonstrate how pacemakers work. We all saw his six-pack.

"Focus, Noor," I tried to encourage myself. Softly, I patted him on his shoulder. "Mr. George, can you hear me?" I looked at his eyes, but they were half-closed, so I couldn't really figure out if he was dead, had suffered from a stroke, or was simply sleeping. I remembered that my younger cousin slept with his eyes half-closed. How was this supposed to help me? It wasn't, so, "Focus, focus, Noor!"

I clapped hysterically. Again I patted him on his shoulder, but harder this time. A loud snuffle broke the silence. I jumped backward, screaming. He was sleeping, thank God. He was snoring. At least he was not dead.

I didn't want to be famous for boring my client to death.

I looked around. His office was not that big, but it was filled up with the clutter of too many business files, books, and hideous metal statues. I leaned against the glass of his office window and watched two of the workers unloading a truck with Bon Bon boxes. The red O was too flashy to be missed. As it was stuffy, I opened the window and took a deep breath of fresh air. A cough from behind me made me realize that Mr. George was waking up. He was stretching and yawning in his chair. I didn't want him to feel embarrassed; hence I pretended nothing had happened. I walked back to my seat and continued from where we had stopped, "So, what have you decided regarding the flavors? Would you like to try them?"

"Oh, Ms. Beyrouti, you're still here?" Mr. George's eyes were fighting his urge to sleep. He separated three flavor bottles from the rest and smelled them, nodding, "The aromas are outstanding. You're right." He winked at me.

"I'll make my first order with DanielCo. Please write down what I need." I held my pen and looked at him like a student waiting for a test result.

"I want twenty-five kilograms of each of these three flavors." He adjusted his eyeglasses. "Numbers 215, 302, and 328. I have a new distributor in Africa who asked me for new flavors. You came to see me at the right time."

I was pleased with the positive news.

"It's needless to say that I need your products urgently. How soon can you deliver them?"

"We can send them by air freight. The flavors would be here in your factory within a week or so," I answered.

"Brilliant." He was pleased.

I looked at him with deep appreciation. My hero, my first client! I promised to offer him reasonable prices and went on to put my papers in my folder, preparing to leave.

"Oops, we didn't discuss the payment terms," I murmured. I stood up, holding my purse and file.

"Mr. George, regarding the payment terms, do you prefer cash in advance or L/C?" I asked him.

He didn't answer. Something told me this was a déjà vu. I kneeled and looked at his face. His eyes were half-closed. Yep, he was definitely sleeping again. I took my things and walked out. I couldn't wait any longer. I had other matters to take care of.

*****

I saw through the glass partition that Mr. Nader was sitting behind his desk, talking to Toni. I knocked on the door and entered. "Mr. Nader, guess what? Today I got my first order. I sold 75 kilograms of flavors to a new client, Bon Bon, and Co."

He raised his eyebrows, answering in French, "Vraiment? I'm very impressed, Noor."

Toni instantly gave me an energetic high five. "Excellent news. Congratulations!"

I told Mr. Nader all the details regarding the flavors chosen, the amounts, and the delivery date required.

"Do they want the flavors in 1kg or 25kg packs? You know that packaging size affects price, right?" He stared at me, waiting for my answer.

I had no clue, but I needed to call my client regarding the payment terms anyway, so I promised Mr. Nader to get back to him on that point.

I sat behind my desk and extended my legs. For the first time, I felt I was part of the sales team. A new era had begun.

I grabbed the phone and called Mr. George. "Hello, Mr. George? It's me, Noor from DanielCo. Noor, yes, Noor from DanielCo. We just had a meeting around two hours ago." Finally, he remembered me.

"I wanted to double-check regarding your order: Do you prefer the flavors to be packed in 1kg or 25kg packages?"

"My order? Which order?"

He seemed confused, so I repeated slowly, "Mr. George, today's order for your new distributor in Africa."

"No," he paused for a few moments, then added, "I don't remember making any order with you."

My heart bounced in my chest. "But Mr. George. Don't you remember the order you made right after you woke up?"

Perhaps I shouldn't have mentioned that detail. I felt him fuming through the receiver. "After I woke up? Are you suggesting that I slept during our meeting?"

I tried to calm him down. "Sorry, Mr. George, I didn't mean actual sleep. You were just relaxing your eyes."

"Relaxing my eyes?! Listen, Ms. Beyrouti, and listen carefully: Never call me again, and tell your French supplier ..." I whispered that they were Italian, but he didn't notice and went on yelling, "... their products are not welcome in my factory, not now, not ever!"

BANG. He hung up.

The conversation was over, and so was my first order, just like that. My dreams were shattered. I didn't expect that coming from Mr. Sleepyhead.

Above all, how was I going to explain that to Mr. Nader? I was dizzy and felt like throwing up. My naturally tanned color turned into an ochre shade. I munched on my Lion bar for self-boost.

Eventually, I went to Mr. Nader's office and closed the door behind me. It took me a few seconds to come out with it and blurt it all out. I told him the whole story.

"It seems Mr. George forgot all about his order because he fell asleep during our meeting."

Mr. Nader struggled to hide his smile. "Let's keep this story between us. Shall we? I'm sure his nap had nothing to do with your sales skills."

*****

The next morning, I was still feeling incompetent and useless. My colleagues at the company noticed that I was not as cheerful as usual. I justified it with all the workload I had.

"Noor, come to my office, s'il te plait (*please*)."

I was on guard when I entered Mr. Nader's office, expecting the worst.

"Good morning, Mr. Nader."

Mr. Nader seemed busy and stressed. He had so many files and papers in front of him. "I'm working on our next year's budget, and we need to bring in new customers, mainly for the food and beverage, which is your specialty. As you know, the best way to make good connections in Lebanon is to be personally introduced to potential prospects. That is why I'd like you to start accompanying Salim, Wael, and Toni for a day or more per week to meet their customers. Salim knows every factory in Beirut, Wael is great for Bekaa, and Toni has excellent connections in the north of Lebanon."

"Great idea," I replied. "When should I start?"

"You're starting tomorrow! Tell Toni you'll join him on his trip to the north," Mr. Nader replied.

Chapter Ten - In These Arms

Mood Music:
"In These Arms" by Jon Bon Jovi

Toni had an old, brown metallic BMW 320 with a roof opening. It was a practical car, nothing spectacular really. At that time, only a few of Daniel Co's employees could afford a luxurious car. The most commonly driven cars were second-hand Japanese cars, with strong enough engines to survive steep mountain roads but small enough to do that with minimum fuel consumption. Naturally, the senior managers played in a different league: Mr. Nader drove a brand-new Saab, and Mr. Daniel owned a black, full-option Buick.

It was the day of our "business development on the go."

While Toni focused on getting his car out of the packed parking, I discreetly checked his car. Brochures were scattered everywhere, and many small bottles filled with chemicals were kept randomly on the floor behind his seat. He had a pile of customers' business cards wrapped with a rubber band around the gear, and there was dust all over his car. The mess didn't seem to bother him at all, but for me, a girl obsessed with organizing and cleaning (potential OCD?), it was a nightmare. I fought the urge to clean it all up.

Toni started our conversation, "Did you know that my sister Maria and your sister are good friends? They were classmates in several business courses."

A friend of my sister Riwa? I raised my eyebrows. "No, I had no idea."

In my head, I tried to put a face to the name. I couldn't remember a girl named Maria.

We got stuck in some heavy traffic. Toni turned the music louder, and my body started moving to the beat. I wanted to remain proper and professional, but when a new song started, not just any song, one of my favorite songs, I couldn't stop myself from singing along. At first, I sang timidly, but right in the middle of it, I sang as loud as I could.

I'd please you
I'd tell you that I'd never leave you
and love you 'til the end of time
if you were in these arms tonight

"Thank God I'm half deaf in my right ear," Toni joked.

I burst out laughing. "Sorry, but I'm in love with the Scorpions, and this song is out of this world. It's as if someone with supernatural powers created it. It's just full of passion."

"You're right. It's full of passion." He winked. "But that's not the Scorpions. It's Jon Bon Jovi."

"Are you kidding me?" I asked.

"I assure you it's him," he replied.

"Oh well, such a pity he died so young." I shrugged.

"Jon Bon Jovi hasn't died! He's still very much alive." Toni exclaimed. At that time, we were driving on the highway going up north.

"But I read about his fatal car crash in the newspaper just two days ago," I explained.

"Well, if you say so." He raised one eyebrow, looking totally unconvinced.

There was an awkward silence until he asked me casually, "Have you had breakfast already? There is this amazing place by the sea that makes the best thyme mankoushe ever, and if you love lemonade, their lemonade is out of this world too." He glanced at me, trying to read my facial expressions. He couldn't. I was sending out conflicting signals.

I was totally confused and had no idea what to reply to. But I had to decide quickly.

On the one hand, I had never had breakfast with a cool guy in a restaurant by the sea or anywhere else for that matter. On the other hand, what if someone saw me having breakfast with him in an obscure place? They might tell my dad, or worse, my mom, or even worse, my sister. I would be in big-time trouble.

"Of course, mankoushe would be great. Let's go!" I told him.

As Toni took a side road, my heart started beating fast. I glimpsed at him; he looked decent enough. I had no reason to be worried.

There was a small wooden gate in-between the trees. On top, "Chez Joe" was written in bold blue font. I waited for Toni, expecting him to open the door, but of course, he didn't. "It's not a date!" I reminded myself.

We entered through the wooden door which led to the terrace facing the Mediterranean Sea. The seating area consisted of bamboo chairs with turquoise cushions overlooking the clear blue water, glittering in the morning sun.

I took a long look around. "Wow, this place is fabulous. How come I've never heard of it?"

He gestured with his hand to a round table under the shade. "It's quite popular among the locals here. On the weekend, it's always full."

We sat on two adjacent chairs, watching the sea. "I'm actually from this area," he said, nodding with his head towards the north. "I'm from a village called Bahra; my dad used to bring us here when we were little."

A wave washed the rocky shore, and I felt tiny water drops on my face. Toni signaled to a waiter who directly came to our table. He ordered two mankoushe and two lemonades for us.

"Right away," the waiter said.

A few miles away, a red fishing boat was swinging slowly back and forth on the distant calm water.

"It's such an amazing atmosphere, the air is so fresh, and the water is so clean and clear, I can almost see the bottom. Can we swim here? I mean not now, I mean not us, someone, can someone swim here and not now?"

Toni giggled. He must have felt my tension. "Someone? Anyone? Yes, for sure, *someone* can swim here. It's an open beach. You know what? We can go swimming here one day. Especially on Saturday afternoons, it's usually packed. You'll love it."

I blushed and ignored his proposal. "Are you here every Saturday?" I asked him.

"No, not really. I prefer to swim at my village's beach, it's similar to this one in terms of scenery and water cleanliness, but it's a few minutes away by car from my home. I go snorkeling during the weekend and even on weekdays, looking for sea urchins and crabs."

"Crabs!" I shrieked, "I'm so scared of crabs. When I was a kid, I went swimming with friends on a rocky beach similar to this one. By the end of the day, when I went to the chalet to change, can you imagine what I found?"

He shook his head. "No, I can't even imagine."

"I found crab legs stuck on the sole of my sports shoes."

"Wait, why were you wearing shoes in the water?" He was confused.

"As a safety measure, of course, you never know what's down there."

"Safety measure? Snorkeling with you must be a lot of fun." He shook his head.

Breakfast was served, and Toni was right about it. It was one of the best mankoushe I'd ever had before. Toni and I resumed our conversation only after our plates were empty except for a few thyme leaves.

"Have you always been in sales of chemicals and ingredients?" I asked him.

"No, not really. I used to be a medical rep for a few years. But I'm so glad I made this move; I'm happier here and making much more money."

"More money? My salary here is barely enough for my basic needs." I was puzzled.

"Of course, mine too, but I don't depend on my salary or sales commissions. Most of my income is coming from my side business," he explained.

"Side business? What side business?" I asked in surprise.

"You didn't know?! We all have our side businesses. Otherwise, how could anyone survive with such low salaries?" He took off his aviator shades and listed the side businesses of each of our colleagues.

Toni himself bought chemicals from DanielCo under a different name and then sold them, at a higher profit margin, to small factories. Then there was Salim, our super-smart colleague, who produced chemical raw materials in his kitchen, which were cheaper than those sourced by DanielCo from German suppliers. And finally, Anwar had a skin and hair care line on the side, producing hair masks and face-bleaching creams.

"Seriously? All of you? I had no idea."

At that moment, Toni's mobile phone rang, and he had a tense discussion with one of his clients. He walked back and forth until finally, he seemed more relaxed and leaned back on the wall next to me. I couldn't hear what he was saying, but I heard him laughing from time to time, which made me smile. He stood tall, holding with one hand his Nokia mobile, which covered most of his profile. His goldish summer tan covered his arms, face, and neck. I felt like I was in the middle of an old romantic Egyptian movie, in which he would naturally be Hussein Fahmy, and I would be the girl fascinated by him.

The phone call had a positive outcome: The customer accepted Toni's offer and agreed to buy triple the quantity of pool chlorine he had initially requested. Toni explained that the international supply of chlorine was going down, and there was a global shortage. This was new information for me. No one had mentioned that in our weekly discussions.

The rest of the day was full of meetings and lots of private chit-chats. Within a few hours, I got to know a lot about Toni: He was a business graduate, five years older than me, and he lived with his family, which included his dad, mom, grandparents, sister, and brother. He liked to eat lasagna and burgers. He had been single for more than a year and thought I was cute!

"What do you mean exactly?" I asked him, but he didn't reply. He just laughed.

*****

I went home with a smile on my face. I felt different, and I couldn't explain why. I didn't want to talk about my elated happiness with anyone. It was my very own secret. Luckily, no one was at home, as my parents had gone to visit my uncle, and Riwa was at the movies with her friends. So I started watching a love-hate Mexican series dubbed in Arabic.

The phone rang, and I answered anxiously, hoping it would be Toni miraculously.

"Good evening." I heard a man's voice.

"Hello, who is this?" I answered, still having hope.

"I'm Riyad." I sighed. In a deep voice, he continued, "How are you doing, my dear?"

"Yeah, right, another prank caller!" I thought.

I was used to these calls. Random callers, bored people with no life, having nothing better to do besides disturbing others.

Me: "I'm fine, thanks. How can I help you, Riyad?"

Riyad: "Is your dad at home?"

Me: "And why are you asking me about my dad, Riyad?"

Riyad: "I need to talk to him."

Me: (in a cynical tone) "Oh, you need to talk to him, of course. And what are you planning to tell him, if I may ask?"

Riyad: (in a serious tone) "Who am I talking to? Noor or Riwa?"

Oops! I was busted. He was not a prank caller. He was one of dad's acquaintances. "Ahh! It's Riwa." I lied.

"So sorry, I didn't recognize your voice. My dad is out, but I will surely tell him you called."

Shoot! How was I going to explain that to Dad?

*****

A loud discussion woke me up. We hardly fought at our house, so I naturally got worried. I quietly opened my bedroom door, still dressed in my Dalmatian pajamas, and sneaked out into the TV room. My hair's curls went upwards as they usually did after a long sleep. Mom was drinking her Turkish coffee and smoking two cigarettes simultaneously. Uh oh, the last time I had seen her smoking two cigarettes in parallel was when we had been obliged to leave our apartment during one of the civil war battles. My dad had found us a safer place to stay, assuring us that it was only a matter of a few weeks before we could get back to our home. Thankfully, our neighbors in the new building were friendly, and I became good friends with their kids because I ended up celebrating three consecutive birthdays there.

Shaking her leg, Mom kept on repeating the same sentence, "But that was over 40 years ago; you don't know how to do it anymore."

Dad, dressed in his blue printed pajamas and holding his full bent pipe in his hand, assured her, "It's not rocket science. Of course, I know how to do it."

"Good morning, Mom, good morning, Dad." I gave them my routine cheek kisses. "What are you discussing so early? You woke me up."

Mom retorted, "You should have been awake hours ago. It's almost 9:00 am. The day is gone." It was pointless to argue with her.

"Your mom is totally against me. She doesn't believe that I can refurbish our oak-wood bedroom closets." Dad explained.

"But he doesn't know!" Mom replied.

Dad fixed his eyeglasses. "I know very well! I learned how to do it in high school."

Mom looked at me while gesturing at him. "You heard what he just said in his own words? Back in high school! That was 40 years ago! He's going to ruin the closets. I know that deep within my heart."

I had to interfere. "What's wrong with those closets anyway?"

"Exactly! There's nothing wrong with them," she said and looked at Dad triumphantly. "See? Even your beloved daughter thinks they're OK."

Dad shook his head. "The closets' color is fading, and the wood is dry; it needs to hydrate. I have to fix them."

Mom stood up and announced in her dramatic voice, "I give up; this is a byzantine discussion." She pointed her finger at him, and with an eagle look, she announced, "Fine by me, you refurbish them, you do whatever you want, but this is totally your responsibility. I'm not going to be part of this."

She grabbed her ashtray and rushed to the kitchen. Uh oh, I knew where this was leading. If my mom was not going to help, it meant that either Riwa or I would have to do the refurbishing. I loved my dad, but he wasn't a DIY kind of guy. He was a typical manager who liked to delegate. I needed a scapegoat.

"Dad, … I'm sorry I can't help you today. I promised Blossom that we'd go to the beach. Sorry, but Riwa should be free today."

He nodded. "Good idea! I'll refurbish the closets with your sister then."

Dad grabbed one of the jazz mixtapes he had personally recorded and put it on his stereo. As I went to my bedroom to get ready for the beach, he turned the volume up. I blushed. The song playing was "Sexual Healing," his favorite.

Chapter Eleven - Balash Tebousni

Mood Music:
"Balash Tebousni"
by Mohamad Abd El Wahab

Blossom's dad was a reputed and wealthy businessman. She lived with her family in a luxurious building facing the seaside in one of Beirut's fanciest areas. Their huge apartment was tastefully decorated with art pieces, ancient carpets, and collectors' items from all around the world. They had not one but two drivers and several maids for domestic help. When I first met her during our sophomore year, it didn't cross my mind that someone as humble as her was raised in such a privileged environment.

The more I got to know her, the more I didn't understand her. I never understood why she wouldn't allow her dad to pay for her master's degree. She worked her socks off to secure her tuition while all she needed to do was ask him.

I honked at the car in front of me. "Just go, for God's sake! What kind of a driver is this guy? Eating his sandwich and checking out girls at the same time!"

I also wondered why Blossom had stopped eating beef and chicken. One day, out of the blue, she announced, "No more burgers, no more kibbe for me! I'm a vegetarian now."

"Why?! What are we supposed to eat when we go out? Only hummus?" I complained.

Eventually, I found a loophole in the vegetarian cause, which she kept on defending. "Aha! So, answer me this: how come you eat eggs but no chicken? Why is it ok eat the baby but not the mother?"

I thought I would challenge her with my question, but she just rolled her eyes and said, "Noor, surely I do! Because eggs which we eat aren't fertilized." I didn't get that. What did sex have to do with any of this?

I double-parked my car in front of the entrance to her building, blocking the way of a brand-new Cadillac, and spoke to someone on the interphone, "Could you tell Blossom that I'm waiting for her to come down? It's Noor."

Blossom came down a few minutes later with a big smile as usual. "Good morning, how are you? Good?" we both said simultaneously, kissing each other on the cheeks three times as is Lebanese tradition.

"So, are you excited to go to the beach?" I asked her. Blossom said she was over the moon. She hadn't been to the beach for ages. The reason for that was Blossom's father. He had imposed the rule on his daughters that they weren't allowed to wear swimsuits in public. Initially, that was not a big problem for the girls because their dad owned a villa with a pool, so they could swim as much as they wanted. But when he sold his villa and they moved to an apartment a few years ago, Blossom was particularly devastated. She was an excellent swimmer and loved being in the water.

Luckily, I overheard a woman at the hairdresser talking about a women-only beach club that had opened in the city. Although it had been open to the public for more than a year,

I hadn't heard about it before. I suggested to Blossom that we check it out.

The ladies' club was a few minutes by car from her home. I parked on the corniche, and we went into the club. My first reaction was, "What the ...!"

In the lobby, there was greenish-black mold all over the ceiling. "Oops, be careful," Blossom warned me as she almost slipped. "The floors are wet." An overly suntanned woman sat behind the reception desk. She checked us out from head to toe. "Two tickets, right?"

"Yes," I said.

She asked us to open our beach bags, and she looked inside. Then she searched for any food or drinks. "You know you aren't allowed to bring along any food or drinks, right? I need to keep this." She took out my aluminum-wrapped sandwich.

"Ohh! But I made that one. It's butter and apricot jam." She wasn't impressed. I felt as if we were going into a women's prison rather than a club.

We went up the stairs which led to the main terrace. The brightness of the place was overwhelming. It was too sunny, and the white walls, which reflected the sunlight, made it even brighter. I put on my brand-new Vogue shades, looking overly dressed for such a modest place. As I was used to eating my breakfast first thing in the morning, I was pretty hungry, so I asked a lady in a black one-piece swimsuit and jeans shorts for the way to the restaurant.

"It's over there." She pointed to a shabby kiosk with a large window.

It didn't look hygienic at all. The closer we got to the kiosk, the worse the smell got.

I grimaced. "I don't think I can eat there. I have a sensitive stomach."

Blossom said hesitantly, "Let's try. We don't seem to have another choice."

"May we have two chocolate croissants, please?" I asked the lady in the kiosk.

She replied with a strong accent, "Habibti, we don't have kerwason (that's how she pronounced it). We only have thyme mankoushe. Do you want two?" I leaned forward, removed my shades, and looked through the window. Their mankoushe had a yellowish color, soaked in oil, and were definitely not freshly baked. From a food technologist's perspective, aka me, those mankoushe had been made at least one or two days ago.

I gave the lady a fake smile, "Thank you, no need. Do you have digestive biscuits, by any chance?"

"Die what?" The lady put her hand behind her ear and came closer. Blossom pulled me back and thanked the lady.

Blossom whispered as we walked away, "Are you serious? How would you expect this shop to have digestive biscuits?" She frowned. "What would have been your next question? Do you have Oreos?" Indeed that would have been my next question.

"I wish I'd hidden my yummy sandwich so the lady at the reception had never found it. "My tummy keeps on growling." I sighed.

We quickly found two adjacent white plastic sun loungers facing the sea. I neatly placed my towel on one of them, took off my beach dress, and laid down in my swimsuit. Blossom did the same. The ladies' club was located on a small cliff overlooking one of Beirut's many mixed beaches.

"That's funny! I thought the club was in a more secluded area," I said as I applied sun cream to my face. Blossom sat up and checked.

"You're right! This is absolutely ridiculous." She pointed at the beachside. "Look at those girls talking to the men on their jet skis!"

I grabbed a magazine, put on my big white straw hat, and shrugged. "Oh well! That's their choice." I started reading while Blossom fell asleep right away. How could she sleep with the loud dance music around? I had no idea. Since she lived in a quiet neighborhood, I would have imagined that even a bit of noise would disturb her. As for me, I was lucky enough to live on a street where being quiet was unheard of.

Noise pollution was caused by almost every resident on our street, including my neighbor's rooster and my sister. Riwa insisted on playing a specific part of a piano piece she was composing – tarara tarara tararaaa – over and over again. One evening, she was forced to stop abruptly as one of our neighbors lost her mind and shouted her head off. "I can't take it anymore. I just can't take this music anymore." Her husband succeeded in soothing her, but it took some time for the atmosphere to cool down. Riwa and I turned off our salon's lights and sat in total darkness, pretending it hadn't been Riwa.

Another example of how our neighborhood was alive 24/7 was my friend Jana's father, one floor down. He was a perfect gentleman, totally in love with his wife for more than 30 years, and he was not shy of showing it publicly (not very typical at that time).

He always gave her compliments. "Look at my wife," he used to tell me, "isn't she the most beautiful woman in the world?" Her eyes started glittering whenever she heard him say that and looked away shyly.

When they were both at home, he sang Mohamad Abd El Wahab's love songs to her, which was so sweet. He was also protective and made sure he was always there for her. Whenever she came back from work, he waited for her on their 6th-floor balcony and helped her park her car. "Go back, go back, stop, a bit to the right, now a bit to the left." He gave his instructions in such a loud voice that it was impossible to have a nap at this time of day.

Taunt Warde, the lady who also lived on the 6th floor but in the opposite building, thought it was normal to air her dirty laundry. She had no issue discussing social events, her daughters-in-law, and grocery shopping from one balcony to another.

La crème de la crème was, however, the gypsy lady who insisted on selling Zaatar herbs (thyme) at 6:00 in the morning (including weekends), carrying the herbs on her back and chanting, "Zaatar! Zaatar! Who wants to buy Zaatar from me?"

Blossom moved, starting to wake up. She checked the time. "Ummm, nice, one hour of peaceful sleep. Shall we go to the pool? It's getting hot. I don't want to get sunburned."

I put down my magazine and answered, "Good point, let's go."

The pool didn't look tempting in any way. Was it the mix of sun tanning oil and sun cream that turned the water milky? I couldn't figure it out. Blossom's eyes bulged as she pointed at the water. "I'm not going to swim in here."

The ladies were doing all sorts of things around the pool, from belly dancing to playing cards and smoking Hubble bubbles.

Blossom nudged me. "Look at that woman in the green swimsuit." She had a mirror in one hand and a pair of tweezers in the other.

"Is she seriously fixing her eyebrows in front of everyone?"

We were both shocked. Then I had a closer look at her. I heard one of the ladies asking, "Warde, would you like another cup of Turkish coffee?"

"You know me. I never say no to coffee!" She laughed heartily.

Yep, that was my neighbor, Taunt Warde. I could recognize that voice in a million. I pulled my hat down to hide my face. We walked back to our seats, totally in denial.

"I thought it was going to be an elegant, relaxing place. How wrong I was!" Blossom complained. "I wish we'd never come here! It was a total waste of time." She threw her stuff back in her beach bag, obviously disappointed. I didn't contradict her as I felt the same.

When we drove back to her house, I suggested going to an ordinary mixed beach. "Ocean Dew is *the* 'in' place nowadays. If we can make it there by 8:00 am, I promise you we'll arrive before the crowd. Should we try it one day?"

Blossom was not easily convinced. "Umm, I'm not sure. You know me, I don't go to mixed beaches."

"But it'll be empty in the morning, and it's big and clean. You'll love it. Trust me!" Finally, she agreed.

*****

A fresh, familiar smell filled up the air of our apartment. It was so intense that I couldn't stop coughing.

"Hello, I'm back. Anybody home?" I announced as I walked towards the bedrooms.

Riwa came out of my parents' room, holding a paintbrush. She threw an angry look at me. "You cheeky, cheeky sister. You went to the beach and left me here, alone, to help dad with his closet project!"

I lifted my eyebrows. "Well, it was only fair, considering that last time I had to saw wood to make a balcony door for your bedroom. We're in the 20th century! Who saws wood nowadays?!"

I entered my room, and she followed me. "You call that sawing? You made an asymmetrical door that doesn't even close properly. Whenever it rains, water comes in!" She crossed her arms, sitting on the leather chair in front of my bed.

"Hey! I just followed your dad's directions, and if it's any consolation for you, it wasn't a great outing anyway." I lowered my voice. "I saw Taunt Warde in her swimsuit, removing her facial hair."

Riwa chortled. "Now that's what I call karma."

I sniffed. "By the way, what's that weird smell?" Riwa headed toward my parents' room and asked me to follow her. "Come and look for yourself."

It was a total mess. There were many small plastic bottles filled with brownish liquids and brushes everywhere. The shiny closet doors were wide open, and my parents' clothes were scattered all over the beds.

"We used olive oil. We tried different years of production, and after thorough experimentation, Dad decided to use this year's edition of extra virgin olive oil."

I was impressed. The closets looked brand new. "I didn't expect this result. Honestly, you make such a good team. So, Riwa, Dad's next DIY project is surely yours."

*****

Chapter Twelve - Oudak Rannan

Mood Music:
"Oudak Rannan" by Fairouz

"Somebody's looking smashing today!" Ruba's small, round eyes were fixed on me.

"Something about you looks different. Not your hair. What is it?" She kept on staring at me, and suddenly her face relaxed, nodding, "I know it's your face, you're tanned, and your clothes! Why are you wearing a skirt? You never wear a skirt!"

"I sometimes do," I insisted. Ruba sat across from my desk, waiting for me to continue. I couldn't wipe the smile off my face. It was funny how people could get nosy for such small things: tan, no tan, a skirt, a pair of pants, who cares?!

I pointed at my face and said, "This is the beach effect, and as for this old skirt, well, no specific reason. I just felt like I needed a change."

I didn't say that I made an effort to look more stylish since I was going to spend the day with Toni – for business reasons, of course.

Actually, both my t-shirt and my long jersey skirt belonged to my neighbor Jana. She had always been the stylish one of us. In college, we had agreed to have an open-closet policy, which meant we could borrow whatever we liked from each other's closets, including our parents' clothes and accessories. My favorite piece was her dad's leather biker jacket; I loved wearing it together with jeans on sunny winter days. Her favorite piece was my mom's green suede jacket. I liked it on her too, as it brought out the green color of her eyes. She also liked our salon's crystal chandeliers, which I promised to give her when I would inherit them one day.

As per Mr. Nader's plan, I was supposed to join Toni for a week, starting from Monday. But Toni, whom I longed to see, didn't show up on Monday. Certainly, I was disappointed, but Mr. Nader explained that he had a private matter to attend to. I hoped he would be back on Tuesday.

On Tuesday morning, around 10 o'clock, we were in the car heading to Jbeil (Byblos), the ancient city where the Phoenicians had invented the alphabet a long time ago. It didn't take me long to notice that Toni was not acting like his usual self. He barely talked, and he kept on clenching his jaws. When Fairouz's song "Nasam Alayna El Hawa" played on the radio, and I joyfully sang and snapped my fingers, he directly changed the music to soft oldies. I asked him if everything was ok. He just nodded. Fine! I decided to give him his space and drifted away in my thoughts. On the highway, almost halfway to Jbeil, Toni slowed down next to an awful car wreckage. One of the cars was turned upside down, and the other was destroyed beyond repair.

"Oh my God! Did you see that?" I asked. "What a horrible accident. Poor guys, I hope no one got seriously hurt."

Toni was enormously disturbed. His voice was trembling, and it seemed as if he was going to cry.

"Two people died." He paused for a few seconds, then added, "One of them was my best friend, Walid. He was in that white car that rolled over."

"Ah …" I didn't say a word.

A few minutes later, I dared to ask, "Is that why you didn't come to work yesterday?"

"Yeah, I was with his family," he mumbled.

He took a tissue and wiped his nose, then leaned forward towards the glove compartment and grabbed a Kodak envelope. "Look, that's him in the pictures. We were together on the day when he had his pictures taken."

I looked closely at Walid's pictures. He was in his 20s and had a strikingly warm smile.

"How did it happen? The accident, I mean."

He exhaled deeply, trying not to break down. "Walid was racing with one of his friends after a party; the other guy was drunk, he lost control and boom. They both died instantly. A witness told the police what had happened."

"His poor parents …," I murmured.

"Noor?" he asked me softly, "Do you mind if we pull over for a bit? I need some fresh air."

"Of course not." I nodded.

He took a side road and parked next to a deserted meadow. We got out of the car. It was a sunny day with blue skies, and only a few clouds were scattered here and there. As he walked in front of me, I heard his slow footsteps on the rocky street.

I sat on a rock along the side, watching him. I could feel his grief. He stood tall, turning his back to me, but I saw that he was discreetly wiping his tears. I watched him with uncertainty, not knowing what to say or do. I was not talented at showing affection or giving support. Ultimately, he sat down on a rock close to me and opened up about Walid.

"We were friends since we were eight years old. We went to the same school, we were both volunteers for the Red Cross, and during the weekends, we were scuba diving buddies. We were practically inseparable."

We ended up talking for more than an hour. He talked and talked while I mostly listened.

*****

I arrived home pale, breathless, and confused. It was not only because of Walid's car crash but also due to another power cut. I was forced to climb seven flights of stairs to reach our apartment.

"Hey." My mother kissed me quickly and went on circuiting around the house as she always did when she was busy. The smoke of her cigarette followed her as a loyal companion.

"Mom?" I followed her trail. "What's for dinner? I peeked in the kitchen, but nothing was prepared except for white rice.

She answered without slowing down, "I'm not done yet. I'm short of coriander and garlic. Wait, I'll write a grocery list for you to give to Abdo."

Abdo was the owner of the minimarket right underneath us. Luckily, I didn't have to go back down the stairs. Lebanese people, being creative as they are, have invented the best delivery system ever. It is personal, practical, fast, and free. We call it the "basket."

The "basket" can be anything from a woven basket to a plastic bucket − anything big enough to be filled with groceries and tied to a long rope. The rope must be long enough to reach the minimarket down on the street. The shopkeeper then fills the "basket" up with the required items, it is pulled up again, and voila, the shopping is done.

In the 1990s, "artificial intelligence" was not yet common. We depended solely on human intelligence, and people were labeled as either smart or dumb. There was no middle way.

Hisham, my childhood friend, was smart, but his cousin was on the other side of the spectrum.

Hisham lent his cousin a sports t-shirt for a football match. Two weeks later, when my friend asked for his t-shirt back, his cousin asked him to pass by his place to pick it up.

He assured Hisham, "If the power is cut, don't bother to come up to our place. I'll put the t-shirt in the "basket" and let it down." His cousin had a plastic bucket, a big red one attached to a rope.

In the evening, Hisham went to get his t-shirt back. There was a power cut as expected, so the elevator was off. Hisham stood on the street and asked his cousin for the t-shirt.

His cousin yelled from the balcony, "Here it comes." But instead of letting the "basket" slowly down from the balcony as he was supposed to do, he threw it directly down to the street. Within seconds, the basket landed on Hisham's head, resulting in a severe cut, excessive blood loss, and possibly a minor concussion.

"Hurry up. What are you waiting for?" Mom asked me as I stood on my bedroom's balcony reading her list: Wella shampoo, Marlboro cigarettes, Arabic bread, khebez frangi (literally meaning "foreign bread"; this is what we call sandwich bread), coriander, and, of course, garlic.

I put the shopping list in our grocery basket and let it down to Abdo's minimarket. Abdo, who was around 150kg and hardly ever moved from his ragged armchair, gestured at one of his teenage workers to get to work. The kid ran to my basket, grabbed my mom's list, and started filling it up. Finally, I slowly pulled it up again, making sure it didn't hit one of our neighbors' heads as they peeked from their balconies.

When Mom later checked the items in the basket, she frowned. "What is this supposed to be?"

She held the shampoo bottle in her hand, staring at the label. "No, this is not the Wella shampoo that I normally buy. The label is completely different! I've bought this shampoo for more than 15 years, and the label never looked like this before." She drew heavily on her cigarette. "Give it back to him. This is fake!"

"Ok, Mom." I ran to the balcony again, turned over Abdo's invoice, and wrote on its back: This is not Wella shampoo. It is fake, and we don't want it. Then I did the basket procedure once again. Abdo sent one of his boys to our apartment to explain that the manufacturing company had changed the label, but we didn't believe him. We insisted on returning the bottle of shampoo.

*****

Chapter Thirteen - I Swear

Mood Music:
"I Swear" by All-4-One

It was 7:30 am, and the whole family was awake. Dad shaved, took a shower, changed, and asked us to join him in the TV room. Mom was sitting beside him, listening to the news on the radio. The news was as gloomy as ever: repetitive power cuts, pollution in our rivers, and stories of how stray bullets killed yet another innocent person – typical depressing reality.

Dad told Riwa, "I need you for a few minutes. We need to talk."

Riwa and I exchanged glances. Dad's serious tone suggested that there was a problem. Mom turned off the radio and asked, "What is it?"

"Yesterday, I had a special visitor, a gentleman you all know well, my friend, Riyad. He asked me for Riwa's hand in marriage."

I cracked up laughing. "Is this a joke?"

Dad was not joking. My tonsils were swelling, and I couldn't swallow properly.

"Riwa, he told me you had a conversation with him on the phone the other day."

Riwa denied it in surprise. I realized just then that this surprise marriage proposal must have much to do with our phone conversation the other day.

Riwa's face turned red. "Dad, without giving it a second thought, my answer is definitely no. He's not the right person for me. His job is a mystery to us, he's a mystery to us, and we hardly know anything about this man, plus he's way older than me."

Dad nodded. "True, true, this is my opinion as well, but it's my obligation to ask you, and it's up to you to decide."

Riwa took me aside and gave me a big lecture in her bedroom. "In a very short time, you've managed to embarrass me in a restaurant, you took the liberty to sign me up for Dad's DIY project, and now this. You'd better stop, Noor, or else you'll be in big-time trouble."

"Ok, ok!" I promised not to bother her anymore.

*****

A week later, at the office, Toni was back to his old giggly self. He asked me if I would join him for lunch because there was something important he wanted to tell me. I was hesitant because, from my experience, whenever a guy declared, "I'd like to tell you something," it was always bad news. It usually meant that this guy liked you. That was not the bad part of it, but rather what came after. I had to say no because I was never ready. How could I say no and not hurt others? That was my dilemma. Facing a conflict and saying no have never been my greatest strengths.

My parents never ceased to remind me of the charming young guy I had met at a family wedding. He was a distant cousin studying architecture abroad. My mom knew his parents well and thought highly of them. After visiting our home a few times and getting to know me better, he officially proposed. He was 24 years old, but I was only 16, and I had big dreams, which didn't include marriage. So, I asked my parents to tell him no.

The following summer, he visited us without prior notice. My parents were thrilled as they considered him the perfect catch. After lunch, my parents left us alone in the salon to talk. He tried to open our topic, but the moment he said, "Noor, I …" I panicked, and instead of telling him how I felt, I offered him our world atlas to read and left the room. Out of the thousands of books my parents had, I chose the world atlas! For five consecutive summers, the same story repeated itself. He would visit us and have lunch with my family. The moment we were left alone, and he would open our topic, I would panic, give him the world atlas and leave the room. I even ensured a new atlas edition following the USSR's dissolution. My parents eventually had to interfere and explain the situation to him.

I was unable to decline Toni's invitation. I ended up meeting him at an Italian restaurant next to our office. After ordering pasta, Toni opened up, "Your support the other day when I was down, well, you were just so helpful. You were the only one who pulled me up when I was down."

He looked straight into my eyes. "I'm not sure how to begin, but Noor, I can't stop thinking of you. The things you say, the way you make me laugh, I …"

"Oh-oh!" The tricky part was about to start. I needed to hide. I needed to be in my cocoon. I closed my eyes, trying to escape.

Toni went on, "I'd like to get to know you more. How do you feel about all this?"

I was terrified. This was not because Toni was not a nice, calm, kind, generous, funny, and handsome guy. He was all that. And it wasn't because we didn't click – we did. I was just not ready. I froze.

"Noor, I know you've never been in a relationship before, and I know you always say you aren't ready, but we'll take it one step at a time. You don't have to worry."

As if he was reading my mind. I started to slowly feel less stressed and reluctantly stepped out of my virtual cocoon. In the end, he invited me to continue our conversation over dinner the next day.

*****

I was turning in bed, unable to sleep, too nervous and confused after my conversation with Toni. For the first time in my life, I had agreed to go on a date. It was not like I didn't have any feelings. Of course, I had feelings, I wanted to be in love one day and get married and have children, but somehow I was not sure how to start. I had no idea how to behave in a relationship. Love had no system. I needed a system.

I woke up earlier than usual, feeling super excited to be going on my first official date, set to be right after work. I had a lot of tedious administrative work to take care of; hence I decided to stay at the office for the day. I felt as if the clock's hands were not moving at all. I went to the canteen, had breakfast, then had a snack, then went there again, had lunch, and then had another snack. In between all the meals, I drank several mugs of hot chocolate, but the day was still barely halfway through.

Toni was not back at the office as he had several meetings to attend with Mr. Nader. By the time my other colleagues were returning from their market visits, I had only one more hour to wait. But that one hour felt like forever. What made it worse was that Toni didn't call or leave me a message. I started wondering if we would go out for dinner after all. The clock on the wall was finally showing 5:30 pm, and everyone started packing their things, getting ready to leave. I grabbed my purse and left too.

It was quite bright outside. The sun wasn't going to set for another two hours, as was always the case in the summertime. Toni was nowhere to be seen.

I sighed as I walked toward my car. I got stood up on my first date!

I lowered my head, fighting the tears that were ready to burst out. "I should have declined his invitation right away. I'm such a fool."

"Hi, Noor. What took you so long?" I turned to the right; it was Toni standing next to my car. Toni's hazel eyes were laughing. "I missed you today. It was boring without you." I couldn't hide my smile. His face suddenly wrinkled when he remembered something, "What was wrong with Mr. Nader today? He didn't leave me for one second. I couldn't manage to call you. So, my car or yours?"

"My car," I stated and climbed into the driver's seat. I placed the key in the ignition and turned it, but my blue Nissan didn't crank at all. I tried to start the car several times, but it was useless.

"Your battery is dead." Toni got out of my car and slammed the door. "Let's take my car. We'll fix your car later," he said, tapping on his wristwatch.

"No, wait, I can fix this," I replied.

The countless times I had watched my mechanic fixing cars had qualified me as a car mechanic. I opened the hood, took off my jacket, and threw it on the back seat. After that, I took a long look at the battery.

"Mmmm, same old problem. All I need is a stone." I walked around my car in circles, searching for a suitable stone. I kneeled and checked under my car. Perfect.

I grabbed a medium-sized stone and rubbed the soil off it. This should work.

Toni watched me, leaning back on a pine tree. I checked my car's battery and the cables connected to it, then repetitively hit the battery with the stone, using all my strength.

Bang! Bang! Bang! Two soldiers in their green camouflage uniforms came running from the nearby military base.

"What's the problem here?" one of the soldiers asked.

"Respect!" Toni said and stood next to them. "It's her battery. She said that she could fix it all by herself."

I took a glance at my live audience. They were doubtful of my mechanical skills, trying hard to hide their snickering. My banging got louder and louder. I leaned closer to the battery and made sure all the cables were connected tightly. The men watching me were all eyes. I automatically stretched my top to cover myself and closed the hood.

"God, please let it start; please don't let me be embarrassed in front of them," I murmured and turned the key slowly.

"Yes! Yes!" A big smile flashed over my face as I saw the soldiers going back to their base in disappointment. Toni sat in the car, grinning. "Not bad, not bad at all!"

*****

The crepe restaurant Toni had chosen was quite popular. I hadn't been there before, but I had heard a lot of positive reviews about it. I was excited to be on an actual date, but at the same time, I was also worried if I was doing the right thing. I looked up at the enormous white statue of Saint Mary facing the Mediterranean Sea. Was she staring at me? I got shivers all over.

"I don't understand this. There's a lot of space right here." I pointed my finger at all the empty parking spaces in front of the restaurant.

"Why did your colleague park my car in the back?" I asked the valet.

He answered sheepishly, "We're sorry, Miss, but we only park the fancy cars in the front." It was totally uncalled for.

The restaurant was more beautiful than I had ever imagined. It was a breathtaking Lebanese villa, beautifully designed and uniquely decorated with Lebanese artisan craftwork and pottery. When Toni gave his name to the lady at the reception, she welcomed us in and automatically escorted us to our table. I looked at my reflection in a huge mirror that was hung on the wall. I looked tense but amicable. My sleeveless, red, V-necked top and white pants gave my body a nice, curvy shape and showed off my bronze tan. My make-up was hardly noticeable, but my large golden earrings were too obvious to miss. I confidently passed the occupied tables, staring at the stylish clientele — and I don't mean only the girls. Everyone was fashionable, girls, guys, and older couples. Everyone looked just glamorous.

Toni softly put his hand on my back as he walked behind me. When we reached our table, he pulled my chair back like a perfect gentleman. I was impressed not only by his etiquette but by the whole atmosphere. Our round table overlooked the sea, and slowly we watched the sun go down while listening to French oldies.

I took a look at the menu and instantly chose the savory crepe filled with creamy chicken, while Toni decided on the chef's signature dish: Steak au Poivre (*pepper steak*)served with Pommes Frites (*french fries*).

"I'm glad you chose this place. It's so beautiful in here."

"I'm glad you like it." Toni's eyes sparkled.

Like it? I was dazzled – beyond cloud nine, to be precise.

The service was quick, and our food came in no time, "Bon appétit." Toni smiled. "I could get used to this," I thought to myself.

Was it the ambiance, the delicious crepe, or his charm that helped me make my decision? Whatever it was, I made up my mind even before getting to the dessert.

"Toni, I thought about what you told me yesterday."

He nodded, being all ears. "And I'm ready to give it a try." I could feel my face turning all red.

Toni laughed, "Great ..." But I didn't let him continue his sentence. I had more to say. "There's only one condition: Our relationship has to be purely emotional, no physical contact, like the puritans, so you can write me poems, send me flowers, and so on."

He couldn't stop laughing; then, he softly held my hand despite my resistance. "Shhh, shh, relax, don't worry now. I'm not going to hurt you; I'm just holding your hand. Don't be scared."

I was agitated, and my jaw hurt. I felt his finger gently caressing my hand as I tried hard to escape his piercing eyes.

In the light of the lantern, I took a long glance at his face. For the first time, I noticed his perfectly arched eyebrows, wide hazel eyes, and tiny lips. His features were sharp and straight, quite the opposite of my round features. He was like a young Clint Eastwood.

We talked a lot that evening, and he shared his innermost dreams with me. His ultimate wish was to sell one of his family's properties and live off the bank interest. He was also planning to retire within a few years to spend the rest of his life swimming and fishing. I thought it was a ridiculous plan, but I didn't mind.

Toni drove my car while I looked up at the starry sky, contemplating. I was happy. I had never imagined that dating would be so wonderful. The song that was playing on the radio was "I Swear" by All-4-one. "From now on, let this be our song." He grinned, showing a charming dimple under his eye.

Chapter Fourteen - Amarain

Mood Music:
"Amarain" by Amr Diab

Riwa and I went down one floor to visit Jana and Haya, our neighbors and childhood friends. Year after year, we kept our tradition of having breakfast together on weekends, public holidays, strikes, 11and governmental mourning, basically whenever we had a free morning. I rang the bell, and Taunt Sana opened the door. "Good morning, Taunt." Her face brightened as it always did whenever she saw us. "They're both in the TV room. Hurry up before the food gets cold."

As I walked along the corridor, she added, "Ah, before I forget, please tell your mom today it's our street's turn for water supply."

"Thanks, I'll remember it."

Public water supply was scarce, so the government had set up a weekly schedule for supplying the different Lebanese districts. When the day of the water supply came up, our building turned into a noisy piazza. All the neighbors called each other from their windows to make sure that everyone knew. When our two water tanks were full, my mom filled up the 20 glass gallons she had bought to have some extra water reserve.

Jana and Haya were each lying on a sofa watching TV. The table in front of them was already set. There were freshly baked manakish, both thyme, and cheese flavored, a platter of foul (fava beans), croissants, and a platter of precut tomatoes and cucumbers. Of course, there was the obligatory tea kettle and juice as well.

After exchanging hugs and kisses, we started chit-chatting right away. It was amazing how quickly news could stack up in just a few days.

I waited for Taunt Sana to finally leave the room to break my latest news. "Girls, listen, there's something important I need to share with you."

Jana turned off the TV and looked at me seriously. "Tell me what happened."

I blushed. "You remember I told you about Toni, my colleague at work, right? Well, I think we're dating!"

Riwa's mouth started trembling. "What do you mean by dating? And who is this Toni? Your colleague from up north? Who is his family? Do we know them? What does his father do? Noor, just to remind you. Gentlemen don't go dating girls behind their parents' backs. A gentleman would knock on the door and ask to meet your family."

"No, I think you've got me all wrong; it's not dating like in the movies, nothing like that, I swear to God. He just said that he liked me, and I said that I did too, that's it," I tried to justify myself, slightly panicking. Riwa used to have this effect on me.

Haya, the logical person among us, tried to calm Riwa down. "She hasn't done anything wrong. Just relax. Noor knows right from wrong, and besides, she's open about it, and she'll tell us all the details. Right, Noor?" I nodded.

Riwa stood up, pointing her finger at me angrily. "Listen to me. I have nothing to do with this, and when our parents find out, and they will, I'll tell them I have nothing to do with it. I disapprove; I'm telling you right now, I disapprove."

*****

"Jocelyne! No, I can't send you one of the workers to the villa now! They're busy! Yes, we're all busy. As you know, I'm running a company here, and people have work to do. What do you mean it's urgent? The balls? Which balls? Fine. I will send you one of my workers." Mr. Daniel rolled his eyes. "Women!" He ended the conversation with his wife and directly asked his secretary to send him one of his bodyguards. He was foaming.

I waited silently for him to give me his directions on our upcoming exhibition. It turned out that Mr. Daniel was impressed by my market study, and for that reason, he included me in his inner circle team. He unofficially extended my job description to include random duties ranging from organizing the company's workshops to preparing market studies and assisting top clients in choosing presents from our luxury department. I felt privileged.

Joseph, Mr. Daniel's driver, knocked on the door. Joseph was a tall, muscular man with a body fit to be a bodyguard or a wrestler, but he had a sweet face, and his heart was very kind. "Excuse me, Mr. Daniel, have you asked for me?"

"Yes, come in. I need you for a critical task. Take the black jeep and go to my villa immediately. Mrs. Daniel is waiting for you."

Then he clarified, "She's having her friends over. First, you need to fetch the tennis balls for them. Obviously, they aren't going to waste their time doing it themselves. Once they finish their tennis game, they'll probably want to swim in our pool. So, you need to make sure that our pool has the right temperature. You squat next to the pool and dip your finger in every 15 minutes. If it's too hot, you turn the temperature down, and if it's too cold, you turn it up. Do you understand?"

Joseph nodded, "Yes, Mr. Daniel, same as last time."

"What are you waiting for then? Proceed immediately. It's an emergency."

I was in complete shock when Mr. Daniel turned back to me. His luxurious life was completely different from mine. He continued our conversation, "So, for our upcoming exhibition, we need to offer our visitors some candies. I don't want to pay too much because random people will pretend to visit our booth for business, and all they want is to steal the candies."

I announced eagerly, "I know Mr. Daniel. How about little mint candies? Our neighbor has a small candy workshop, and they make those little candies. I've tried them. They're tiny and yet refreshing at the same time. They're wrapped beautifully, and the best part is the price: They're extremely cheap because they're sold per kg and not per piece. You'll end up paying almost nothing per candy, and that's even without my special discount."

"Brilliant!" Mr. Daniel banged his palm on his desk. He called his assistant and asked her to join us immediately. "Send a memo to all the divisions' managers informing them that from now on, they have to consult with Mlle Beyrouti for any upcoming company event, particularly regarding food menus, refreshments, etc. We need more people at DanielCo with this spirit."

A big smile flashed over my face. My mentor loved my ideas.

*****

On Sunday at 7:55 am, Blossom and I got out of her convertible Wrangler, the only car parked on the fenced parking lot of the trendiest beach in Lebanon, the Ocean Dew Beach Club. Birds were singing and fluttering around us as we headed toward the gate. The Mediterranean water glittered from a distance, and I had a strong urge to jump in at that very second. "I love the beach," I almost screamed.

We walked into Ocean Dew's main lobby, but there was only a cleaning lady. "We haven't opened yet. Come back at 10:00 am," she uttered carelessly.

Blossom and I looked at each other. This lady ruined our plan. The whole idea was to swim before everyone else.

"Ummm, excuse me," I asked her kindly, "could you please call your manager? I'd like to talk to him."

She gave me a thorough look before she disappeared through a wooden door. A few minutes later, a young man in blue shorts and a plain white t-shirt joined us in the lobby. His smile was all over his face, and he said in a cheerful voice, "Good morning, ladies. What can I do for you?"

"We've just discovered that the club is still closed at this time of day, but we came all the way from Beirut. Is there any chance you could let us in now?"

He gazed at our desperate faces and nodded, "No problem! I'll let you in, but at your own risk. The lifeguard shifts start at 10:00 am, so don't swim out too far, please. Stay close to the shore."

"Of course, we promise," we said simultaneously. He didn't take any money for the tickets and said we were his guests.

"I can't believe it. We have an endless sandy beach all to ourselves. Aren't we lucky?" I nudged Blossom.

Blossom was dazzled by the beauty of the place. She had no idea such a heavenly hideaway existed in the south of Lebanon. We strolled between citrus trees and wooden cabanas, splashing sand and small pebbles with our feet until we reached several nicely designed pools. The largest one had a waterfall and a pool bar. "It's stunning!" Blossom exclaimed as she blocked the sun with her hand. She gestured at two wooden chaise lounges with two white mattresses that shared a bamboo umbrella. "Shall we sit here near the water?" "Sure," I said, putting my towel on one of the chairs.

First, we walked on the white sand but couldn't resist running into the clear, shallow water. When we finally relaxed on the sand, I thought it was a perfect opportunity to open up about Toni. "Hey, Blossom, you won't believe what has happened these last few weeks."

"Why? What do you mean?" she asked in surprise.

"You remember Toni, right? My colleague at work, I mentioned him last time I saw you." I stopped to see her reaction.

"I'm all ears. So, what happened?" she asked.

"He's hilarious and generous and excellent at sales. And guess what?! We started dating." Blossom giggled. "What are you saying? You're dating? Well, congratulations!"

I chuckled. "It's been a few weeks now, but I feel like it's been a year. We've become close friends. I see him every day at work and sometimes after work. I feel like he's my buddy; I can tell him anything. What else? We always have an amazing time together. We laugh so much, and I feel I can be myself with him."

Blossom propped her sunglasses up. "Wow! All of that in a few weeks! I'm impressed. I want to meet this guy who swept away my friend's heart so quickly!"

I beamed. "Of course, I'd love you to meet Toni. I've already told him so much about you." We agreed to organize something soon.

After our long dip in the sea and thorough relationship discussions, we laid down on the golden sand to tan. Our feet were tickled by small waves hitting the shore.

All we could hear was the soothing sound of the waves and the squawking of seagulls flying above us. Suddenly, I felt the sun being blocked from my face. I opened my eyes, and I saw a man staring at me. I gasped. Blossom and I sat straight and looked around us. There were two young men in red trunks, resembling the lifeguards from the Baywatch series.

"Hi, you're quite early! I'm Jad, and this is my friend Kasem. We're the lifeguards on duty today," he explained while Blossom searched for her cover-up.

"The manager let us in. He's very nice. I'm Noor, by the way, and that's my friend, Blossom."

"The beach is amazing at this time. We always come early to surf. Would you like to join us?" Jad gently ran his fingers through his black hair.

"The two of us?" I exchanged looks with Blossom. I had never been invited to join in any adventurous activity, not to mention by a cool, young guy. I wondered if my black shades had anything to do with it. I didn't know how to surf, but I decided to go ahead and try – there was nothing to lose.

I looked at Blossom's reluctant face and took the initiative to answer for both of us, "Sure, we'd love to join."

I put on my shorts and followed them. Blossom pulled me back and whispered in my ear, "Are you crazy? We don't know how to surf, and you know very well that I'm not comfortable wearing a swimsuit in front of men. How could you do this to me?" She had a point, but I managed to convince her to take it easy and enjoy the moment, "This is a once-in-a-lifetime adventure. Come on, don't be a chicken."

"Noor, sit behind me and hold on tight. Don't worry about anything. I'll do the paddling. All you have to do is enjoy." Kasem winked at me. He was perfectly right. It didn't take us long to relax and enjoy ourselves. Blossom and I ended up being on surfboards with two strangers. They paddled slowly next to each other so we could all get a chance to chat.

It was a lovely ride, and there was no need to be worried at all.

Blossom told them that we studied food science and were doing our master's degree. "Food science? So, what do you study exactly? Do you learn how to cook? Can you make a lasagna dish for me?" Jad asked.

We cracked up laughing so hard that I fell off the surfboard. "Not really; we are no chefs," Blossom clarified and gave details about the courses we took, ranging from food engineering to food chemistry.

We kept on chatting, mainly about the beach and life in Beirut versus life in the south. In the meantime, it was getting hotter and sunnier.

"We need to get back, girls," Kasem announced as he turned his board.

I peeked over his shoulder. Ocean Dew, the enormous beach resort, looked like a tiny maquette with miniature trees and cabanas.

Once we reached the shore, Blossom and I thanked the two guys for the lovely trip and went to pack our stuff.

Blossom put on her long flowery dress looking at the horizon. "I don't know what to say!" She couldn't wipe the smile off her face. "I can't believe that I enjoyed the ride. I was on a surfboard in the middle of the sea with a total stranger, but I had the time of my life. Those guys were so genuine."

*****

Chapter Fifteen - Common People

Mood Music:
"Common People" by Pulp

When you meet someone in Lebanon, the first question that comes to mind is, "What's your family name?" This piece of information opens Pandora's Box. A family name offers a general perspective on the person's background, area of origin, religion, and sect. Sometimes, it can even expose the person's financial situation, domestic violence history, and level of generosity or stinginess.

Lebanese family names vary a lot. A family name can be an adjective like victorious (Naser) or happy (Mabsout) or reflecting a royal position such as king (Malak) or Sheikh. In many cases, family names reflect one of the ancestor's jobs, such as blacksmith (Haddad), baker (Khabaz), drummer (Tabbal), and jewelry designer (Al Sayegh). Other family names reflect the area where a family originates from, for example, Beyrouti (originating from Beirut).

Then there are those unique Lebanese family names which I have no idea how they were created: Wazze meaning "swan," Sharshouh meaning "low class," Ajeeb meaning "bizarre," Foustouk meaning "pistachio," Timsah meaning "crocodile," Toufeili meaning "parasite," Bateekha meaning "one watermelon," Hashash meaning "junkie," and the best of the best is Yamout which means "dying."

Imagine a doctor's clinic, where a nurse calls the next patient's name, "Mr. Dying, the doctor would like to see you now."

No matter what the family name is, there is always a story behind it. Toni's family name was Charity, and I needed to know its story because once my parents heard about him, my interrogation would start. Naturally, their first question would be, "What's his family name?" Then they would bombard me with questions such as, "Charity? Did they give charity, or did they receive it?" But it wouldn't stop there. They would ask about his family tree, background, and family history dating a few 100 years back.

My parents were not that picky. They were just like other parents who wanted the best for their daughters. Maybe my mom was not totally like any other parent. Because of her origin, she had an extra interest in those matters. My mom had a "princess title"; she was a direct descendant of Salah al-Din Al Ayoubi. Family roots meant a great deal to her.

To be proactive, I checked "The Origin of Lebanese Families," a book I found at home, but nothing was mentioned. I was hoping to discuss the matter with Toni before our families met.

*****

Toni invited all our colleagues for a weekend lunch at his family house. The smile didn't leave my face as I was getting ready, doing my hair, and putting on perfume. In my head, that lunch meant only one thing: Toni was indirectly introducing me to his parents. The next natural step would be that he would visit us at home, then both families would meet, one thing would lead to the other, and then da da doumm da da doumm, we would get engaged.

I rushed down. Ruba, who had offered to pick me up, was already waiting down in her Renault. Her car was brand new with a super cooling A/C, perfect for Lebanese summers. Just before Jbeil (Byblos), she took the exit that headed up straight to Toni's village. We turned off the A/C and opened the windows to enjoy the fresh air. The view of the sea beneath us got more visible as we went up the hill. The area was still virgin, beautiful, and green. We drove between fruit trees and passed sheep grazing next to the road.

"Good morning, please join us for coffee," a lady in her garden greeted us, and other locals waved as we passed by.

When Ruba announced, "We have arrived," my tummy went swirling and twirling. I put on a big smile and walked towards Toni and his dad, standing at the gate of their stone house. "Hello, hello," Toni's father shook my hand and kissed me on the cheek.

"Your visit is an honor to us," he told me. That was not a special welcome for me. It is how Lebanese people welcome their guests. "Thank you, Ammo (uncle). The honor is all mine."

My colleagues parked their cars one after the other next to Ruba's car. Our loud voices must have attracted the attention of Toni's mom, who rushed from the kitchen, laughing, hugging, and kissing each one of us. I gave her the sweets Ruba and I had bought on the way, saying, "Very nice to finally meet you, Taunt. Toni talks a lot about you."

After a thorough explanation of who is who, many hellos, and numerous welcomes, Ammo asked us to join him in the front garden. It was a small, cute garden directly by the roadside. The floor was made of beautiful mosaic tiles, and the plant pots were full of flowers and roses with enchanting smells. Living in Beirut had made me forget the scent of blooming roses because the odor of car fuel and power generators suppressed any other smell.

From the strategic position on my bamboo chair, I observed everyone closely: Mr. Nader was having a lot of fun, leading a circle of Daniel Co's employees and telling them inside jokes, including those about the big boss himself. Toni and the rest of my colleagues were chatting and laughing while having fizzy drinks and crunching mixed nuts. Toni's mom kept coming and going, giving instructions to her husband and daughter to set the table, while his grandparents were sitting on a double swing chair watching everyone. I was dividing up my time between the different groups. From time to time, I also helped Toni's mom set the table and prepare the food, but then I would sneak back into the DanielCo circle to not miss any jokes.

"But Mr. Nader, I honestly found it outrageous to receive such ridiculous memos from Mr. Daniel. Which company specifies the minimum number of papers per paper clip? I mean, how did he even come up with five papers? So, if I need to attach four papers, should I use a stapler instead of a clip?" Ruba complained, waving her hands frantically. The rest of us burst out laughing, but she was seriously annoyed.

"I managed to accept that memo, but then came the second one saying that for any document that I photocopy, I need to note down the reason why I had to photocopy it," she added.

Mr. Nader circled his finger next to his temple, saying, "Yes, he's loco sometimes."

Ruba smirked. "You might think that was no big deal. But wait until you hear about the third memo he sent yesterday, just before we left the office. That memo is a pure disgrace."

All eyes were on Ruba. "Mr. Daniel wants all the girls at the company to inform the human resource division whenever we get our menstrual period. He needs to double-check whether we're faking the dates to take our legally granted sick leave."

"What are you saying?" My eyebrows went up. "I'm not telling anyone anything of that sort," I commented.

The guys were laughing hysterically. But Salim, one of our oldest colleagues, took it way too seriously. "This time, Mr. Daniel has crossed the red line. We're a conservative society, and such topics are not to be discussed in public. If my sister's boss would dare to ask her about her menstrual cycle, I swear, I'd kill him with my own hands." He kept punching his palm with his fist.

"Relax, relax now." Toni and the other guys quickly tried to calm him down, rubbing his neck and asking him not to take it too personally.

We all knew that underneath Salim's conservative appearance – he was in his early thirties, half bald and with a traditional mustache and a calm attitude – he hid an enormous amount of rage. Perhaps it had to do with his previous career helping his dad in manufacturing gun silencers. Salim insisted he had a normal childhood, but how on earth did he learn how to open car locks with hair clips and start a car with wires? He was like a big brother to whom I went whenever I was in trouble. If I stapled my finger with our office stapler, he always managed to take it out without blinking an eye.

Finally, Ammo invited us to their buffet. The table was full of various Lebanese meze such as tabbouleh, fattoush salads, hummus, stuffed vine leaves, meatballs, spinach pastry, cheese spring rolls, spicy cubed potatoes, etc. I could see that the food was prepared with love. We were all done eating when Toni's mom joined us, carrying a tray of Turkish coffee and a sugar bowl. When she started to serve us, I automatically stood up and took the coffee tray, offering to help. Ruba helped serve the fruits, and Toni's sister was getting the tea. Toni's mom stopped abruptly before putting the Baklavas on the table. "Oh no! I forgot to bring Sweet'N Low for those of you who are on a diet." She rushed back to the kitchen.

I moved to the swing chair as soon as Toni's grandparents went for their nap. Toni joined me on the chair that could barely fit two. It was cozy and warm. I could feel Toni's arm rubbing at mine as we swung. He turned to me and whispered in my ear, "I wish we were alone." My heart skipped a beat. I was too scared someone would overhear him.

*****

I checked the time. I had never woken up at 6:30 am before, but I was super hyper and full of energy. I couldn't wait to go to work to see Toni, my official boyfriend. After all, I did meet his family, and we had been going out regularly for a few months now.

As it was too early to leave the house, I made a mug of hot chocolate and made myself comfortable in the rocking chair on our balcony. "What a beautiful day!" I kept on telling myself. It couldn't get any better.

I sat there watching our vivid street: Neighbors were getting ready to start their day, some were having Nescafé in mugs, and others were eating breakfast. Our neighbor below was singing love songs to his wife as he was watering his plants. I loved our street! I stood up to look at my beautiful Nissan.

"What the ...? Why is a black Mercedes blocking my car? How am I supposed to get my car out?"

I stood there watching, hoping the car owner would show up, but there was no sign of salvation. Finally, it was time for me to go to work. I dressed and sat in my car. I honked repetitively, disturbing the peaceful morning atmosphere. I expected the car owner to notice the commotion and remove his car, but no, nothing happened. I asked a few passers-by if they knew who the vehicle belonged to, but everyone said the same thing, "No, we've never seen that car before." I also asked the neighbors who were standing on their first-floor balconies. Those were usually the most alert type of neighbors. Nothing happened on our street without them knowing about it.

As they say, "Desperate times call for desperate measures."

I went home and called the police number in our address book.

Man: "Security department of Beirut, yes?"

Me: "Hello, I'm Noor Beyrouti, and I'd like to speak to General Farid, please." This name was mentioned in the address book.

Man: "Where are you calling from, Ma'am?"

Me: "From my house."

Man: …

Me: "Please, can you connect me? It's quite urgent."

Man: "Please inform me about the sort of urgency. Do you hear any gunshots?"

Me: "Of course not. My neighborhood is the safest in the city. Well, except for that one incident when we had a shooting on the street, one man was shot in front of his mom. Rumor has it that it was an honor crime among drug dealers …"

The man on the phone interrupted me impatiently, "Please describe the critical situation to me, Ma'am."

So I did, but when he heard my car being blocked story, he was furious. He even had the nerve to tell me never to call that number again.

"Ma'am, note that this is not a 911 call center. You've called a government number intended for high-security emergencies. Who gave you this number in the first place?"

*****

Chapter Sixteen - Maria

Mood Music:
"Maria"
by Leonard Bernstein from West Side Story

As I had expected, the office was already empty. I was late, thanks to the black Mercedes. Everyone on the sales team had already left for customer visits, except Ruba, of course. I greeted her and sat at my desk, preparing for my day. Lately, I was getting better and better at sales, and I managed to close a few deals. Joining Toni at his business meetings helped me a lot. I learned how he bonded with his clients and managed to close deals. I had also read several books on negotiation skills, common sales mistakes, and body language. I worked on improving my sales skills in every way. I didn't only get the hang of it, but I also started to enjoy it.

"Bonjour," I smiled at one of the security guards at Sunny Juice, one of our top clients. He let me in right away since I was a daily visitor. I informed the receptionist that I had a meeting with their MD, Mr. Jean-Paul, and went straight to his office. Mr. Jean-Paul was a young CEO and the founder's son, coming from a well-known political and influential family. He was a kind-hearted person with temper issues. I couldn't blame him, he was under enormous stress from his family to expand the business further and further, but at the same time, the Lebanese market was shrinking continuously.

The office door was open, and Mr. Jean-Paul was on the phone. I knocked, and he gave me a sign to enter. I sat facing him and got my notebook from my bag.

He shouted, "Listen, bro, this is not what we agreed on. If you don't stick to your initial offer, I will cancel the whole deal, yes, the whole deal. I'm busy now." He hung up.

I observed Mr. Jean-Paul's facial expression. He was so angry to the point of explosion. Naturally, it was the worst time to discuss my price offer, but it was too late to leave. According to his body language, it was evident that he was not ready to have a conversation. Mr. Jean-Paul started working on some files in front of him, completely ignoring my presence. I wanted him to relax, so I decided to give him some space. I also had a lot to do, so I grabbed a pen from my bag, some of my files, and my super big calculator and started working on some other projects. It was quality working time for both of us. No one dared to bother us. Time passed quickly, and frankly, his office was excellent for work. He had a nice view overlooking Beirut, comfortable furniture, and most of all: silence. After half an hour, I managed to take care of several pending issues.

"So, Noor!" Finally, Mr. Jean-Paul was ready to talk. I smiled, "Bonjour, Mr. Jean–Paul, how are you doing?"

He asked me in a serious but rather warm tone, "What's on our agenda today?"

"Discussion of our latest price offers for orange concentrate, pineapple concentrate, and some fruit-vegetable premixes, which your R&D team has agreed on. I've sent you all the offers by fax, and here are additional copies."

I handed the documents to him.

He read them in a few seconds and asked hastily, "Are these the best prices you can give me?"

"Yes, Mr. Jean-Paul, I assure you of that. I can't reduce them any further." He made some calculations, finally commenting, "Ok, ça va (*ok, fine*)."

He grabbed his Montblanc pen and signed my offers, confirming the order of three containers of orange concentrate, four containers of pineapple concentrate, and 5 tons of a veg-fruit mix. In the end, he asked me to finalize the deal with Mrs. Maria, his purchasing manager. "Bro, remember that we needed these containers yesterday, so you're already late!"

I smiled. I knew that was coming. Mr. Jean-Paul called everyone "bro," even me, and always requested his shipments to be delivered ASAP. His style caused everyone severe stress, but I was ok with that.

Our meeting was over. I stood up, tidying up my papers, while he went to check his emails.

"Noor, when you return to the office, please call your German supplier to confirm this deal. I don't want any delays."

How could I tell him that Mr. Daniel was too stingy when making international calls and that I had to get at least three approvals before making an international call?

Mr. Jean-Paul must have sensed my hesitation. "Look, bro, if Mr. Daniel doesn't allow you to make international calls – I know how much he loves his money – you're welcome to use my office and make your calls from here. Not only for my Sunny Juice orders but for any other juice factory as well."

I was speechless. He handed me the phone saying, "Here, call them now."

I knew our supplier's number by heart. Since joining DanielCo, I had memorized more than a hundred business phone numbers by heart, national and international (with and without extensions).

I directly called my colleagues in Germany and confirmed his orders asking for an urgent shipment. He listened carefully as I explained the situation on the phone. Finally, I saw a smile of satisfaction on his face.

As I was about to leave his office, I remembered an important issue. "Ah, by the way, Mr. Daniel told me once again that he'd like to have a meeting with you …"

He interrupted me with a wave of his hand. "No, I don't want to see him."

"Ok, no problem!" I said, smiling, and went to his purchasing manager. I needed to make sure to align with her.

"Bonjour, Mme Maria." I knocked lightly on her door. She looked busy behind her golden-framed eyeglasses. But her looks did not get affected by the loads of work she had. Her blond hair was perfectly blown, her nails shimmered red, and her golden necklace perfectly matched her stylish outfit.

"Bonjour Noor. Please, please come on in." She took off her glasses and leaned back in her swivel chair." I'm so tired. You know it's the high season, and our factory works several shifts daily to fulfill our ice cream and juice orders. I'm exhausted. I don't even have time to eat." She stood up abruptly, lifting her top. "Look!" She showed me how loose her skirt had become.

I raised my eyebrows. "That's not ok. You've lost so much weight. You need to take care of yourself. If not for you, then for your son. Don't stay without food. Eat something, have a banana, an apple, even a bar of chocolate," I pleaded.

"I'm having coffee most of the day, no appetite, I'm too stressed. Anyway, Mr. Jean-Paul just called me and said that he confirmed new orders with you. I'll photocopy them for my records." I handed her the signed documents. She added that she would send me all their requirements by fax later today.

"Great, thanks a lot." I was ready to leave when I remembered something, "By the way, I thought of you this morning. In my car, I was listening to the song "Maria" over and over again. Mariaaaa, I just met a girl named Maria. Do you know it? It's from West Side Story. I just love it."

Mrs. Maria's face lit up, "Habibti (*my sweetheart*), you have it in your car? That's such an old song. It brings back so many memories. Noor, would you be an angel and lend me the tape?"

I laughed, "Of course! I'll fetch it for you. You can have it."

*****

Toni and I had officially gone steady since the end of June. Those few months introduced me to a new world full of romance, love, fights, internal tourism, and culinary trips. In our free time, we went out to restaurants or cafes, watched movies, or discovered Lebanese villages and towns. We were two peas in a pod. We enjoyed doing activities together, such as hiking, snorkeling, and shooting. Snorkeling was the best. I loved being in the water and observing crabs and starfish.

I once had a horrible experience when we went hiking though. Our guide got lost, and our 2-hour beginner's trip ended up being 6 hours of pure torture. The nails that a shoe repairman had used to fix my shoe sole poked my heel all the way, causing me extreme pain. I was so tired and exhausted that I couldn't lift my head anymore.

Back home, Riwa asked me, "How was your hiking trip? How was the view from up there?"

"It was exhausting! I can't believe I made it back alive. After three hours of hiking, I was already done. The only thing I remember was the hiking boots of the man walking in front of me. It was a Timberland, just for the record." I replied.

When Toni suggested that we go shooting, I was thrilled. I had joined my Dad a few times on his morning hunting trips, so I was kind of used to rifles.

Toni placed a few coca-cola cans on the edge of the wall in his back garden. He demonstrated how to hold a rifle correctly, which eye to close and how to shoot. I thought it was unnecessary as I had held a gun many times before. Perhaps it happened because I was nervous in front of him. I tried too hard. When it was my turn, Toni fixed the cans and shouted, "Now, shoot." His command startled me, and I ended up shooting in between his legs instead of shooting the cans. Thankfully, he was not injured, but he freaked out and refused to continue. He decided that we should focus more on touristic outings.

Toni held my hand tightly, ensuring I didn't slip as we strolled on the concrete walkway in Jeita Grotto. I couldn't believe my eyes. Jeita was even more beautiful than anyone had ever told me. I had meant to visit that renowned cave for a long time, but somehow it had never happened before I met Toni. When Toni suggested taking me to all those places I'd never been to, I was more than thrilled.

I was fascinated by every stalactite and stalagmite formed over hundreds of years. I tried to figure out what each looked like: I imagined towers, mushrooms, mothers, older men chit-chatting, and lovers. The options were endless.

All the visitors were quiet, and there was a serene peace inside the grotto. None of the visitors wanted to miss the sound of water drops as they formed new creations.

"Noor, are you done here?" Toni whispered in my ear. I nodded.

"Good, then let's go down to the lower cave. We'll take a boat." He confidently led the way.

The lower cave was chilly and dark, and the light projections dancing on the water. From time to time, the tour guide briefed us about the cave's history. When we returned, Toni held out his hand as I stepped carefully out of the boat.

We walked back to the entrance, and I grabbed my purse from our locker. I gave Toni his mobile. No mobiles were allowed inside the cave. "That was one unforgettable trip!" I said enthusiastically.

"Best Noor ever!" He laughed. When he turned on his mobile, he received countless missed call notifications.

"Wow! So many missed calls! Who's so insistent on talking to you on a Saturday? Was it your Dad?" I asked him in surprise.

He turned it on silent mode. "No, it's only Mira," he said as he tucked his mobile into his jeans pocket.

"Mira? Again?" I rolled my eyes dramatically.

"Aren't you going to call her back? It seems rather urgent," I said cynically.

He put on a poker face, so I couldn't figure out how he felt.

"I know why she's calling. She'll ask me about one of their orders, and I don't want to discuss business now. Ok?" His tone was firm as he walked away.

I followed him. "I don't get it. Why does Mira call you on a Saturday afternoon? Doesn't she know it's your weekend, and you're spending it with me?"

"Come on! Don't make such a big deal out of it. It's just a phone call, a business phone call!" He was starting to get angry.

"No," I insisted, "it's not just a business phone call. I've noticed how she keeps flirting with you. She has no decency at all. She knows you have a girlfriend. She knows me, and still, she doesn't stop. You seem to like it, don't you?"

He laughed. "Sure, I like the attention; why not? She's kind of pretty, and her father is my biggest client. They're loaded!"

I couldn't believe he would joke about such a topic. I fixed my purse on my shoulder and stormed off. He didn't follow me, and a few seconds later, I slowed down voluntarily for him to catch up. Toni smirked. He knew that I couldn't just leave. I needed a ride back to my car. There was no Uber back then.

He held my hand, grinning. "Look, I was only teasing you. I swear I don't care about her. I only care about you. You should know that by now."

I didn't say a word.

He held my hand and squeezed it tightly. "How about we grab some sandwiches and just relax by the beach." I agreed.

"Behind every joke, there is always some kind of truth." This saying stuck in my head as we drove back to his village. I felt completely and utterly empty. Nothing seemed to fill me up, not even the chocolate ice cream we had.

When the day was over, and I drove back to Beirut, totally alone, I let my tears flow freely. As fast as I was driving, the 45-minute trip home felt like seconds to me, and before I knew it, I was standing in the lobby of our building.

*****

Chapter Seventeen - Another One Bites the Dust

Mood Music:
"Another One Bites the Dust" by Queen

I wiped my eyes with a tissue as I waited for the elevator to reach the ground floor. As usual, it took forever to arrive.

"Good evening, Taunt Im Abed" (*literally meaning: Auntie, the mother of Abed*). In Lebanon, it is common to call a mother by the name of her eldest son. I greeted our neighbor, who wasn't particularly one of my favorites. Her style was appalling with her shiny ensemble and exaggerated makeup.

"Hello, Noor. How are you, my dear? How are your mom and Riwa?" She kissed me on the cheeks.

"All is well," I replied.

The elevator arrived, and, out of respect, I opened the door for her to enter first. Then I stepped in, covering my nose with a tissue.

"Why is it always smelly in here?!" Taunt Im Abed's face wrinkled as she tried not to breathe.

"Of course, it's smelly. What do you expect? As long as all the corpses and garbage remain stacked down there, the smell won't go away!" I pointed to the shaft underneath.

She automatically looked down as if she had bionic eyes to see through the elevator's metallic flooring.

"Corpses? What corpses? Do you mean from wartime?" The elevator stopped on the third floor. She stepped out but held the door wide open, waiting for my reply. "From wartime?" she asked again.

I rolled my lower lip and shrugged. "Maybe, but the corpses of mice and rats must be piled down there. It's really about time that our building committee gets this shaft cleaned. Don't you think?"

She sighed in relief. "Rats and mice?! God! I thought you were talking about human corpses."

Taunt Im Abed held the door open while looking at me from head to toe. "Darling, what do you do for a living?"

BANG BANG. "Close the elevator door!" someone yelled from one of the floors above us.

I answered quickly, "I work for a big company selling food ingredients, and I'm doing my master's degree along the way."

Her face was expressionless for a moment, then she commented casually, "Well, it's better than staying at home doing nothing."

I kept pressing the button for the 7th floor to escape, but naturally, the elevator couldn't move with an open door.

She insisted on continuing our chit-chat. "My darling Noor …"

I interrupted her, "Taunt, someone needs the elevator.

They're banging on the door."

"Let them wait! What's the hurry? Now, where was I? Yes, you're still young, and you have a job which means you earn money; in a way, that's a good thing. Look, you're the same age as my daughter Natalie. As you know, she already has a son, and the next one is on the way. Take this advice from me, don't let your job distract you from your ultimate goal."

"What do you mean, Taunt? Which ultimate goal?" I asked.

She looked surprised. "You know a girl's ultimate goal is to find a husband and settle down. "She winked at me. "I'll keep you in mind in case one of my friends is looking for a bride for her son. Bye, bye, and say hello to your mom from me."

She was finally gone. The elevator went up, but my mood kept on going down. I had already been sad because of Mira's phone calls and Toni's joking about it, but after listening to my neighbor's lecture, my feelings were bouncing between fury and sadness. What did she mean by saying that she would keep me in mind? Who told her I needed a suitor?

*****

Summer was over, and yellow autumn leaves covered Sawfar's roads. The bare trees stood tall when Dad and I walked along the corniche. My dad was in his black wool coat, covering his partially bald head with a beret. I was dressed in jeans, an oversized brick raincoat with a small white fur collar, and Timberland boots. Only the rustling of leaves and the howling of the wind broke our silence.

I rubbed my hands together. "It's quite cold today, Dad. I don't remember Sawfar being this cold."

Dad laughed and held me tight. "Sawfar is more than 1,200 meters above sea level, plus it's December." He chuckled. "When you were kids, you loved coming here to build a snowman. It seems times have changed. Shall we go back to Beirut, my sweetie?"

"No, no, it's nice. I just expected it to be warmer, that's all."

We continued walking, looking at the beautiful, deserted houses. Sawfar was mainly a summer place. At that time of year, many of Sawfar's residents had abandoned their cold homes and moved back to Beirut for a warmer winter.

"What's new with you, Noor? It's been a while since we've had a good talk." His voice was full of love. He knew me well, and he must have sensed that I was hiding something.

"All is well. I love my job, it's fascinating, and there's something new every day – new workshops, new brands to sell, meeting new clients." I kicked a pile of leaves as I walked. "Dad?"

He smiled and replied warmly, "Yes, sweetie."

"Well, it's about one of my colleagues at work, his name is Toni, and his desk is next to mine. He's a business graduate, a few years older than me, and ..."

"Do you like him?" Dad interrupted in a serious tone.

"Yes, sort of. I would like you and Mom to meet him, but I want it to be casual, so I thought of ..."

"Yes?" he asked, slowing down.

"Well, I thought of organizing a New Year's dinner at our place, nothing fancy, just a few friends and some music, and I could ask him to come over. What do you think, Dad?"

I looked at him, trying to guess what he was thinking, but his face was emotionless. He didn't say a word. I felt hot despite the cold weather, but Dad kept on walking silently. When we were almost at the end of the corniche, he cleared his throat and stood facing me, putting both hands on my shoulders. "Noor, you're not a little girl anymore. Your mom and I have raised you well, with moral values. We're open-minded, but only to a certain degree. After all, we're Lebanese people and having a boyfriend/girlfriend is a sensitive issue. We have our culture and traditions, and if a man wants to get to know you, he should have known better how to behave. He should have done it the proper way. I mean, he should have called me and asked for an appointment to visit us at home, together with his family."

He opened his car door and turned on the heater as we drove back to Beirut. "Of course, I'll meet Toni at our home. I'll leave it up to you how and when you'll organize a meeting with him."

I bit my lip. I didn't dare to tell Dad anything else. I had initially planned to ask Dad's opinion about our relationship and tell him that we had been dating for more than a year. I was going to talk about Toni's positive sides and the things that drove me nuts. But to be realistic, it was neither the time nor the place, so I decided to drop it.

*****

Riwa's big day finally arrived. My sister was going to fight some of the country's best female karate athletes at the

Lebanese Karate Championship. The sports stadium was packed as if it was an international basketball game. "No wonder we couldn't find a place to park!" Riwa murmured, watching the excited crowd as she rushed to join her team. I squeezed myself in among other AUB club fans.

"AUB...AUB...AUB!!!" The audience was cheering, shouting, and whistling. The beat of their drums was so intense that I felt like it was coming out of my stomach.

The tournament started, and it was not long before Riwa's name was called. My sister walked confidently in her white karate gear and blue belt. Her black hair was tied back in a ponytail, allowing her big black eyes to sparkle. She looked focused.

Riwa was fearless, making all the right moves, kicking, and punching. I was surprised when the referee ended her match only a few minutes after it had started. Riwa's name was called again, and once more, her match ended quickly.

I asked a guy next to me, "What's going on? How come the referee ends Riwa's matches so soon? I don't understand."

He pointed at Riwa. "Is she your sister?" I nodded.

"She's amazing! She's winning all her matches and in record time too."

One victory after the other. No matter how tall or strong her opponents were, Riwa knocked them out within moments. It was unbelievable. The audience was astounded, cheering even louder than before. Unlike everyone else, I was neither happy about her victories nor the gold medal she eventually won. I made a grumpy face.

My sister was already known for being intelligent, but after such a victory, I was worried people would see her as "the smart girl who can kick an ass." And who would marry her with such a reputation? I had often tried to convince her to take ballet lessons, telling her, "Why not? I know you love watching Swan Lake."

Right before we had left for the stadium, Mom had taken me aside, "Take good care of your sister and be fully prepared for any type of sports emergency."

I assured her that we had everything under control. But, frankly speaking, what did a sports emergency even mean? And what was I supposed to do if it happened? The only emergency I was ever trained for was a war emergency.

When a battle was about to start, I knew exactly what to do: I had to open the windows of our apartment so the glass wouldn't shatter due to pressure, then I had to close the oven's gas bulb for safety reasons, and finally, within seconds, I had to grab my rucksack and run to the shelter. My war rucksack was light and professionally packed, including only essential belongings such as official documents (e.g., passport, school degrees, etc.) and a few pieces of clothes and underwear. I never needed to pack any shoes because, during war periods, I wore my shoes even at night for quick escapes.

After the tournament, I joined Riwa's team for the celebration. They went to Bliss House to have ice cream. Riwa was super excited about her triumph, and I was super excited about my chocolate milkshake. Our excitement didn't last long, as Riwa's colleague accidentally hurt her arm when he demonstrated a sidekick. She screamed in pain and held her arm tightly, unable to straighten it anymore. It seemed serious. I called Mom and informed her that we would be late as we had to go to the emergency hospital. She insisted that I should get Riwa the best doctor I could find. "And don't worry about money. We'll pay in cash." Mom never believed that our insurance company paid for our medical treatments.

As we walked into the emergency room, I stopped a nurse, "Excuse me, Miss, my sister hurt her arm doing karate. We think it's broken."

The nurse looked at us from behind her eyeglasses. "Very well, come along." She asked Riwa to wait for the doctor in a small, white room and gave me a pile of admission papers to fill out.

"Ok, Riwa, I'll take care of all the administrative stuff and come back as soon as I can." It took me more than half an hour before my mission was accomplished. I pushed the white curtain aside and walked into Riwa's room. She was sitting comfortably on her bed, telling two young doctors about the latest movie she had seen.

"Seriously?!" I thought to myself. Naturally, both doctors were taken entirely by her story. Riwa was the Shahrazad of storytelling, captivating her audience by adding imaginative scenes and descriptive details, making them crave more. She has always been creative in narrating a story to the extent that even if the original author heard her version, he wouldn't recognize it as his story.

I hoped she would be brief because I had no intention of spending my whole evening at the emergency hospital. At this very moment, Riwa announced, "That was the end."

"Excuse me, what do you think about her arm? Is it broken?" I asked straight away, so Riwa wouldn't start again.

One of the doctors nodded confidently, "Absolutely, it's broken."

He stood up, about to leave. "Don't worry. Dr. Ahmad, one of our top orthopedic surgeons, will come and check it as soon as he's free." He turned to my sister, "It's been a pleasure meeting you. Such a pity we have to leave you now, but we hope to see you again soon."

Riwa laughed. After they left, she explained to me, "I just had to tell them the story of that specific movie because it's also about this doctor who ..." I interrupted her.

"Please not now. I need to explain to you what we still need to do regarding your insurance claim." She agreed.

It wasn't long before Dr. Ahmad, the orthopedic surgeon, arrived. He checked her name on the file, "Hi Riwa, how are you today? I heard you're our karate champion?"

"Yes, thanks. I love karate. It's more than sports; it's a way of life," Riwa replied.

"Of course, of course," he mumbled as he checked her x-ray. "Ummmm, your arm is broken in two places, here and here," he said, pointing at her wrist and ulna bone. He moved her arm softly in different directions. "Are you right- or left-handed?"

"Well, I use my right hand for attacks and my left for defense."

Dr. Ahmad shook his head in surprise. "No, no, I mean for writing, my dear, not for martial arts."

She blushed. "I'm right-handed."

"Perfect! Then you'll have no trouble adjusting." He patted her on the shoulder. "You'll need a cast. I'll explain the procedure to you."

It was after midnight when we finally left the hospital. A security man, who was drinking tea and chatting with his colleague, waved to us. "Bye, champion! I wish you a quick recovery." The other watchman added, "You were great today. I saw you live. You make us all proud."

Riwa thanked them. When I looked at her, she was glowing. And so was I, feeling very proud of her. Not all sisters need to be ballerinas, after all.

*****

Chapter Eighteen - Only When You Leave

Mood Music:
"Only When You Leave" by Spandau Ballet

My start to the New Year was not that impressive. It was a disaster, to be specific. Toni's New Year's Eve meeting with my parents was not what I expected. They were not impressed by him at all. My mom sensed that he was not an honest man. After the meeting, I had a lengthy argument with my family and insisted that Toni was the one for me. I was stressed and worried, which affected how I behaved toward Toni in the following weeks.

In the meantime, Mr. Nader told me that I would have to go to Germany in April to meet our potential new supplier. I was over the moon. I would go on a business trip to Germany, a country I was dying to explore, all expenses paid.

While I was checking my wardrobe, Mom shouted from the kitchen, "Noor, open the door."

"Yalla, coming." I ran to the door and looked through the peephole. To my great surprise, it was my uncle with his wife and three children and my oldest single auntie who lived with them.

"Hello, hello." We all kissed and hugged.

"Please come in. It's freezing outside," I pleaded.

The landing outside our apartment became wet because of the water dripping from their hair and clothes.

My mom removed her apron and quickly came to welcome her guests, while my dad helped my little cousin Youssef take off his coat.

"Welcome, welcome." My Dad chuckled as he pinched Youssef's cheek. "Do I see the first signs of a mustache here?"

My uncle's wife hung up her coat, laughing. "The kids are growing older, just like us."

My auntie's face grimaced when she saw Riwa. "Habibti, how's your arm? Are you still in pain?"

"I'm fine, auntie. The doctor assured me that I could resume karate in no time," Riwa said, holding the flower bouquet my cousin had given her.

My uncle laughed. "Riwa will never change. Karate comes first!"

While discussing Riwa's karate career, my mom gave me a sign to follow her into the kitchen, where she asked me to get a large cake from the pastry shop downstairs quickly.

When I came back, Dad was already roasting chestnuts on his unique Aladdin Heater. Due to the many power cuts in Beirut, Dad got a power generator for our private use at home. Unfortunately, it was not that powerful and had a limited power supply. That was the reason why Dad bought an Aladdin Heater that ran solely on fuel. It looked old even when it was new. Frankly, I didn't know anyone else who had a similar device, but my Dad loved it. He used the heater during winter to warm up our TV room, for roasting nuts or toasting bread, and sometimes Mom used it for cooking.

I put the Black Forest cake on a silver platter and served it to our guests with Turkish coffee and black tea. I made sure to use our silver teapot and flowery china cups, which we only use for guests. I also got our elegant silver cutlery and china plates and placed them all on the table.

"What's wrong with Sofia? She's quiet today?" Dad asked, flipping the chestnuts with a BBQ clip.

Her mom winked at him. "You know her tooth is aching." There was a moment of silence before we all burst out laughing. Sofia, my teenage cousin, turned all red. It was not difficult to decode our family's "tooth pain" as a girl's monthly cycle.

Auntie Lamia opened her purse and took out a flowery pouch filled with all types of medicine.

"I have the perfect medicine for your pain here. Take two pills now and two more in six hours, and you'll be fine."

Sofia resisted at first but finally gave in and took the medicine.

My uncle's wife gasped. "Lamia, good you reminded me. I forgot to ask you at home. Do you have your medicine for heart palpitations? I feel like my heartbeat hasn't been normal these last two days." Auntie Lamia replied proudly, "Of course, here you go."

The doorbell rang. Two other aunties and their families came to see us. "Hello, hello, welcome, welcome." My mom opened the door with a cigarette in the corner of her mouth. I had to quickly go to the pastry shop again and get another cake. Our TV room was full. Everyone was talking simultaneously, discussing big hot topics such as my cousin's growing mustache, Riwa's broken arm, and bird hunting. The doorbell rang again. It was my other uncle and his family. Before we knew it, we were around thirty Beyrouti family members. There were too many to fit in our cozy TV room, but we didn't move to the salon. It was too big to be warmed by our Aladdin Heater. Some of us sat on the carpet, and a few cousins moved to the kitchen.

One of my uncles asked Dad, "Have you heard about your cousin Hajj Ali's sons? Their business is doing very well. May God protect them."

"Of course," Dad replied, "I saw Hasan a week ago, and he updated me on their new business projects. Quite impressive."

I nudged one of my cousins sitting next to me. "Who are they talking about?"

"It's the other branch of our family," he explained. "Their belated father, a cousin of your dad, was a wealthy businessman. He died a few years ago, and his sons inherited his business and wealth."

He leaned closer to me. "Rumor has it that at one point in time, he owned 20% of Lebanese land."

"Seriously?! I smirked. "Don't tell me you also believe this nonsense."

"No, it's not nonsense; it's a fact." he insisted.

"Let me get this straight. According to you, my dad's cousin owned 20% of the Lebanese land, and according to my mom's cousin, their grandfather owned 40% of the Lebanese land. With simple calculations, we conclude that my relatives own more than 60% of the country! I find it extremely hard to believe, and it's simply not true."

*****

April 7th

"Only when you leave, I need to love you." This song could have been written for Toni and me. The moment he heard I was going to travel, and even though it was just for ten days, he turned into prince charming, following me like a shadow, giving me extra love and attention as if I was leaving for good.

Toni scowled. "Nounou, will you think of me when you're in Germany? I'll be devastated without you."

I felt guilty and selfish to be excited about my trip while leaving him in such a state. "Do you have any doubt? I'll miss you a lot. I miss you already. You understand I'm only going because this trip is crucial for my career."

Since my trip was scheduled for the following day, we decided to make the best of my few hours left in Lebanon and attend all our business meetings together. Toni parked his car on the ramp next to Faith and Sons, a medium-sized company producing detergents. Because they were one of his most important customers, he took extra care of their business and made sure to visit them at least two to three times per week. I wished he wouldn't. I was not too fond of Mira, the owner's daughter. She was flirtatious.

When we stepped into their administration office, Mira's face lit up. She sat behind her desk wearing a confident smile. She wore a blue and white striped t-shirt and light blue jeans. Her long, fair hair flowed over her shoulders. She welcomed us enthusiastically, and I noticed how she couldn't take her eyes off Toni.

"Hi dear." She kissed me.

I smiled back. "Hi."

"You're traveling tomorrow, right?" She smirked. "Toni told me you're going to Germany."

I turned towards Toni, wondering why he would share such personal information with his client, but he avoided eye contact and pretended to be busy with his files.

"Would you like a cup of coffee?" she asked me as she walked towards the coffee machine.

"No, thanks," I replied, but she prepared coffee anyway. She made two cups of cappuccino, one for her and another for Toni, without asking him. That surprised me because he hated all types of hot beverages, as far as I knew.

I watched them as they discussed their business. Mira kept on flicking her hair backward, blushing and giggling. Toni tried to act naturally, but I could feel he was not himself.

I waited until we were in the car before bursting out, "What was that all about? Mira was flirting with you nonstop, and you didn't have the decency to stop her. It's obvious. The girl is in love with you."

Toni looked surprised. "You think so?"

"Hello! Yes, of course, I think so. But that's not important. What's important is what you're going to do about it. We can't continue like this."

Toni thought about it for a while, then he looked straight at me, saying, "You're right. We can't continue like this. I'll fix it. Never doubt that you're the only one in my heart."

Chapter Nineteen - Conquest of Paradise

Mood Music:
"Conquest of Paradise" by Vangelis

"Your ticket, please." A lady in a blue uniform and a scarf around her neck wished me a lovely flight. I thanked her and hoped her wish would come true. I was anxious and worried. I reckoned that I must have developed some kind of flying phobia. I sat in a window seat and double-checked that I didn't forget anything important: my passport was in my purse, my ticket was in my hand, and the airline had my suitcase. I took a deep breath. There was no reason to be worried at all. So far, everything was going as planned.

I reread my itinerary:

Beirut to Amsterdam at 3:30 am – MEA
Amsterdam to Frankfurt at 9:25 am – KLM
Train from Frankfurt airport to Heidelberg at 12:35 pm

"It's going to be a long day!" I sighed. The night flight to Amsterdam was easy and smooth, but I didn't enjoy one bit of it. I couldn't because I was too focused on the plane's right wing, checking if its lights kept blinking as they were supposed to. I didn't want any surprises.

I arrived at Amsterdam Airport completely drained, but at least I was safe and sound. The airport was well-lit, clean, and organized, but it was too spacious for me. I felt lost. Bizarre thoughts circled in my mind, such as, "What if I have a heart attack right here next to the shops? What if I drop dead at this moment?" I was panicking.

On the flight from Amsterdam to Frankfurt, the flight attendant was friendly and helped me find my seat, "There you go, seat number 23F."

After storing my purse in the cabin above my head, I buckled my seatbelt and started flipping through their inflight magazine. Flying was not my favorite thing, and I had to take two flights in one day. Right next to me, there was a well-built young man. I assumed he was Dutch or German. By looking at his multi-pocket backpack, I presumed he was a frequent traveler. He was my complete opposite: calm, totally relaxed, and had no problem being on a plane. He seemed to be enjoying it.

"Excuse me," I said.

"Yaa?" he asked in surprise.

"I don't travel very often, and I'm worried I'm on the wrong flight. Do you know for sure if this one is going to Frankfurt?"

He paused for a few seconds to grasp my question, then shook his head. "Yaa, this flight is heading towards Frankfurt Airport. The airline won't allow you on the wrong flight, don't worry!" I felt relaxed.

The plane took off on time and flew over the clouds amid a blue and sunny sky. Contrary to what I expected, the flight was bumpy, too bumpy. I panicked and held my seat tightly. I took the chance to contemplate my life, my good deeds, and my sins. On that day, I made many promises to God and many promises to myself. I pledged to become a better person if I just lived through this flight.

*****

After more than one long hour of turbulence, I arrived at Frankfurt Airport feeling blessed and excited about my new life opportunity. At the airport train station, I immediately realized I had no idea how to take a train. We had had no working trains in Lebanon since my grandparents' time. I hoped someone at the information desk could help me out. I stood in a long and slow queue, waiting for my turn. The big clock hanging on the wall read almost half past 12. My train was set to leave at 12:35. I had plenty of time by Lebanese standards because come on, the train wouldn't go at 12:35 sharp!

When it was my turn, the time was 12:38. I stood in front of a man wearing an earring. That was a surprise for me.

"Hello, I need to take the train from Frankfurt to Heidelberg. It says here: platform 8, leaving at 12:35. Please can you tell me where platform 8 is? And what time will the train depart?"

He looked at the screen in front of him. "The train should have left at 12:35 as it says on your ticket, but you're lucky, there's a delay of 15 minutes. We apologize for that."

He pointed towards the right. "Go straight until the end, then take the first escalator on the right, go down one level, and you'll reach platform 8. Please, you need to hurry, yaa?"

I ran as fast as I could. I jumped on the train and sat down breathlessly on the first empty seat I laid eyes on.

"That was close!" I remembered my dad.

He always had a high opinion of Germany and the Germans. "The Germans are disciplined, correct, organized, and have the best football players, like Beckenbauer and Völler," he used to say.

He never ceased to try and convince me to learn German. "The German language is the language of great minds, Einstein, Nietzsche, and Beethoven."

The train departed, and Frankfurt was getting way behind us. It was my first time on a train by myself, and I felt proud that I had managed.

An older man dressed in a uniform approached, disrupting my train of thought, "Fahrscheine, bitte (*ticket please*)," he said. He looked like a train conductor from the movies, so I showed him my ticket, but he refused to stamp it as he did with the other passengers around me. He frowned and said, "Nein! (*no*)" with a wagging finger.

I heard the words "Shyte" and "nicht," but I didn't get what he was saying. As he looked mean, I decided to get out of his sight. It was annoying to leave my clean, comfy leather seat, but I had to.

I carried my suitcase and purse and walked toward the back of the train. I walked and walked until I found another beautiful, clean leather seat. It was also by the window. I grabbed a book from my purse and started reading a novel about love and revenge. Around 15 minutes later, out of the blue, a dark shadow crept slowly over my book. I looked up. It was the same angry train conductor. I gasped loudly. Why was he after me? I was a good Lebanese citizen! I did have a ticket, and I did show it to him. "What's his problem?" I thought.

He started blabbing in German again, but his voice was tenser than before, so I interrupted him politely, "Excuse me, but I don't understand you; I don't speak German. Do you want to see my ticket again? No? What do you want?" I exhaled and looked around for help. It was an impossible situation.

An elegant-looking lady, who must have overheard our conversation, intervened, "Miss, your ticket is for 2nd class, and this is the 1st class. You need to go to a 2nd class car."

"Ohhhh! So you have different classes on the train?! I had no idea."

Dad was right. The Germans were meticulously organized.

*****

Walking through the old streets of Heidelberg was like being captured in a postcard. The beauty of the city was beyond my imagination. The houses were gorgeous; I couldn't pick a favorite. I loved how the balconies were decorated with colorful flowers in beautiful pots instead of empty powdered milk containers as we used in Lebanon. The trees had a striking green color, and the streets were clean. The people looked healthy as if they came out of a sports catalog with their colorful jackets and practical hiking shoes. To my surprise, I didn't find one power cable dangling from a rooftop as is the case on my street in Beirut. I also wondered where the Germans hung their laundry. Their balconies had no clotheslines.

My taxi parked on the right side of the road. "We've arrived.

That's your hotel."

I grabbed my bag and excitedly stepped into the hotel lobby, but what I saw made me freeze. The hall was packed with men. All sorts of men, young, old, fat, thin, all dressed in dark suits. "I must be at the wrong place," I thought. I turned around and left the hotel without a word.

I stood outside on the pavement, clueless about how to get to my hotel. I asked a pedestrian for directions, "Can you help me, please? I'm looking for Motel One."

"You're standing right in front of it. This is the hotel you're looking for." the man replied. I looked up at the hotel sign again and decided to give it another try. I walked hastily into the lobby, pretending to be confident. I felt that several men were checking me out, probably wondering what a young girl dressed in jeans was doing at their solemn gathering.

The lady at the reception desk smiled at me. "Your room is on the second floor. It's bright and has a panoramic view. Ah, I almost forgot, someone left a message for you. Here it is. Mr. Toni called you 30 minutes ago and asked you to call him back."

The first thing I did when I was alone in my room was to return his call.

"I miss you so much, Nounou. I've felt so lonely since you left." His voice was warm. "Don't worry about Mira, by the way. You were right about her," he added.

"What are you going to do? She's one of your most important customers," I asked.

"Forget about that; you're more important to me. I told her today how much I love and miss you and that you and I will get engaged soon."

I was positively shocked. I had imagined us getting engaged, but we had never discussed it.

After our phone call, I felt so much love, and I promised myself to stop doubting him and have more faith in our relationship.

*****

After unpacking my bag, I got ready for my meeting with the sales manager, Mr. Schmidt. According to the fax from our German supplier, he would meet me in the lobby. The men's reunion was still going on.

"How will I recognize him? There are so many people in here." I wondered.

I looked around for a familiar face. I couldn't find anyone I knew, but I saw a few women and at least one celebrity. Tom Hanks was there too. He looked as handsome as ever, dressed in a light grey suit. He seemed to be in a good mood as he didn't stop laughing.

"Oops!" He saw me staring at him. I pretended to look the other way and continued searching for Mr. Schmidt.

I went around in endless circles until, finally, a hand tapped on my shoulder. "There you are, Ms. Beyrouti."

I turned around to see who it was, and to my shock, it was Tom Hanks himself. "It's almost impossible to get hold of you," he said.

My mouth opened in disbelief. "Of me?" I was star-struck.

"I was waiting for you. We're supposed to meet here in the lobby. Didn't you get my fax? I'm Jan Schmidt."

"Ohhh! Sorry, Mr. Schmidt, I got confused for a second. I thought you were someone else."

"No need for formalities, please call me Jan. Did you mistake me for Tom Hanks, the actor? It's normal. Everyone does. When I was in China, they asked me to sign autographs." We both laughed.

I pointed at the men standing around in the lobby, "By the way, which political party has organized this reunion?"

"Does it seem like a political reunion? It's not. These men are our clients having a drink before the company's gala dinner. You're joining us, right?"

"Yes, I'm coming with the company owner and his wife," I said.

Then Jan showed me and a few other international guests (Ricardo from El Salvador, Silvina from Argentina, Silvia from Peru, Mr. Kapadia from India, and Rekaya from Thailand) around the old town of Heidelberg. He briefly gave us some interesting facts about this famous city.

"Heidelberg is directly on the Neckar River. Here to the right, you can see part of its famous university, one of the oldest in

Germany. It was founded back in 1386. It is well-reputed for its law and medicine programs. Heidelberg is a romantic and very tourist city. As you see, it's already evening, and tourists are still visiting its old town and castle. Our gala dinner will take place tonight at one of the ballrooms of Heidelberg's charming red stone castle."

We strolled under the moonlight along the dim streets in the vibrant city center. The stone-covered pedestrian area was full of tourists who came from around the world to feel what it is like to be in the romantic city of Heidelberg. I saw a Chinese group taking photos of each other in front of the Rathaus (townhouse) and an American family standing at the corner as they were eating Turkish Doener. I noticed many young couples walking hand-in-hand or having a drink in one of the street cafes. To add to the place's charm, a Native American band played ethnic music on one of the streets. They had musical instruments and pipes that I had never seen in my life before. We stopped and listened attentively. Their music was out of this world. It was captivating. Many other pedestrians also stopped and dropped a few coins in the basket in front of them.

During my first encounter with the international business society, I discovered a few exciting things:

1- Some Chinese people prefer to use international names instead of their Chinese names to fit better in the business community. Our Chinese colleague Wei chose to be called Sunny instead. He had a valid point.

2- Mr. Kapadia told me that in India, a girl's family asks for a man's hand in marriage, which is opposite to our Lebanese traditions.

3- People from Thailand were hilarious.

4- Latinos were emotional and could be mistaken for Lebanese.

5- Germans had their unique sense of humor, which only those of a certain IQ level could understand.

6- Argentina has a lot of penguins.

However, the most important thing I learned was that no matter where people came from, they were genuine and friendly, and I could always find something in common with them.

*****

The gala dinner at the ancient Heidelberg castle was like no other dinner I had been to before. It was huge. We attended a show with acrobatics, magicians, singers, and dancers. The food selection was enormous and elegantly served. Jan and I chit-chatted nonstop. How wrong I was to think that Germans didn't open up. Within minutes, I knew all the essential information: He was married, in constant fights with his wife, and had no kids.

"Who are these Russian warriors?" Rekaya pointed at a couple coming in our direction. I looked at where she was pointing, and I bit my lip. It was Mr. and Mrs. Daniel. I could understand why the lady from Thailand was shocked. The couple looked totally out of place. Mr. Daniel was wearing a genuine fur coat and a brown Ushanka on his head as if he had popped out of a Russian war movie. Mrs. Daniel, also wearing a fur coat, had her pants tucked into her knee-high boots.

Parading elegantly, they waved and smiled at guests as they got closer to our table. The murmur in the room vanished only to be replaced by a song playing in my head: "Conquest of Paradise," the war song typically used for cake cutting at Lebanese weddings.

On their way to our table, the Daniels took the opportunity to take pictures with some important society figures, business people, and politicians. At that moment, I understood how my mentor's office was filled with celebrity photos. He didn't necessarily know all of them. They just took pictures together.

I whispered to Jan, "By the way, that's Mr. and Mrs. Daniel."

*****

Chapter Twenty - Hasta Que Te Conoci

Mood Music:
"Hasta Que Te Conoci" by Juan Gabriel

At 1:00 am (or 3:00 am in Beirut), I was already exhausted and freezing. I continuously rubbed my arms to warm up. All I wanted to do was go to bed, but I had to wait for a taxi. At least I wasn't alone; the Daniels were standing beside me. We shared a cab back to the hotel. On the way, Mr. Daniel shared some important news, "I've met their CEO, Mr. Stephan, at dinner, and he asked to meet you in person. He heard that you're handling their day-to-day business, and he wants to talk to you. I agreed with him that you'd be at his office at 7:30 am."

"7:30? Sure, Mr. Daniel." It was annoying to know that I would only have a few hours of sleep before my meeting. Unfortunately, I couldn't do anything about it. I had to go and be there on time.

My comfy hotel room was perfect. The moment I lay down on my bed, I fell asleep. I didn't know how long I had been sleeping when I woke up to a horrible noise. Rrrringgg. My heart started pounding. It was dark, and I panicked.

Was it the fire alarm? Was there someone at the door? For the first few moments, I had no idea where I was or what was going on. The constant ringing eventually made me realize that I was in my hotel room, and the ringing was just the phone.

"Noor Alo," I said automatically.

The voice on the other end was talking nonstop, "Add to that another 100,000 USD for rent and other expenses, including those of the lab, and yes, tell them we have three food technologists besides you." The man wouldn't stop talking. He had a loud voice, and I had no idea what he was talking about. I needed a moment to think, to understand what was going on.

Finally, I interrupted him, "Hold on for a second, please. Who are you again? What do you want exactly?"

There was a long pause. Then the man said slowly and firmly, "This is Mr. Daniel, Mlle Beyrouti. Are you still sleeping? Do you know that it's almost time for your meeting?"

I jumped out of bed and grabbed a notebook and a pen. "Mr. Daniel, I'm sorry; I'll be ready in a minute. Please could you repeat what you said before, I mean, at the very beginning?"

He took a deep breath and started all over again. "You have to exaggerate our expenses. Tell them our rent is excessive, double the number of our employees, and add that we invest in research and, of course, in our employees. Be sure to make our company look very impressive. Let them feel fortunate to have us as their agent."

My early meeting with the CEO went very well, and luckily, I didn't have to lie about anything. There was no need as Mr. Stephan didn't ask me about any work-related matters. He just wanted to get to know me personally; what I studied at the university, what my future ambitions were etc.

*****

My ten days in Germany passed so quickly that I couldn't believe it was already time to go home. I had daily meetings and lab work (with no accidents!) from 8 to 6, followed by business dinners and outings. Whenever I had spare time, which was very rare, I called my parents and Toni. They were all counting the days for me to get back.

On my last day in Germany, I made sure to spare some time to pass by Jan's office. Of everyone I met in Germany, I knew I was going to miss him the most. It was our last chat before I departed. He started by telling me how much I had left an impact on him and that he was sure their business would flourish because of me.

Before I left, Jan opened a white cabinet behind his desk and grabbed a book. "This is a small gift for you. It's one of my favorite books, "The Perfume." Have you read it?"

"No, I haven't. Thank you very much. I look forward to reading it." I was a bookworm specializing in novels by classical Arabic authors such as Amin Mahfouz and Ihsan Abd el Koudous. I looked at the cover and was excited to read an English book for a change.

I grabbed my purse and hugged him, saying, "I'm so glad I've met you. I hope to see you in Beirut soon." His eyes twinkled.

*****

My trip to Beirut was via Italy, as it was cheaper. I didn't mind. I was okay with any route that took me back home.

In the check-in area of Milan Airport, a Lebanese man introduced himself to me as Walid. "Have you enjoyed your stay in Milan?" he asked.

"Unfortunately, I didn't get to see it. I have a transit flight from Frankfurt." I shrugged.

"Shopping in Milan was amazing. I bought a lot of branded clothes and shoes." He smirked. "But I ended up with three suitcases, and I don't want to pay overweight charges. Could you check in one suitcase under your name?" he asked me.

Did I have the word NAIVE printed on my forehead? I was nice, but not that nice. My mom made sure to remind me of one important thing: Never, and under no circumstance, take anything from anyone in an airport. I refused and stood as far away from him as possible.

My flight back to Beirut was a different experience altogether. I talked to the lady sitting next to me, she was a young girl my age, and we had many friends in common. We talked and talked until I completely forgot about the airplane's blinking lights and the storm blowing around us.

When I left the plane, all I wanted to do was kiss the Lebanese ground. Finally, I was home. I missed everyone, all my friends and family. I missed our apartment and our food. Ten days of traveling felt like a decade for me. Our airport seemed too old and super tiny compared to European airports. However, it was a sweet reflection of our country; it was loud, warm, and welcoming.

The airport staff greeted passengers with "Hamdellah ala Es saleme," which literally means "thank God for your safety." I stood in line at passport control, waiting for my turn. The airport was busy at that time of day. I was getting restless and impatient. I just wanted to go home. Was that too much to ask for? I was fed up with being a career girl; I just wanted to be with my family and friends.

Then I heard some men shouting at each other and a loud voice yelling, "Come with us!" I asked the man standing in front of me, "Excuse me, what's happening?" He had no idea.

I leaned to the left to get a better view. I saw three policemen arresting a man who was struggling and giving them a hard time. Everyone at the airport was watching silently. It was not a joke; an actual arrest occurred before our eyes. When the man was dragged along next to me, I shrieked. It was Walid. I wouldn't have expected an elegant man like him, who loved shopping, to be in trouble with the law. I couldn't tell for sure, but I reckoned that his arrest had something to do with his suitcase. Moms are always right.

*****

On Wednesday morning, I was back at work, kissing and hugging my colleagues. I told them about my trip and business meetings, astonishing Germany, and my new international friends.

"Mr. Daniel was very impressed by our new German supplier. He said he had some fruitful meetings." Mr. Nader informed me. "Their management agreed to grant DanielCo an exclusivity-sales agreement for Lebanon, and they promised to consider the MENA region as well," he added.

Toni arrived later that morning, bringing along a European guest. He smiled when he saw me. "I missed you, Nounou." he whispered, "I'm so glad you're back. We'll talk later, ok?

I have to rush to Mr. Nader's office. Our guest is waiting for me there."

"Sure." I nodded.

Later, Toni told me he couldn't meet me after work as he had to take his guest out for dinner. I was fine with it since I was sleep-deprived and needed rest.

After driving home on autopilot, I threw myself on the first couch in our TV room. Mom and Dad were not back from Mom's doctor's appointment yet, and Riwa had her karate class. I forced myself to change into something comfier, had a light dinner in front of the TV, and went straight to bed.

*****

"Nooooo!!!" I screamed and sat upright in my bed. Tears were running down my cheeks. My body was trembling, soaked in sweat. I had woken up from a nightmare, not a kid's nightmare with witches and monsters, but it was just as scary. My fluorescent mouse clock showed 2:10 am. It was pitch black in my bedroom, and I could hear my blood rushing in my head. I sighed when I recalled my nightmare. It was horrible. I saw a busy airport with many passengers walking back and forth. Behind the barriers in the arrivals hall stood a man holding a rose bouquet and constantly checking his watch. From my position (floating up in the air), I could only see his back. He looked familiar, though. The airport glass doors opened widely, and a young woman walked out confidently as if she owned the place. She looked around, searching for someone; a tempting smile was on her face when she spotted the man holding his bouquet. Her step became faster as she got closer to him. He rushed to meet her halfway. They passionately hugged and kissed each other. I could hear the girl's distinguished laughter as he covered her face with his smooches. Their image enlarged and became more detailed. Suddenly, the man turned his face staring into space as if he sensed I was watching him. His face was as clear to me as the sun. It was Toni, my boyfriend, kissing Mira, his client.

"Oh my God. What a nightmare!" I sat in my bed, sobbing. It was a vision rather than a dream. I felt like I had witnessed Toni's infidelity with my own eyes.

*****

I could barely sleep that night. I couldn't wait for the sun to rise so I could go to work. I didn't know what to expect, but I needed to see Toni's face and read his body language. I needed to know if my nightmare was real.

I walked into the office pale as a ghost. The dark circles under my eyes were obvious and scary; at that time, I hadn't discovered concealers yet. Toni was on the phone, as usual. I waited a few minutes until he hung up, then I went to his desk. "Good morning, sweetie."

"Hello, my beloved Nounou. Book yourself for lunch today. I miss you. There's so much to talk about," he said happily. I felt like he was going to jump for joy.

I wasn't sure if I should tell him about my nightmare, so I decided to test him first. "Guess who I dreamed of yesterday?" I said while casually drinking my hot chocolate, "Your client, Mira. Imagine? I dreamed that she had come back from a holiday trip. Was she traveling?"

Toni flinched. "Wow! Your sixth sense is startling."

My eyes grew wide, and my breath became faster.

"Yes, she went for a weekend break with her friends," he mumbled.

"Well, is she back?" I asked with a shivering voice.

"I don't know," he answered hastily, "Let me check."

I waited impatiently as he dialed her business phone number.

"May I speak to Ms. Mira, please?" he asked the person on the phone. He listened for a few seconds, then covered the receiver, whispering, "Yes, it seems she's back. She arrived in the early morning."

*****

Another Friday evening, I spent at home reading. I couldn't help wondering how I ended up spending another weekend alone, at home by myself. All my friends had plans, but I didn't want to join in their activities. Riwa was getting ready to meet her friends for dinner, and my parents left to visit my uncle. Officially, I had had a boyfriend for two years, and a logical consequence was that we should be out having fun, but somehow our plans always got canceled last minute. Toni had called me in the morning, saying, "I'm so sorry, my sweetie, I'll be busy this evening. Dad asked me to do his accounting, but I promise to make it up to you next weekend. Would that be ok?" He had sounded miserable and frustrated, so I had decided to stay at home out of solidarity.

After 30 minutes of utter boredom, I decided to surprise Toni and stay with him at home while he worked on his Dad's accounting. But first things first. I had to hide the book I was reading. I didn't want anyone to know that it even existed. I couldn't keep it in my room because I didn't want to be in trouble. I had to keep it somewhere safe, where no one else would find it. But where? We had 1,000 books neatly organized on bookshelves all around our home. Despite that, it was almost impossible to find the perfect place for the book. We didn't have any other books of this sort. We had political and history books, novels, atlases, and geography books. We even had my grandfather's Turkish law books dating back to the 1890s.

After thinking for a while, I found the perfect hiding place for my book: under my sister's bed. I slipped it there without anybody seeing me and then went back to my room to get ready. By the time I had opened both closet doors, my sister had ambushed my room, shouting, "What the hell is this?" She was holding my book in her hand, the one I had just hidden in her room.

"Can you explain to me why this rubbish is under my bed?" She read the title aloud, "' Intimate Relationship Tips for a Married Couple.' Why on earth are you reading such a book? Confess NOW. Are you having an intimate relationship with your jerk boyfriend before you're even married?"

I gasped. "What? No, I swear to God,"

She interrupted me, "Then why are you reading this?"

"Because I don't know much about this topic. Of course, I know the basic things, but I don't know the details. And I need to know them for when I get married. Don't judge me. It was your idea in the first place." I replied innocently.

She was fuming. "You were the one who told me to read more books, remember?" I added.

Riwa's expression changed from surprise to plain disgust. "How dare you associate me with such rubbish! I suggested that you read more books to broaden your horizons, but I meant substantial books, bestsellers, for example, by renowned authors."

She pointed at my book. "Tell me, do you know who wrote this book?"

I shook my head. "Here! Check for yourself." She handed it to me.

I looked at her, then read aloud, "An expert couple."

I rubbed my chin, staring at her. She had a point; it was a cheap book. At this moment, a storm broke into my bedroom. Riwa gave me a lecture on books and being intellectual, and how a girl should be conservative, protect her honor, abiding by our religious and social rules.

Riwa looked at her watch. "I have to stop now as I'm running late." She pointed at the book, yelling, "This is not over yet. We will continue our discussion another time." It took me some time to calm down and get a hold of myself again. Riwa's lectures had a significant impact on me.

Before I left home, I took a final look at myself in the mirror. I looked pretty and nervous. I wore my special long, flowery, bordeaux-colored dress — the one Toni had chosen for me.

*****

There are two sad chapters ahead.
If you prefer happy stories, then please feel free
to skip directly to Chapter 23.

Chapter Twenty-One - The Boy Is Mine

Mood Music:
"The Boy Is Mine" by Brandy and Monica

It was a long trip to Toni's home, but I enjoyed every single bit. The music was mind-blowing on every radio station, including Light FM. I felt like nightclubbing. I had never been to a nightclub before, but I was going to suggest that to Toni.

It was dark on the curvy road going up to his house, and I was the only person driving at that time, but the moonlight lit my way. The first thing I noticed when I reached his home was a strange car parked in his garage. I rang the bell, unable to hide my grin.

His dad opened the door and greeted me in a surprised yet polite manner, "Hello, Noor."

I kissed him on his cheek, asking him, "Is Toni here?"

"Sure, please come in." He moved to the side, letting me in. The moment I entered, everyone fell silent. Toni looked like a defeated tiger. I didn't know if he felt embarrassed or angry. Mira, who sat next to him on the sofa with her hand on his thigh, seemed relaxed, not caring too much about what was happening. Toni didn't say a word while I froze in my place, motionless.

His dad saved the situation. He pulled me to a side room, closing the door behind him. "Noor, you're like a daughter to me. I won't lie to you. Toni and Mira have been dating for quite some time now."

He told me many things that I didn't hear and, what's more, didn't understand. My brain blocked everything off. It was too much to take it all in. I ran to the main door and left Toni's home as fast as I could without looking back. I was devastated, shaken beyond description, but above all, I felt ashamed. Toni should have been the one to be embarrassed, but I was.

I drove back home like a maniac, splashing other cars as I sped on the highway. I didn't care that it was raining and that the wipers barely swiped water off the windshield. I wanted to be home.

"What's wrong?" Riwa followed me into the salon as I was mumbling incomprehensible words.

"She was there at his house!" I shouted, going around in circles.

"Who was there? Stop moving! You're making me dizzy."

"Mira," I yelled. "His client. She was there watching TV in their living room. He sat beside her, and she had her hand on his thigh."

"Are you hundred percent sure?" she asked.

"Of course, I am. I saw Mira with my own eyes, and his dad told me everything. He said they're dating."

Riwa was very angry. She never liked him. She detested him more like it. She had tried to convince me a million times to leave him, but I had never listened to her. Instead, I accused her of being jealous that I had a boyfriend, and she didn't.

I ran about our salon aimlessly while Riwa started removing our daggers from the wall. "They need cleaning," she muttered. She also locked all of our windows and balcony doors.

"What are you doing? I'm suffocating in here. Open the window! I need some fresh air!" I shouted. "I promise you I'm not going to jump from the balcony if that's what you're thinking of."

She made me sit down, saying softly, "Just relax now, I'll make you a hot chocolate, but first I'll get you a glass of water. You need hydration."

I was sobbing nonstop. "No. Stay here. I need you. I need all of you. Where are Jana and Haya? Why aren't they with me?" I burst into tears again.

"Ok, I'll get them, but stay calm and don't do anything crazy while I'm gone."

Before I knew it, the three girls were all sitting around me. We intensely discussed the latest news. I was see-sawing between a wild dog ready to attack and a helpless little girl biting her nails and cursing her misfortune.

"We told you not to trust him. He was a liar all along."

"He's after her money, that's it."

"He's after her looks, and don't forget she's a few years younger than you."

"Probably, his mother pushed him into this. She never liked you anyway."

"What?" My eyes turned into saucepans.

"Stop, please. You're making things worse."

I couldn't decide what was more disturbing, the fact that she was younger and came from a more affluent family or that he had lied to me. The answer wasn't important because new questions that were more psychologically disturbing came to my mind. "Am I not lovable? Am I unattractive?" I said out loud.

Riwa handed me a mug of hot chocolate. "What nonsense! Of course, you're attractive, and of course, you're lovable. Use your brain now. Why are we all sitting here with you? Because we love you dearly." They all hugged me.

Jana was my age, and she knew Toni the best. He considered her a close friend. I reached for her, desperately hoping she could tell me something to make me feel a little better. She pressed her lips together.

I freaked out. "Jana, are you hiding something?"

"I'm sorry, Noor, but I didn't want you to get hurt. Mira's childhood friend just joined our office two months ago, and she showed us her holiday pictures from Cyprus. She went with Mira and some other girls ..." I didn't let her finish her sentence.

"Yes, I know. And?"

Jana mumbled, "It seems Toni and Mira have been dating for months now. He even picked her up from the airport when she arrived. They kissed and hugged as if there was no one looking. Obviously, my new colleague had to tell Mira to slow down her public display of affection because people were staring at them."

"OMG! Just like in my nightmare!" I screamed.

Jana moved closer to me and held my hand gently. "For some reason, Mira thinks you two broke up a long time ago."

*****

Later that night, when Riwa entered our salon, I didn't notice her as I was still pacing the room. She stopped me, insisting that I should go to bed. "It's 1:00 am, for God's sake." I tried to object at first because I was hyperactive, and my mind was going crazy. But Riwa was stubborn. She dragged me to my room and tucked me into bed. She kissed me on my forehead, assuring me that things would get better.

"My sweetie, you got it all wrong. Subconsciously, you always wanted to break up with him, but you didn't want to hurt him. Now you have your life back. You should be celebrating instead of crying. He wasn't the right one for you. You knew it. How often did you tell him it wasn't working out?" I nodded. "How many times did you want to go to the U.S. to do your Ph.D., but he persuaded you to stay?"

As she spoke, I felt better and less hysterical. She promised me that I was destined for great things. I hoped she was right. I finally closed my eyes and slowly dozed off.

*****

My mom and dad must have felt something fishy going on, but whenever they asked me, I assured them everything was fine. Usually, I wouldn't have hidden such a big thing, but Mom was already overwhelmed by her health issues, and Dad was terribly worried. Mom had been diagnosed with atherosclerosis, and she needed to undergo an operation.

I went to bed late every night and discussed with Riwa what had happened. She told me exactly what she had told me the day before, that I was destined for great things and so on. Then I dozed off and slept.

On one of those days, at dawn, I woke up feeling miserable. I snuck into my parents' room and lay down between them, hugging Dad with my arm. Dad opened his eyes and caressed my hair softly. "Are you ok, my love?" My voice shivered, and I couldn't say a word. Tears were running down my cheeks. "Shhhh, come with me."

He asked me to get ready as he wanted to take me for a walk. He whispered so we wouldn't wake up Mom.

It was Sunday morning, and it was his favorite routine to drive his old Mercedes to the seaside corniche. He parked and got out of the car. We leaned on the fence, gazing at the orange horizon. The wavy sea was dark and deep. Fishing boats were scattered beneath us. Except for a few sports lovers, the corniche was almost empty at such an early time.

"My sweetheart, tell me, what's bothering you? I've never seen you down like this before," he asked me in his loving voice. I told him what had happened and that Toni had been cheating on me.

He was not surprised. "I expected that to happen sooner or later. He isn't an honest man. I don't understand why you went out with him in the first place. He's not the one for you. Frankly, I'm glad this is over. You deserve a much better person, a man of integrity, intellect, and ethics. You're beautiful, Noor, a smart and funny girl. Trust me. You'll find a decent man who will be worthy of you. Just give it some time." Dad stared at the wavy sea with his arm around my shoulder.

During our long walk along the corniche, I opened up to Dad. I had never imagined sharing my worries, fears, and insecurities with him the way I did. At the end of our walk, he looked into my eyes, smiling. "Come with me. I'll take you to a special place where you'll appreciate all your blessings."

He drove to an overcrowded area full of slums and poorly maintained houses. He parked at the corner of a street, and I followed him into a small bakery. I noticed that Dad knew his way around well.

"20 bags of Arabic bread packs, please," he told one of the bakers.

When a man at the counter realized that the packs were for charity, he charged my dad only half the price. "If it's for charity, then I'd like to contribute as well," he explained.

I helped Dad carry the bags and walked behind him through a narrow alley leading to an old mosque. He asked a small boy playing in the square to call the imam. The boy ran inside the mosque instantly. While we were waiting for the imam, a bunch of kids dressed in torn clothes – barely enough to cover them on such a cold morning – gathered around us. They asked us for help, begging for food or money.

Dad opened one of the big plastic bags, grabbed a few bread packs, and started distributing them. I did the same. I always heard about people living under the poverty line, but I had never realized before that poverty was right next door, only a few kilometers away from my own home. I looked into the kids' eyes. They smiled at me with gratitude. A little kid, maybe ten years old, took his bread pack, thanking us, "My mom will be thrilled. I got breakfast for the whole family."

When I was about to cry, the boy asked me, "Why are you crying? Is everything alright?" I was astonished and moved by this little boy's compassion. He was asking *me* if I was alright!

An older man with a bright face and a well-trimmed white beard gracefully received us at the gate, smiling and greeting my dad warmly. I understood from their conversation that he was a regular visitor. Strangely enough, I couldn't recall Dad ever mentioning the imam. He prayed the rosary with wrinkly fingers. Then he led us to a warm side room whose walls were covered with yellowish, decayed stones. A few wooden chairs were perfectly placed around a shabby carpet. Dad whispered a few words in the imam's ear.

The pious man looked at my face gently, then softly laid his hand on my head and began reciting verses of the Holy Quran. His voice was deep and peaceful. In my old school, religious studies were a major part of the curriculum, so hearing the Holy Quran was by no means new to me, yet my reaction was intense. I felt my dad's strong presence by my side. I started crying again, but I didn't bother wiping my tears away. At this place, it felt ok to be weak. It was a serene place where nobody would judge me. The imam didn't stop reciting until I finally calmed down and stopped crying.

*****

Chapter Twenty-Two - Frozen

Mood Music:
"Frozen" by Madonna

Toni suggested meeting up and talking. First, I refused, but on his third attempt, I accepted. We met at a small cafe not far from our office. I felt as if I was sitting next to a total stranger. His mask fell off, and his true self got revealed.

"Please listen to me. I've been trying to talk to you since that horrible evening. Probably, you think I'm cheating on you, but believe me, that's not true," he pleaded.

I laughed in disbelief. "And what was Mira doing in your house on a Friday evening? Buying chemicals?" I asked.

"I told you, she's stalking me. I've told her off many times, but she's not getting it. What can I do? I don't want to upset her. She's my client." Toni tried to hold my hand, but I pushed him away.

"Are you kidding me? Do you think I'm stupid? I know everything. Your dad told me ..."

He interrupted me, "Don't listen to him, my sweetheart. I love you."

Instead of falling for the "love" word as I used to, I was appalled. How could this be love?! I didn't expect my reaction to being physically harsh, but it was. With all my might, I slapped him on his face leaving a red mark on his left cheek. "Not only are you a liar but also a big-time coward."

*****

I called those days "the era of self-imprisonment." I was stuck in my car and didn't know where to go. At home, Mom was sick and busy going from one doctor to the other. At work, Toni and his new girlfriend performed "La Vie En Rose." Mira either sent Toni red roses every week or popped up in our office, bringing them herself. Their romantic meetings at our office were beyond normal, to the extent that one of our senior managers finally scolded Toni for his behavior. "This is a business office, not a dating cafe," he told him.

I found my escape from all that turmoil in different ways. After attending our daily morning meetings at work, I drove 80 km to Tripoli (in the north) and back. I should have taken passengers on board; at least they would have paid for the fuel. Besides driving, I read tons of self-help books. My favorite one was *The Road Less Traveled* by Scott Peck, which starts like this:

"Life is difficult. This is a great truth, one of the greatest truths. It is a great truth because once we truly see this truth, we transcend it. Once we truly know that life is difficult – once we truly understand and accept it-then life is no longer difficult. Because once it is accepted, the fact that life is difficult no longer matters."

He was absolutely and utterly right. My life was very difficult. I needed to accept that and stop whining for the sake of everyone's mental health. I realized that my perception of life was unrealistic. People were neither heroes nor villains, and life was neither black nor white.

To repay Mr. Scott Peck, the author, I decided to name my newly adopted cat after him: Nouna-Scott (I couldn't figure out if the greyish street cat was male or female, hence the double-gender name). Soon, it became my Saturday ritual to read parts of the book to Nouna-Scott while sipping a hot chocolate. He/She loved it.

The paragraph in *The Road Less Traveled* that had the most impact on me was about taking one's own decisions and accepting the consequences. When Mr. Peck, a psychiatrist, mentioned to his boss, Dr. Mac Badgely, that he was tired of working long hours, his boss' reply was enlightening:

"I told you, Scott, you do have a problem." This was hardly the response expected. "Yes," I said, slightly annoyed, "I know I have a problem. That's why I came to see you. What do you think I ought to do about it?" Mac responded: "Scott, apparently, you haven't listened to what I said. I have heard you, and I am agreeing with you. You do have a problem."

"Goddammit." I said, "I know I have a problem. I knew that when I came in here. The question is, what am I going to do about it?" "Scott," Mac replied, "I want you to listen. Listen closely and I will say it again. I agree with you. **You do have a problem. Specifically, you have a problem with time. Your time. Not mine. It's not my problem. It's your problem, with your time.*"*

How come I never thought of that? How come, for years, I blamed the world for anything that went wrong? Dr. Badgely's response changed my perspective on life and how I handled my responsibilities, decisions, and actions. Those were all mine and mine only. Reading that book was the reason for my decision to work on my "character disorder," as Mr. Peck called it. Whenever I was "… in conflict with the world, the world was not at fault."

Both driving up north and Scott Peck's book pushed forward my transformation, but I was still not totally at peace with myself. I decided to be the new Forrest Gump: Run, Noor, run!

Every day, I ran lap after lap on the AUB Green Field. I ran until my legs ached, and I couldn't run anymore. My enthusiasm for running grabbed the attention of some professional runners. One of them was an army general who ran on the AUB Green Field every evening. He offered to teach me how to run correctly, and I agreed. It was a challenge for me because he was fit and disciplined and took jogging very seriously. With time, I found excuses to stop running with him. I had some valid reasons for that.

First, his conversation topics were unorthodox. "If you were a terrorist and wanted to hurt as many people as possible, what would you do, and where would you attack?" How on earth would I know about that? Then, during our running sessions, he kept shouting at me, "Good boy. Go faster!" or "Good boy, do 50 pushups!"

In which way exactly did I resemble "a good boy"? Were my curves not speaking for themselves? I constantly tried to remind him that I was not one of his soldiers, but my attempts were in vain. When he insisted on making me exercise like a soldier, I tried to trick him. "Since you consider me one of your soldiers, can I jump from an army helicopter?"

"No."

Then, things became way too intimate, "Try running without your underpants. Believe me; it's liberating." Woohoo!! He had crossed the line. It was over.

Afterward, I started running with an older Cabinet member, who, as I found out later, was my dad's classmate at school. Due to our significant age difference and different level of political knowledge, we didn't have any common topics. So we stuck to socially accepted "knee injury" conversations, recommending knee doctors and exercises to prevent knee injuries.

*****

On one of my rides to the gym, I noticed a black Mercedes Coupe in front of me. I loved Mercedes Coupes. What a mix of elegance and power! It was one of those new models that stood out, especially next to all the old Mercedes taxis filling up the streets. It was my dream car and the dream car of many other Lebanese people back then. We even came up with a nickname for it: "The Ghost." Lebanese people often used nicknames for new car models such as Mercedes "The Ghost," Mercedes "The Beast," or BMW "The Bat." We also created a color nomenclature system for our beloved cars, e.g., Wazwaz yellow (flashy) or Demon's blood red.

For more than 15 minutes, the car was driving in front of me. It was as if the driver was heading to the same place I was going. After another 10 minutes, I was sure he was also going to AUB. He even had an AUB sticker on his bumper. The Mercedes went inside a tunnel; I did the same. Then we both continued straight. He went left, and so did I.

I saw the driver's eyes in his rearview mirror. He was looking at me, probably wondering why I was following him, which

I was not. He turned right, and I followed suit. AUB was getting closer, and we both had to park.

"What's his problem?" I wondered, "Why is he speeding up? We've arrived at AUB; we need to park now. Shoot! We've missed all the good parking spots."

I followed him to see where we would end up. "Paaap paap, move!" I honked at the car in front of me so he would let me pass. I didn't want to lose "The Ghost." Then I was back on his tail. He drove for quite some time, trying to lose me while constantly glimpsing in his mirror, but he couldn't. Abruptly, he parked his car on the right side of the corniche. I did the same and parked behind him.

Oops! I looked around. Why did I park here? I was too far from AUB. The Mercedes driver locked his car, staring at me in his mirror. Then it hit me. He was scared of me. He must have thought I was stalking him. But I was not a stalker. I was sleep-deprived and heartbroken and not thinking straight. I got out of my car without paying him any attention, as if I had intentionally chosen to park in the middle of nowhere. I carried my sports bag and walked all the way to AUB.

I definitely needed to get over Toni. It was already one month since the cheating incident.

*****

Days passed slowly and meaninglessly. I split my time between work and taking care of my mom. Although she had had a successful operation to widen her arteries, her condition got worse. True, her face had a healthy pinkish color, but she could barely walk or talk. On top of that, her fainting became more frequent.

One evening, Riwa and I took her to see my cardiologist cousin. He recommended that we take her to the emergency hospital immediately. It was a cold, windy December evening. After several check-ups, the doctors at the hospital informed us that Mom had had several minor heart attacks and that she had to spend the night in the ICU for surveillance. "Please go home and rest. You can't help her waiting here," the nurse said.

As we said goodbye, my mom reminded us with teary eyes, "Don't you want to kiss me goodbye?"

"Mom, we'll be here tomorrow morning to take you home. You're here only for monitoring." I leaned down and gave her a quick kiss.

Early the next morning, the hospital called home, asking us to rush to the ICU. My mom had recurrent heart attacks. By the time we reached the hospital, it was over. My mom had already passed away.

May God rest your soul in peace, Mom

Chapter Twenty-Three - Hasta Siempre

Mood Music:
"Hasta Siempre" by Nathalie Cardone

"May God rest her soul in peace. We all loved her dearly," one lady said as she stood on her toes to kiss me.

"Thank you," I murmured, wiping my eyes.

"May God rest your mom's soul. She was such a kind woman." Another lady hugged me tightly. Ladies lined up one behind the other to console my sister and me.

During the Azza period, three days of mourning, family, friends, acquaintances, neighbors, friends of friends, and even politicians visited us to pay their respects and offer their condolences. The first day of Azza was by far the hardest for us, as it was my mom's burial day, only one day after she had passed away. Suddenly, we had to accept the fact that our mom was not at home anymore. She wasn't there to tell us what to do, which juice to serve, or which cake to get. For the first time in my life, we were hosting such a massive event at home with hundreds of people attending, yet she was not there to be the hostess. Riwa and I aged several years within a few hours, but my dad seemed to age more than a decade.

Riwa and I sat on our three-seater couch facing the visitors, and my eldest aunt sat between us, having her hands on our hands. She didn't tell us bluntly, "I'm here for you, I love you," but her actions said it all.

As was Lebanese tradition during Azza, women, and men had to be in separate rooms, but temporary mixing was quite common. The women were seated in our TV and dining room while Dad, my uncles, and cousins welcomed visitors to our huge salon.

Both Mom and Dad were well-known figures in society, and thus many people came to support us in those difficult times. Almost all my colleagues from DanielCo came to pay me their respects, including Mr. Daniel himself. Aziz, Ruba, Wael, Salim, and the truck drivers came, but Toni didn't show up. I didn't expect him to.

We offered our guests an open buffet lunch and dinner during these three days, including starters, main dishes, and desserts. Throughout the day, we served black Turkish coffee. We hired a specialized catering company to supply food and provide waiters for setting the table and serving food and coffee. For most Azza events in Beirut, this catering company would send the same waiter, Asem.

Asem was a serious, middle-aged man who did his job to the utmost perfection. Since he had been on many such sad occasions before, he was familiar with the Beiruty families. He knew who was the cousin of whom, who had diabetes, hence took no sugar in his coffee, and who had high blood pressure, hence took no extra salt in his stuffed vine leaves. He knew most of the visitors, at least by their names.

On such occasions, Asem brought hundreds of plain white plates, glass cups, and cutlery to make things easier for the mourning family. Additionally, we hired two ladies to help him out. The job of these ladies was mainly to prepare coffee and clean the dishes. Typically, visitors stayed for around 30–40 minutes, after which they left, thus giving room for new visitors. Only close family members and friends stayed for a longer time.

"Riwa, can I talk to you in private? Noor, you too." Malik, my sister's best friend, gave us a sign as he walked toward the kitchen. We followed him quickly as he seemed upset.

He looked straight into Riwa's face and said with a bossy tone, "I've been watching you all day. Can you tell me why you're introducing yourself to the women who come to console you? Do you think they don't know who you are? Or do you think they're here for a business meeting?" His upper lip was shivering as it always did whenever he was upset.

Malik getting crazy with Riwa's unconventional behavior was not unusual. "The only thing you have to do today," he addressed me too, "is to sit down, relax, and take your time to grieve. No one is expecting anything more of you."

I looked at Riwa's blushing face. It was unlike her to be quiet and obedient.

I didn't know most of the ladies who visited us. I depended on my auntie, my dad's sister, who knew every woman by name. Whenever I glanced at her discreetly, trying to grasp the woman's name, my auntie raised her eyebrows in surprise and said right in front of the lady, "Madam Anisy?! Didn't you recognize her?" She would hold the lady's hand and explain her position in our family tree, "She's the wife of my second cousin who lives in Achrafieh. How's his hip, by the way? I hope he's better after his operation?"

I didn't have a clue about my family tree, but I shouldn't be blamed. I had a huge family from both sides. My paternal grandmother's side alone were more than seventy direct relatives. That was without counting my dad's first and second cousins or uncles and aunties; that would be several hundred. My maternal grandmother's side was impressive in number as well. My mom's sister married a relative and moved to Curacao in the Dutch Caribbean, where she had many children and grandchildren. She once showed us their pictures. It turned out that I was a member of the Benetton family: I had second cousins from the whole color spectrum, ranging from dark black to snow white.

My main problem during the Azza was my mom's relatives from the north, as neither my auntie nor I knew most of them. "You don't seem to remember me. Of course, you were a little kid in diapers when I last saw you. I'm your mother's first cousin from her dad's side. We used to run and pick fruits in the orchards together," a sweet old lady told me. "You remind me so much of your mother. I can smell her in you."

I smiled lovingly and thanked her for being there for us. When she left, I sniffed my shirt and whispered to Riwa, "Do I smell like olive oil soap?"

Riwa rolled her eyes. "That was metaphorical."

When it got a bit quieter, I decided to peek into the salon to see who was there. I noticed my mom's cousin, Uncle Awad, was sitting next to Dad, whispering in his ear. My dad and Uncle Awad never got along, so I wondered what they were discussing. Uncle Awad was a well-built man in his 60s and looked like he was coming from the 60s too. He had retired a few years back, but he never stopped taking care of himself, dressing up as if he was going on a date. His black hair was always in the best shape, dyed, waxed, and combed back. His black handlebar mustache was also waxed and dyed. He was a copycat of one of his uncles, a former pasha in the Ottoman army. My mom once spilled a family secret, "Do you know that the pasha kept his long, well-groomed mustache in a special wooden mold overnight to make sure it was always perfect?"

Riwa poked me. "What are you looking at?"

I pointed with my head. "Look! Uncle Awad hasn't stopped talking to Dad for the last ten minutes. What do you think they're talking about?"

Dad finally got up and signaled Riwa and me to follow him to his bedroom.

"Girls, Uncle Awad took the initiative for your mom's funeral. Since your mom had a royal title, he thinks she needs to have a VIP burial."

Riwa protested, "What are you saying? Mom wouldn't have liked that." But Dad wouldn't listen.

"Let me finish. Uncle Awad managed – don't ask me how – to get two police escorts for your mom's coffin on her final ride to her hometown in the north."

"Police officers? Please, Dad, tell him no. We don't want that kind of attention." Riwa pleaded with Dad, but he refused, saying that it was too late to do anything now the convoy was already on its way.

As my dad and the other men were getting ready for their trip to the north for my mom's burial, I went to my bedroom for a short break. I laid down on my bed and closed my eyes, imagining my mom, her voice, her ideas, and our funny discussions. It was hard to accept that we had lost her forever. The day before, she had still been at home.

Riwa flung open my bedroom door in a panic. "We're in big trouble. The convoy is ready, but they're unable to move."

I was puzzled. "Why not?"

"Mom's death certificate is missing. We can't bury her without it."

"Oh, that's strange. Who had it last?"

"I had it last, and I remember very well that I put it on the dining table a few hours ago, but now it's gone."

"Ummm, let me think." I stood up and opened one of the drawers in my wooden filing cabinet. I ran my hand along the identical dark green files, reading each tag aloud; "School certificates, birthday cards, medical bandages, original paintings, articles written by Malik," I winked at Riwa when I read the last tag. "Just in case you two end up together one day." I said.

"For God's sake, what are you doing? This is not the time to show me that you are obsessively organized. My mom needs to be buried. Where can I find the certificate?" she shouted.

I looked at her. "Will you wait for a second? Aha, here it is just as I expected, filed under 'death certificates.'"

I handed her a freshly printed document. "Isn't that what you've been looking for?"

She skimmed the document. "Princess Amal Al Ayoubi was declared dead on the ..."

She looked me straight in the eyes. "Are you kidding me? You filed our mother's death certificate before she was even buried. You need help!"

*****

The third day of Azza was by far the busiest. People who had missed the first two days made sure to pass by our home on this last day. Besides that, many visitors who had been there on the first and second days came again on the third day.

Rania and Blossom, my classmates from university, came to see me too. When I saw them, I felt relieved. They were my excuse to take a break. Accepting condolences for several days was an exhausting and stressful exercise. "Let's go to the kitchen," I whispered in their ears.

There was barely any space to stand in our kitchen. Asem and the maids were there, and so were some of our cousins. The whole apartment was packed, including my bedroom. Asem offered the girls some black Turkish coffee. Rania took a cup, but Blossom, who was more of a chocolate person, declined, "No, Asem, thank you."

He looked up and pointed at her. "I know you. You're the daughter of Mr. Sulaiman. What a man! Your father hired me several times to serve at his fancy pool parties. He trusted me with the most important mission, opening his selected champagne bottles."

Rania choked on her coffee the moment he said the word "champagne." I patted her back while Blossom looked around to see if anyone else had heard that. Even in an open society like Lebanon, alcohol was considered taboo at religious events like Muslim funerals, and there was no need to shock our visitors.

No one noticed when we were back to our seats. Our female guests attentively listened to a man giving a speech. To my surprise, that man was none other than Uncle Awad, who took a strategic position in the middle of our TV room for every woman to see and hear him well.

"Sisters and daughters," he started, "I need to talk to you about something important …"

I asked Riwa, frowning, "What is he doing?" She shushed me.

Uncle Awad said, "I ask you all tonight before you go to bed to take off your bras and feel your breasts. It doesn't matter whether your breasts are big or small. I urge you all to do it."

I stood up in an attempt to stop him, but Uncle Awad continued, "I beg you, don't neglect your breast check-up. Breast cancer is a silent killer. I know this because I've lost my wife to it." He grabbed a white handkerchief from his pocket and wiped his eyes, "She was my angel, but now she's gone."

"May God rest her soul in peace," many women consoled him.

A long period of silence followed.

Once life returned to the room, an elegant lady wearing a black drape dress and a diamond necklace softly addressed

Uncle Awad, "I've always wanted to meet you, Mr. Prime Minister. I'm so sorry about your wife's death."

The lady mistook Uncle Awad for our former prime minister!

The situation was getting awkward, so Riwa and I stood up. Riwa escorted Uncle Awad back to the men's section, and I accompanied the lady back to her seat. "Would you like to have some coffee, Auntie?" I asked her.

When the Azza period was over, Dad, Riwa, and I recalled the disasters that had taken place on this last day. Besides Uncle Awad's speech, two other misfortunes happened.

First, a high-ranking religious man stumbled over his long robe when he had gone down our building's dark stairwell during one of the usual power cuts. He had broken his hip and had had to be brought to the hospital.

Second, Uncle Nizar, a man in his late fifties who had lived with his family two floors down from us, had died of a heart attack directly after paying his respects.

May God rest his soul.

*****

Chapter Twenty-Four - Moonlight Sonata

Mood Music:
"Moonlight Sonata" by Beethoven

My mom used to tell us a joke about this little boy whose parents didn't pay the school fees on time. When the school principal asked him for a reason, the little boy answered innocently, "My father said he would pay you when the season starts."

The puzzled principal replied, "Which season is your father talking about?"

"Autumn! You see, Sir, my dad works as an undertaker."

I never laughed at that joke, as I didn't find it particularly funny. Ironically, years later, the joke turned on me. Autumn had already started off with Toni's infidelity. Our love had withered away as the leaves turned yellow and fell on Sawfar Corniche, to put it dramatically. Despite this misery, I wished autumn had lasted longer. When winter took over, the tragedy got more intense. My mom passed away, followed by my auntie two weeks later.

I had often heard people say that home would never be the same again when a mother passed away. I understood the meaning of it when I experienced it first-hand. After losing my mom, our home changed tremendously. It was no longer the warm, vibrant home we were used to but changed into a disturbingly quiet place no matter how noisy we tried to be. It became dark even in bright daylight, and it turned into a sad cocoon despite our joint efforts to keep going on. Our family's hearts had been torn out.

Riwa and I often described that time as a black cloud lingering above our apartment and refusing to go away. It was too much for anyone to handle – even for me, a naturally positive and happy person. Riwa expressed her grief by playing Beethoven's Moonlight Sonata on our piano over and over again while I sat next to her in our salon, writing poems about punishment, death, and doomsday.

> *Afflicted land ... wasted*
> *Mortal life ... decayed*
> *Where do we hide from our fate?*
> *There is no escape ... we need to wait*
> *Our lives are wasted on materialistic things*
> *Unfortunately, we accept whatever life brings*
> *Will we have time before our endless night?*
> *Or will our healing come with bright light?*

I was surrounded by a loving and supportive family, friends, and a cat, but it was still too hard to bear, and I finally hit rock bottom. I prayed a lot and asked God for help, for answers to all my questions. Why did I have to suffer so intensely in such a short period of two months? Was I being punished? For what? Was I a bad person?" The most important question was: Did God still love me?

I felt it was time to let go of my earthly life and move on to the next one. Being a firm believer in God, I could never take my own life, so I had to wait for the right moment.

The moment came on a hopeless, rainy day.

I drove to the seaside corniche, got out of the car, and stood facing the rough, wavy sea. I had a plan: If a wave decided to pull me into the deep sea, I was not going to resist, though I was never going to jump myself. I waited for a few minutes. There was a heavy storm, and the sky was cloudy and dark. The sea was unpredictable and angry. It was the perfect weather, and it couldn't have gotten any worse than that. I watched a crazy wave approaching the shore. I felt like that was the right moment. My time was near. I closed my eyes and prayed, waiting for the wave to drag me along. Then it splashed me with icy water all over. I felt its strength, its power. I opened my eyes. I was still standing on the corniche like a wet chicken. It was not my time yet. It was merely a wet wake-up call.

It didn't take long for my questions to be answered. One evening after my running session at AUB, I saw a small note on my windshield. I grabbed it carefully. It was a small white card that only had three words printed on it:

"God Loves You"

I turned around to see who had put the card on my car, but there was no one. I sat back in my seat, reading and rereading those three powerful words. I counted my blessings: my health, my family, my friends, and my life. God had already answered my questions a long time ago.

*****

I would never have imagined that my new colleague would turn my life upside down as she did. I first met Naya, a "Snow White" type of girl, when she was appointed our Marketing Executive right after I broke up with Toni. I got to know her better at my mother's Azza. She visited us for three consecutive days together with her parents and siblings, although we had never met them before.

She was raised in UAE, France, and Canada, which justified her poor spoken and written Arabic and extreme open-mindedness. We didn't share the same background, interests, hobbies, friends, or family. Yet, we became best friends in no time.

At first, our symbiotic relationship was based on pure need: She needed a translator, while I needed answers to my *how could he* question, which was still lingering in my head. Luckily, Naya's passion was psychology, and her favorite book was *Chicken Soup for the Soul*. She read it out loud all the time, in my car, in her car, at home, at work, and during lunch breaks. Naya tried to answer all my questions, using mainly this book as a reference. When she couldn't help, she encouraged me to open up and find the answers myself. She asked me to tell her about my childhood and teenage years.

"The first two years, I lived in my grandmother's house because my parents thought it was best for me. For years, I doubted my parents' love because of that decision, and I'm still unable to overcome my insecurities," I explained. A new question then miraculously came up: "How could they?"

*****

Mr. Nader asked my colleagues and me in the chemical division to take Naya along to our clients' visits for on-the-job training. She had to learn our business inside and out to develop a marketing strategy for our products. I asked her to join me on my trips to different juice factories. Coming from a business background, she had no idea how food or juice was produced. Contrary to what she had expected, she saw with her own eyes that whole cucumbers could never go through typical juice processors. Juice factories used massive machines that cannot be compared in any way, shape, or form to home juice processors. She also learned that when one of my clients offered her a bit of cheese to taste, she should not ask them to make her a sandwich.

My sales job was not easy at all. I had worked hard to build a trust-based relationship with my clients. I realized that the only way to offer the most suitable products at the best prices was to understand their business deeply. They had to trust me fully and know for sure that their secrets were safe. Having a visitor with me at meetings, even if it was another DanielCo employee, was not always welcome.

Naya understood the secrecy required in my job, and she was cooperative. For specific meetings, I asked her to wait for me in the car or a nearby coffee shop, but sometimes meetings took place in faraway villages next to the Lebanese border, where literally there were no places for her to stay. In those cases, she had to compromise.

Once I asked her to wait for me on the grass in the middle of nowhere. Obviously, she couldn't attend that specific meeting because my client needed my opinion on a confidential matter. After I left her, wondering if I should be worried, a shepherd grazing his sheep passed by. He sat down next to her, and I felt better. I saw that Naya grabbed a book from her purse and started reading passages from *Chicken Soup for the Soul* to him.

During our lunch breaks, we ate our sandwiches sitting on the stairs of a Roman Orthodox church next to our office. We loved those stairs. As we smelled burnt incense drifting by from the inside, we analyzed our love relationships purely from a psychological perspective as if we were experts! Whenever the priest caught a glimpse of us from his window, he opened the church gate for us and invited us in. We always declined politely as we preferred to have our tuna sandwiches outdoors.

Day after day, we resumed discussing life while eating the same types of sandwiches. It must have been the serenity of the place mixed with good food that finally gave us the clarity we needed to find answers.

Around our 100th sandwich day, I declared that I was finally healed. "Now, I can say confidently that I understand both the *how could he* and the *why did he* questions. I feel better, and I'm ready to move on. As proof, I will stop driving my car to the north every morning. I'm done with that. It's actually quite costly."

To be honest, it was about time. Three months had passed since Toni, and I had broken up. But it still occupied my mind and kept me from properly mourning my mom's loss. Naya decided I needed some "maintenance recovery" before being out in the big wide dating world again. We continued eating sandwiches on the church steps and discussing human nature until one day, I came up with a motto for my life: "Happiness comes from within."

*****

I was ready for a new chapter in my life, for a new ME. There was so much in life that I wanted to experience and learn. I didn't want to be in a bubble anymore. To be completely ready to face the world again, I first had to make some changes. I started to love myself again, and that had to be reflected in the way I looked and the way I lived.

I looked ok: brunette, lollypop body shape, black eyes, big cheeks, round nose, perfect skin, perfect teeth (thanks to my cousin, the dentist), pretty lips which were always smiling. I only had one major problem: my rebellious and out-of-control hair.

I summarized my goals on an A4 piece of paper, adding a few inspirational phrases (Go Noor! You can do it!), and hung it on my closet door:

> Noor's goals
> 1. Be a knockout
> 2. Be stylish
> 3. Be cool
> 4. Be more knowledgeable
> 5. Get a new car

*****

Chapter Twenty-Five - You Gotta Be

Mood Music:
"You Gotta Be" by Des'ree

Goal 1: Be a knockout

My hair never grew long. I used to blame my long legs for taking nutrients from my hair before discovering that it was purely genetic. My hair had one unique characteristic, though: it predicted the weather. If my hair went frizzy, the humidity in the air was high. Riwa depended on such information for choosing her daily work outfit.

When my mom was my age, she had a different type of hair. Her hair was silky, straight, and glossy, like a fairytale princess. Once I asked her for her secret, and it wasn't a surprise for me when she answered, "Olive oil."

For mom, olive oil was a magic potion. She grew up watching farmers harvesting her dad's olive trees and workers pressing olives to make oil and later soap. She believed in the effectiveness of olive oil, and therefore it was her solution to any problem:

"Mom, my tummy hurts a lot. Which medicine should I take?"

"No need for any medicine, I'll massage warm olive oil in your tummy, and you'll be just fine."

"Mom, my ears are blocked."

"Pour in some olive oil."

"Mom, I can't turn my neck. It hurts!"

"Olive oil."

"Mom?"

"Olive oil."

"If olive oil helps with all these problems, why not try it as a hair mask?"

It worked. Initially, my hair turned sleek and shiny at home, but the moment I stepped out in the fresh air, my hair went crazy again.

Naya promised to book me an appointment with her fancy hairdresser. "Celebrities seek his advice. He's not just a hairdresser. He's a visagist," she told me. I had no idea what a visagist was, but I trusted her.

I loved my new "à la française" short hairstyle!

Naya's mom took it upon herself to introduce me to the world of makeup – not any world, but specifically that of Chanel.

I never liked heavy makeup and layers and layers of colors on my face, but she said, "My darling, a girl is never elegant enough unless her hair is done and she wears makeup." She was a beautiful woman who looked more like a Spanish actress than a mom. She knew what she was talking about.

She spent a lot of time explaining all the steps I should follow, from cleaning my skin to applying a foundation base, and then all the colors that go on top of it and how to blend and blend.

In the end, and after hours of training, I said, "Nope, sorry taunt, I am just not bonding with makeup."

Goal 2: Be stylish

Naya loved intense colors. Her favorite pair of pants were flowery red. She also loved polka-dot dresses and wore a wool cardigan over her swimsuit. The girl's sense of fashion was unheard of.

As for me, I mainly had two types of clothes in my wardrobe: either jeans or business suits. Interestingly enough, my sister shared my fashion sense, and although I was a bit more daring when it came to jacket cuts, our suits were more or less the same.

One Saturday evening, Riwa and I surprised a shoe salesman when we entered his shop wearing identical navy-blue suits. "Bloody hell! What kind of bank do you work for? They should be ashamed to make you work late on the weekend!" He assumed the suits were our work uniforms. Riwa and I didn't explain to him that they hadn't been imposed on us but wearing them was our personal choice.

My old style had to disappear, and a new Noor had to be born. At that time, personal shoppers didn't exist. I hired Naya for help. My master plan was to mix her colorful fashion with my dark conservative style to find a middle ground. I thought of something like Jennifer Aniston's style.

Thanks to Zara, my mission was accomplished, and a new Noor was born.

Goal 3: Be cool

I had never been a party girl and had never been to nightclubs or pubs before. According to my self-improvement plan, this had to change. I needed to check things out to decide whether I liked the nightlife or not. When I discussed this with Naya, she was startled, "Are you kidding me? You haven't been to Pacifico, B018, or Amore Libertat? Why? Beirut's nightlife is out of this world." She listed around 50 famous nightclubs, lounges, and pubs that were a must-see, and she volunteered to be my guide.

Every day after work, we made it our mission to visit at least three cool places. It was more like going on an expedition rather than hanging out. Within three months, I visited every cool place in town.

Goal 4: Be more knowledgeable

I had a lot of interests – among them tiles, art, and glass manufacturing. It wasn't easy to find courses on such topics, so I started with two available classes: scuba diving and photography. My open-water diving course was disappointing. All I could see were worms, worms, and worms. I knew our marine life was threatened but to such an extent?! Come on!

I loved my photography course, which a professional press photographer taught. He taught me how to take pictures and develop them afterward. I was privileged to develop news pictures before they were sent out to the media.

I also tried tennis lessons but chose to give them up due to inconvenience. As a teenager, I played basketball for many years. It was my passion. I played seven days a week with an extra-long session on Sunday. I was talented, and my team won awards. But obviously, basketball and tennis are totally different. To me, the main difference was the design of the balls. Basketballs are big and orange, while tennis balls are small and yellow. To my brain, tennis balls were invisible. My tennis coach served the ball countless times. "Watch the ball; it's coming now." But I couldn't spot it. After several unsuccessful attempts, he suggested I stick to basketball and forget about tennis.

*****

Goal 5: Get a new car

"I'm looking for a Nissan car, something small, suitable for a girl," I informed the car dealer. The car showroom was located on an outdoor plot in the south, exhibiting more than 100 cars which all seemed in excellent condition.

"Sure, look around. Do you like anything specific?" He asked me in his strong, southern accent.

"Not really. They all look the same to me." He pointed to several cars, but I wasn't excited about any of them. Each one had a defect. "This one is too dark, this one is too big, and this one looks cheap."

As I was wandering around the showroom, I saw the most beautiful car I had ever seen in my life. My face brightened up as I rushed towards it. "What can you tell me about this BMW?"

He scowled, "You don't want that! It's not a girl's car. It's a fast, sporty car …"

I interrupted him, "It looks gorgeous, four doors, roof opening. Which model is it?"

"It's a BMW 318, 1993, full option: roof opening, A/C, leather interior, but … I'm telling you, it's not a girl's car."

"Please open it," I demanded.

Then I did the car pre-purchase assessment myself: I checked if it had any previous accidents, compared the two sides, and checked its mileage. I even opened the hood and checked the engine, wires, battery, etc. I had learned one thing or two from the many breakdowns I used to have with my old car.

According to my initial assessment, the car was in good condition and had not been in a major accident. "I like it, but my mechanic has to check it first," I told the dealer.

I grabbed the giant calculator from my purse and did some calculations. "Ok, here's my deal: my Nissan plus this amount of money." I showed him the five-digit number on the screen. "What do you say?"

After a few rounds of going back and forth, he accepted my offer. We signed initial agreements, and I promised him to come back with my mechanic the following week to finalize the deal. I left my old car there and took the bus back to Beirut.

*****

Chapter Twenty-Six - Goodnight and Thank You

Mood Music:
"Goodnight and Thank You"
Evita Perone, the Movie

"Please come in." I tried to kiss Naya on her cheeks three times, as are our customs, but she insisted on hugging me tightly, squeezing me until I started coughing. "You need to learn how to hug properly ... like this." She hugged me again. "Please stop it," she demanded.

"Stop what?"

"Stop patting me on my back. You are not my grandma. Noor, I love you. You're my best friend."

"You're welcome."

"How come you cannot say 'I love you' back?" She couldn't believe how unaffectionate I was.

"I don't know. I never learned it, I guess. Love was always implied rather than said," I explained.

These past few months, Naya and I had become inseparable, 24/7 friends. Our differences and opposite interests made our friendship stronger.

"Look, no, don't look, I mean, look. A gorgeous guy is walking towards us," Naya whispered as we were walking on the street. I turned 360 degrees and looked in all directions. "Where? Where?"

"He's facing you." She nudged me.

I didn't find him good-looking at all. And we had other ongoing discussions like that. For example, if Naya loved a top, I would hate it, and if I loved a song, she would think it was crazy.

Over time, we succeeded in creating a middle ground that fit both of us. I jogged while she walked and read while she played ping pong. We always went to McDonald's first, then to my favorite Italian place.

Naya walked into our apartment, dressed in a long flowery dress and a white cardigan on top. She justified wearing wool by constantly feeling cold. Funny coincidence! Because I was always exothermic. As kids, Riwa used my feet as her hot water bag to keep warm. Naya brought along a bag full of mood boosters, including various chocolates and cookies.

"Are you still feeling bad about Toni's wedding card?"

"Yeah. He's getting married. He's moved on with his life. And I? Well, I'm still my old self. Nothing has changed ..."

"Forget about him. Who cares! He's a liar, and you should be happy for them. They deserve each other! You'll soon find an amazing guy."

We sat on the three-seater wooden carved sofa with our feet up on the coffee table. As she spoke, I ate three Oreo packs. "Naya, sorry, but I'm still not feeling better. Anything else you can add, perhaps?"

"No, not really!" she replied. Then her eyes began to sparkle, and she stood up. "Let's have fun! I have a great idea. I need two big plastic bowls filled with water."

We carried those big bowls, which I usually used for laundry, and placed them on our dining table. We sat on adjacent Louis XIV dining chairs, each facing a bowl. Acting like a guru, she explained the procedure in English mixed with broken Arabic, "It's a simple exercise. It will help us relax and improve our creativity as well. Just do what I do."

She dipped her index finger in the water, twirling it slowly in all directions. "Make any shape you want. It doesn't matter. Let yourself go, be free," she mumbled.

I twirled my fingers in the water, designing beautiful imaginary ribbons and butterflies. The water was neither hot nor cold, just perfect. The blue color of my plastic bowl implied a pool of ambiance. At first, my ribbon designs were liberating. I also made a heart shape, a UFO, a chicken, and an egg. The egg, however, turned into a never-ending vicious circle. I was stuck and terribly disturbed.

I stopped abruptly. "Is that it? I'm more bugged now than before."

Naya stared at me with her big black eyes and handed me a chocolate bar, "Here! Have a KitKat."

I gobbled it up without tasting it. Then I gobbled up the second and the third. In no time, the chocolate bag was empty, just like me. I had every right to emotional eating. If being cheated on and lied to weren't enough excuses for emotional eating, then I wondered what would be.

Finally, Naya turned to her last resort. "You know what? Let's go to your bedroom. I'll teach you how to meditate. I'm sure this will help."

Riwa overheard us. "Meditation?! I'd like to join." She followed us, crunching on an apple.

Naya and I lay down on the floor while Riwa took the meditating position on my bed. Although my flowery curtains were already shut, a ray of light penetrated the corridor.

"You need to stop eating your apple now!" Naya said. Riwa's munching instantly stopped.

Naya gently closed my bedroom door and lay next to me on my fluffy carpet. "Shhhhhh, we all need to be quiet. Listen to your breathing; slowly breathe in and breathe out, in and out. Slowly, try not to think of anything. Just breathe in and breathe out. Now imagine you're going somewhere far, far up, you're leaving earth, and you're going up to the sky. Imagine you're going even further up to reach space. You're still breathing in and breathing out very slowly."

In a few minutes, my bedroom was quiet. Only the sounds of our breathing could be heard.

Minutes passed. We were all quiet. Then Riwa whispered, "Naya, what's next? I've been in space for quite some time now. Should I land on a planet?"

There was no answer. Riwa's voice got louder, "Naya, I'm floating aimlessly in space. What's next?" Impatiently, Riwa got up from my bed and turned on the light.

Naya quickly covered her eyes with her hands. "Please turn it off! I'm sleeping."

"Are you kidding me? Both of you are sleeping! I thought we're supposed to meditate." Riwa was shocked.

I didn't bother to answer. My fluffy carpet was so comfy, and I was emotionally exhausted. Riwa opened the door and left my bedroom, blabbing, "It's not your fault. It's my fault to waste my time with you two."

*****

Mr. Daniel considered me his knight in shining armor, so he selected me for his special missions.

"Noor, organize this exhibition and that workshop. Ah! Before I forget, why don't you check the potential market for electric fly zappers on your way?"

"Gladly, Mr. Daniel," I would answer.

"Noor, conduct a market analysis on car brakes, car oil, sausage-producing machines, water chlorine, dried garlic, bleaching agents, bicycles, and cappuccino powder mixes."

I loved it! I loved all these special missions. Being up for new challenges, I was more than excited to take on all those projects, plus long working hours made me feel special and needed. Clearly, it was all for no extra benefits whatsoever, except the respect and appreciation of my mentor, Mr. Daniel.

To add a further new thrill to my work, I decided to be an ISO expert. I took a week off from work and participated in an ISO lead assessor course in Jordan. Of course, I paid for the trip and the course using my savings. When I came back, I surprised Mr. Daniel.

"Mr. Daniel, no need for you to get an extra ISO consultant. I can help. I'm officially an ISO lead assessor now." I proudly showed him my certificate. "Do you mind if I take charge of Daniel Co's ISO system at absolutely no extra pay?"

Instantly, he banged on his desk. "Yes! Excellent! This is the spirit we need in this company, proactive employees. From this moment onwards, you'll work together with Rawad Jameel." Mr. Daniel asked Rawad to join us.

Rawad and I were good friends, so he already knew about my new ISO certificate but pretended to be impressed.

Rawad smiled. "Great news; I'll brief Noor later on because I have an internal meeting with my team in 10 minutes. Anything else, Mr. Daniel?"

"Yes, I need your opinion on an important matter. Have a look at your new medical team business cards. I asked for a new revolutionary design. What do you think?"

Rawad looked at a few card prototypes raising his eyebrows, "I've never seen anything like this before!"

Mr. Daniel nodded with pride.

"Ummm, Mr. Daniel, these job titles don't match our actual jobs nor our job descriptions," Rawad added.

Mr. Daniel closed his eyes as he always did when he assumed that the person in front of him was not up to his thinking level. Rawad moved restlessly in his chair, hesitant to say what was going through his head. Finally, he said, "According to this new design, you've divided our 30 medical engineers into a big machine and small machine specialists." Rawad couldn't hide his smile anymore. "It doesn't make any sense. Who decides if a machine is big or small? A diagnostic device for osteoporosis, for example, is it a big or a small machine ...?"

Mr. Daniel interrupted him, shaking his head, "No, no, don't bother me with such details. This is your responsibility to decide. Merci for now."

He increased the volume of the "Evita" soundtrack playing in his office, which meant thank you and goodbye.

*****

Chapter Twenty-Seven - Volare

Mood Music:
"Volare" by Gypsy Kings

Naya caught me on the wrong foot when she invited me to her birthday party. "Are you kidding me? Out of all the days in the year, your birthday happens to be on the exact same day as Toni's wedding! And if that wasn't enough, you chose to have your party at the same venue as his. You must be kidding me?" I shouted, going back and forth in her salon.

"What does it matter?! They won't see you. True it's the same building, but our party will be in a different hall, it's a huge place," Naya explained.

"Huge or not, I don't care. There's no way I'm going to that place."

"But it's the trendiest place these days," Naya insisted.

"I am NOT going," I said.

Naya finally got the message and decided to have her party at a nightclub as far away from Toni's party as possible. In fact, she chose a lounge in a different town, Kaslik.

On the evening of August 1st, I wore tight black pants and an open blacktop. I had my hair and makeup done, and I was ready to party. I had visited several nightclubs on my "nightclub excursions" to accomplish my "be cool" goal, but this was the first time I was going to party and not merely tour the place. Naya picked me up at 9:00 pm. We had to leave Beirut early in order not to get stuck on the highway at rush hour.

The nightclub she had chosen was a Latino nightclub called "Libre". It was famous for its vibrant music and fun ambiance. Since I was a fan of Spanish and Flamenco music, I was looking forward to dancing. And I was relieved that something would finally distract me from thinking about Toni's wedding.

After handing the car keys to the valet, we walked through a small dark corridor that led into the actual nightclub. The crazy lights coming from the ceiling and the loud music made me feel out of place. It could also have been my bad mood. A lady at the reception led us to our reserved table. Naya had invited 20 people. It was 10:00 pm, and the table was empty, but some of her friends were already going wild on the dance floor.

"Yalla! Let's go." Naya rushed to them, and I had to follow.

I walked hesitantly to the dance floor, but when I looked around, I thought, "What the heck! Nobody seems to care." I went wild too.

When a young girl dressed in tight pants and a bra passed by us, I immediately turned the other way, assuming she was a drug dealer who wanted to sell me some pills or God knows what. But Naya assured me that she was an ordinary girl wearing a stylish "bustier," not a bra and that the girl was one of her guests.

Later on, Naya introduced me to the star of the show, a young man with a muscular, hairless body, wearing sparkly pants and an open, short vest. She explained, "He's an amazing belly dancer." I had no idea belly dancing could also be a man's career.

Coming from a conservative background, I was shocked by all that: the stunning dance floor, the freedom, the revealing dresses, and the public display of affection. But I was still fine until a guy, one of Naya's guests, asked me if I would like to have "Safe Sex on the Beach." I was offended and about to give it back to him when Naya calmed me down, saying, "Relax! That's just the name of a drink."

I ended up trying that drink, and it was not bad at all. The night as described by the belly dancer, was "Caliente *(hot)*." Dancers were jumping and singing on the floor, holding their drinks up in the air. I had a blast! I had never felt so free.

When I looked at my watch, it was around 1:00 am. I had never stayed out that late before. I went up to Naya, who was dancing in the center of a circle. "I have to go." I pointed at my watch.

Naya understood my panic. Her parents would be mad at her too. She asked a waiter for the bill, which took him ages to get. We were seriously late.

One hour later, I finally reached home. I opened our apartment door slowly, hoping that everyone would be fast asleep. It was already 3:00 am. To my greatest surprise, Dad was sitting on his chair waiting for me.

"Was there an emergency? An accident?" he asked.

"No, we're all fine," I answered sheepishly.

"Are you out of your mind? My own daughter going dancing in a disco until the morning?" I had never seen Dad as angry as he was that night.

I tried to explain, "Dad, I'm so sorry, but honestly, it wasn't my fault. It took the waiter a long time to get the bill. Then we had to split it up among all of us. And there was a lot of traffic on the way back. By the way, Dad, it turned out that it's not called 'disco' anymore. Nowadays, they call it a 'nightclub.'

At that very second, Dad exploded like a volcano, "I don't care what they call it, and I also don't care if there was traffic on the road. My daughters are respectful girls who come back home at a decent time. I'm extremely disappointed in you. I expected you to behave better than that."

I stood with my eyes on the floor, not daring to say a word. In the end, Dad made it crystal clear that I wouldn't be allowed to hang out with Naya anymore unless I would change my lifestyle and followed our home rules. For the next three days, Dad didn't speak to me.

*****

Toni went on his honeymoon somewhere in the world. I didn't want to know anything about him. Anyway, I already had many things to keep me busy, my regular work, my ISO assignment, and my new job. Mr. Daniel had appointed me as a Food Manager for all of the Middle East. We didn't have any international business in the Middle East yet, but I managed that too. He decided that I should open new markets and develop new businesses – at no extra pay, of course.

One morning, as I was writing the report on my latest trip to Syria, the phone on my desk rang. I heard a soft male voice saying, "Bonjour, I'm Chady, your colleague; I just wanted to wish you a lovely day. I watched you in the morning while you were parking your BMW ... I felt the need to wish you a beautiful day."

"Oh!" I mumbled, totally surprised by his lovely gesture. "Thank you so much, Chady."

We didn't know what to say, so he said goodbye and told me he would call later. I checked the list of employees at DanielCo. "Chady, Chady, Chady," I murmured as I moved my finger down the long list. "Ah, here he is. Well, that's a surprise!" He worked in the medical division, so I immediately called Rawad. I asked him about Chady, the mysterious caller, but he refused to tell me anything on the phone. "There are many people around me. I'll talk to you later during one of our coffee breaks tomorrow or after tomorrow. Let's see when I get some free time."

*****

Chapter Twenty-Eight - Happy Together

Mood Music:
"Happy Together" by The Turtles

"Beyrouti, are you free for coffee now?" Rawad asked me. "Sure, I'll meet you down at the entrance." I had been waiting for this "get to know Chady" coffee for two days. Who would know him better than his boss?

In a small coffee shop next to DanielCo, we sat at a round table drinking our cappuccino. Rawad tapped on the table. "Beyrouti, as I understand, you're interested to know more about Chady?"

"Exactly, he's been calling me for the last two days to wish me a lovely morning or a lovely afternoon. What can you tell me about him?"

"If you want me to be honest, he's not the one for you," Rawad told me without any initial introduction. I opened my eyes widely. "But why not?"

"Mark my words: He's not the one for you. I can't explain why, but I'm ready to answer all your questions." Rawad told me that Chady was five years older than me, well-educated, a scuba diver, and his family was known and well-off.

"I don't understand. You didn't say one bad thing about him. What's the problem then?" I asked.

Rawad shook his head. "It isn't a problem per se, but since I know you so well, I'm sure you two won't click."

Rawad parked in front of DanielCo, and as we were about to cross the street, he waved to a young man with a goatee. I had never seen that young man before, but he waved back, saying, "Hi, Noor and Rawad."

I smiled back. Rawad whispered to me with a sly smile on his face, "That's Chady."

I turned and watched him as he went to his car, which was miraculously parked next to mine. He was neither tall nor short, neither fat nor slim, neither gorgeous nor ugly. He was midway through everything. He looked nothing like Toni, who was a Don Juan wannabe. He seemed more down-to-earth and friendly. I didn't get stomach cramps or feel my heart beating extra, and I didn't see any fireworks. When I was back at my desk, Chady called me and asked me out.

"I saw you when you came back with Rawad. Are you free to go out next Saturday?"

"Saturday? Ooops, I can't make it this Saturday as I've already made other plans, sorry!"

"No worries. Let's make it Monday then?"

"Monday for sure," I answered directly. I hung up, confused between being excited about a new date and worried because he seemed too pushy.

*****

While I was lost in my life's turmoil, being single, and working with no extra pay, Riwa was getting a firm grip on her own life. Her consultancy work was going at full speed. Since Mom had died, Riwa took care of every little thing at our home perfectly, which was stressful for her but far more stressful for my dad and me. Her new rules limited my freedom. "Make sure you're home before midnight, don't forget to get the groceries, and by the way, you turned into a vegetarian today!" she told me.

"What do you mean? Why?"

"I've decided not to cook meat anymore. You know animals' rights and so on."

I told Dad that she was becoming too bossy, but Dad had to take her side because of her cooking talents. Her soup and her salads were to die for. One day, however, something shocking happened that opened Dad's eyes as well. Ho-ho! Riwa crossed her line big time. Dad was watching an American movie on TV when Riwa put a cup of hot milk with a pinch of orange blossom water on the table in front of him and said, "Dad, after drinking your cup of milk, you can go to bed."

What did she just say? That was our dad she was talking to, not a little kid. Dad told her right to her face and made sure she understood who the boss in our home was.

From then, Dad and I agreed that Riwa needed to start her own family and leave us in peace. But despite our extensive network of family and friends, we couldn't find "the one" for her. Riwa's standards were too high. She refused guys for reasons such as, "He hasn't read Atlas Shrugged," or "Can you believe it! He doesn't know who Loreena McKennitt is."

We always tried to change her mind, except when she indicated that her last suitor was suicidal. Ok, that was a valid reason.

*****

When I asked Naya for her opinion on Riwa's disastrous love life, she suggested that I should visit one of those famous TV fortune tellers who could reveal the secrets of the world beyond and unfold its mysteries. Personally, I never believed in that hocus-pocus nonsense, but it was my last resort. I wanted to eat meat again.

His office was located on the 1st floor of a shabby-looking building next to the airport area. His young, plastic-surgery-transformed assistant welcomed us in, "Please have a seat. Dr. Zaynoun will be with you in ten minutes."

Restlessly, I whispered to Naya, "Are you sure we should be here?"

She nodded. "He's a famous fortune-teller! What are you worried about? He'll help Riwa."

After almost an hour, Dr. Zaynoun, dressed all in black, escorted an elegant, middle-aged woman to the door. "Rest assured, madam, that your son will leave his girlfriend. Trust me on that." The woman left full of hope.

He asked me to follow him. My voice was quivering, and my heart was beating fast. I knew I would not ask him to change Riwa's fate and find her a groom. I wanted to know what her problem was. Why wasn't she falling in love with anyone? Deep in my heart, I was not convinced that he knew anything. I decided to test him. I planned to have a constant thought in my head, not related to my family or me, to forbid him from reading my mind. Well, just in case, he was able to do so.

"Would you like to have some Turkish coffee?" Dr. Zaynoun asked me politely.

"No, thanks." Yeah right! As if I would ask to be deliberately drugged on my first visit.

"What can I do for you?" he asked me, looking straight into my eyes with a cocky smile.

"I'd like to ask you about my sister; her name is Riwa. She's in her late twenties, and she isn't married yet. I want to know if she's ever going to get married. Can you tell me that?" I instantly searched for something to think of to avoid allowing him to read my mind. I thought of his desk's golden corner. "Golden corner, golden corner," I wouldn't stop repeating that thought in my head.

"What's her date of birth and full name, please?" he asked.

I gave him the information and went back to my "golden corner" thought.

He squinted his eyes and started mumbling incomprehensible words. I watched him, making sure I stayed strong in order not to give him any information in my mind.

Finally, he opened his eyes and announced, "According to my supernatural sources, your sister is never going to get married."

"But why?! Are you sure? Can you double-check with your sources, please?"

He took a deep breath. "The problem is your mom."

"How come?" I wondered if my mom could have any influence from her position in the other world. He cleared his voice and said confidently, "Your mom is in a constant fight with your dad, and all this screaming and arguing has affected your sister's view on marriage. But luckily, I can help her."

What the hell was he talking about? My mom was dead, and besides that, she rarely had any arguments with Dad when she was still alive, except when he had started his DIY projects. The fortune-teller didn't have a clue what he was talking about. I needed to leave his office right away before he could do some hocus pocus and hypnotize me.

I stood up hastily. "You know what? I'll come back for this particular problem another time. I have to leave now." I paid his enormous fees and rushed out of the building.

A few weeks later, I had the urge to call that cheating fortune teller and announce the big news: Riwa and Malik, her best friend, got engaged. I wanted to tell Dr. Zaynoun, "You didn't see that coming, did you?"

Frankly, no one could see that coming, not even Cupid. Riwa announced one day that she was in love. As she was walking around the AUB campus with Malik, she saw fireworks in the sky, and at that moment, she knew that Malik was the one – just for the record, there was the opening of a five-star hotel that night. It turned out that Malik had had feelings for her all along. After all their disputed tennis matches and endless arguments, Dad and I couldn't have imagined in our wildest dreams that those two rivals would end up being in love. Dad was over the moon, and so was I.

*****

Chapter Twenty-Nine - You Are My Home

Mood Music:
"You Are My Home"
by Vanessa Williams and Chayanne

My sister asked me to help her hand out her wedding invitation cards. I needed at least two whole days to hand out each card personally. By Saturday evening, I had managed to hand out more than 2/3 of Riwa's invitation cards. The rest were easier to deliver, mostly to close family and my friends.

The only worrisome issue on my mind was Chady. I had not accepted any of his invitations to go out. I always found excuses. He was too pushy for me. I was not ready to be on an official date. I needed to know the person first, to be his friend. Sure, there was no way to know him unless I went out with him. It was a kind of vicious circle. He started calling me at home, driving me further away from him. I never found out who had given him my home number.

His emotions were overwhelming. It was too much passion in such a short time. I tried to avoid him as much as possible, hoping he would get the message by himself. Ultimately, I felt he got it because he reduced his calls and invitations.

My problem with Chady also affected my ISO work with Rawad. Whenever we had a meeting, I had to call Rawad first to check if Chady was in the office or not. I didn't want to bump into him and then have all the phone calls and messages start up again. Rawad found the perfect solution to my problem: Whenever we needed to meet, he sent Chady on a long-distance mission outside Beirut for the whole day.

In my mind, Chady was out of the question. At the same time, I heard that Lebanon had one of the highest percentages of unmarried women among the Arab countries. I didn't want to become part of a statistic. My relatives and friends considered me a top candidate for eligible bachelors. Everyone in my entourage, and I mean everyone – including gas station employees, car mechanics, neighbors, and ladies at hairdressers – tried to hook me up with potential husbands. The guys' advantages: coming from a known family, having a good job, and owning an apartment.

Frankly speaking, I loved those one-time blind dates. What was there not to love about it? Meeting new people? Wonderful. Going out to new restaurants? Perfect.

I was fine as long as only my date and I were involved, and our date took place in a restaurant. But things got tricky when those blind dates took place at our apartment and involved two whole families.

A visit to our home meant it would happen in our salon, not in the TV room. Like many Lebanese families, we used the salon only for special occasions to impress our visitors with our lovely furniture and decorations. In honor of our guests, we would also use our expensive silverware, which we usually wouldn't use. Within an hour or so, both families would be deeply engaged in conversation to gather the maximum amount of information about each other, education, hobbies, and anything really. My potential husband –and his mom – would check me out as I served them coffee. Was I pretty enough? Conservative or outgoing? Introvert? Well educated?

*****

I went to see Rania, one of my close friends from AUB.

"Welcome, Habibti; it's been a long time," Rania's mom greeted me warmly. I handed her Riwa's invitation card. "It would be our absolute honor if you and Rania would join us."

"Congratulations!" she giggled and put her hand on my shoulder. "Noor, you know, I stopped attending weddings when my husband passed away a few years ago, but I'm sure Rania would love to attend."

She led me to their garden, where Rania was relaxing on a bamboo chair, reading a magazine. The table had already been set – glasses, teacups, plates, napkins, and matching cutlery. After several hellos, welcomes, and kisses, Rania brought various French pastries and freshly squeezed orange juice from their kitchen.

"How nice! It looks beautiful."

She was thrilled and cautiously removed Riwa's invitation card from the envelope. "I'm so excited about her wedding. Who would have imagined that Riwa and Malik would end up getting married?"

"I know. They were cats and dogs for as long as I can remember."

Their landline rang as we spoke, and her mom answered it from the kitchen.

Rania stopped talking to check out who was calling. "Hello, thank God we're very well. Yes, he's doing well. She's also doing well, thank you," her Mom said. "Who is this, if I may ask? Oh! Hello madam, how are you? How's your mom? How are your children?"

Then she paused, listening, before she said, "Rania? No. She's not engaged yet. If he's from a good family, then why not? What's his name? Zaki White. Please tell me more about him and his family."

At this moment, Rania jumped off her seat and got a black notebook. She stood next to her mom, flipping the notebook pages. Finally, she gave her mom a thumbs-up sign. I was confused. Rania's mom continued the conversation, "This Thursday, madam? Yes, we're free. You're all welcome at 6:00 pm."

Rania came back to the garden.

"What was that about? Why did you check your notebook?" I asked her while she was pouring tea for me.

"This is my invention! A secret, it's a summary of years of hard work. I've made a register listing all the suitors who have already visited me. On many unfortunate occasions, a suitor who had already visited us ended up revisiting us, assuming I was another girl. It was kind of embarrassing for both of us, so to avoid any misunderstandings or mutual embarrassment, I came up with this system. Look."

I moved closer to her. The book said:

February 1998

Groom	Age	Education	Link	Why not?
Hasan Hasan	30	MSc, UCLA	Taunt Samia	Has an American girlfriend in L.A.
Omar Jamal	32	gynecologist, Paris	neighbor, Uncle Akram	Nice. He didn't call back. Update: married to cousin Zeina
Toni Nadim	29	dentist, Lebanese uni	Cousin Hala	Charming, but is he gay?
Nadim Jallal	34	MBA, AUB	saw me at Najla's wedding	Interests: just cars!

The list had more than fifty names. "That's funny! I've met a few of those guys as well. You're right. The dentist was quite charming. I've heard he's married now." I took a sip of my tea. "I should take advantage of this amazing summary. Next time I get a call about a suitor's visit, I'll check with you first for your opinion."

*****

It was the final countdown to Riwa's wedding, and we had a week full of lunches, dinners, outings, and a bachelorette party for Riwa. On her wedding morning, I asked her to come to my room. I gave her a navy-colored velvet box. "Is this for me?" she said in surprise. "You've already gotten me a lot of presents."

"I know, but this one is different. I think you'll like it the most." I couldn't wait for her to open it.

She gasped, almost speechless. "That's our mom's diamond necklace. It was broken and old, but now it looks amazing!"

She put it around her neck and looked in the mirror.

"I took it for repair at the same shop where our dad got it for mom 40 years ago and asked them to redesign it to suit your taste."

Riwa hugged me warmly. "I absolutely love it and can't wait to wear it tonight."

*****

After a day of running around, from the hairdresser to the makeup artist, I was running late. Initially, I had planned to be at the wedding venue by 7:00 pm to help Riwa before the guests arrived. Unfortunately, there was traffic everywhere; it was a typical Saturday evening. I got nervous, tapping on the wheel, and continuously changing radio channels. I couldn't believe I was running the risk of missing my only sister's wedding entrance (Zaffe).

Zaffe is the opening of a Lebanese wedding, usually involving traditional singing and dancing. I didn't want to miss any moment and knew I had to take quick action. Politicians' convoys always pushed their way through without having an emergency. I had watched their drivers a million times zooming off while I was stuck in traffic. They got away with it by acting confidently and arrogantly. And, of course, they had the political power to back them up.

I didn't have any power, but I had an emergency. I squeezed my BMW in between two cars and honked until they gave me the way. I heard the drivers shouting and blabbing as I passed, but I ignored them.

I sighed when I finally got out of that congested area, but it was not over yet. I had to drive like a maniac to be at the wedding on time. I bypassed cars to my right and my left, driving like an ambulance. Then I looked in the rearview mirror and saw a car following me. I wondered if it was the police. I kept on speeding, as it was an urgent situation, and I was sure the police officers would understand. When I left the highway, I slowed down to make a right turn. The car behind passed me slowly, and I noticed that the driver almost stopped to wave at me. No way! I laughed my head off. It was an official European embassy car. The driver must have been new in Lebanon and confused about getting out of traffic. No wonder he followed me all the way.

*****

I went directly to Riwa's room to glimpse her before anyone else. Riwa looked pretty and classy. She reminded me of Audrey Hepburn with her chic hair updo and my mom's 60s diamond necklace. Her inner beauty even outshined her naturally beautiful face. She was happy, genuinely happy.

I had never seen my dad as proud as he was that evening when he escorted Riwa into the ballroom. His eyes were full of tears. He fixed his eyeglasses with one hand, and with the other, he held Riwa's arm tightly. He cherished every second with her before he had to let her go. His little girl had to grow up. Malik hugged my dad and took Riwa's hand. He was also beaming. They were both beaming.

I wasn't emotional at the wedding at all. Quite the contrary, I was excited and happy for them and myself – finally, a joyful celebration in my family. We needed that! I danced until my feet ached.

I bet Malik didn't expect his correct and by-the-book lifestyle to turn into a kind of Seinfeld series by marrying my sister. At least not from the first dance! Miraculously, the music CD, "Spring" by Vivaldi, which Riwa had carefully selected, broke just before they started dancing. Riwa had always mentioned that playing "Conquest of Paradise" at weddings was ridiculous, so she had insisted on Vivaldi. Still, she ended up dancing to "Conquest of Paradise." Perhaps Riwa's frustration stressed Malik out because as he started dancing – robustly, I must say – his wedding band fell off and was lost forever.

When Riwa and Malik returned from their honeymoon in Italy and France, I rushed to see them. I was startled by Riwa's face. She looked gorgeous. Her fair face glowed, contrasting her black hair. She was relaxed and calm. She spoke softly and almost glided rather than walked. It was clear Riwa had finally found her home.

*****

Chapter Thirty - I Want to Know What Love Is

Mood Music:
"I Want to Know What Love Is" by Foreigner

Update:
Riwa had been married for three years. Dad and I spent a lot of time together, forming a stronger bond. I kept myself busy at work and with extra activities and classes. I got a mobile phone, and I was still single.

*****

I took out an evening gown from my closet, well protected in a garment bag. It was the same sleeveless burgundy dress I wore at Riwa's wedding. True, it was several years old, but it was still a classic, plus I looked pretty good in it. I put it carefully on my bed. I was invited to the wedding of two of my classmates. Leila was a dietician and her fiancé Dany was a pilot. What a sweet couple! They fell in love back in kindergarten.

Leila's map to her husband's mountain villa was perfect. She wrote excellent directions for such a rural area. I passed next to the goat tied to a fig tree which was indicated on the map. Then, later on, I saw a group of men playing backgammon. They waved to me. Finally, I passed by a rusty, broken truck from the 1940s, as mentioned on the map as well. Of course, I was stuck in traffic on the road leading to the villa, as Leila had predicted. Through the window, I noticed beautiful lights glittering and sparkling on the fence. I knew about this before. When we were still in school, Leila had already told us about every detail of her big day.

I parked right in front of the Spanish-style wrought iron gate, and a valet took the keys of my BMW. The smell of jasmine flowers filled up the entrance of the elegantly designed stone villa. I held the rim of my dress as I slowly climbed the few steps, making sure not to stumble. Having had my hair and makeup professionally done, I felt all eyes on me as I walked in confidently to guitar music.

"Congratulations," I told an older, glamorous-looking lady standing in the line of family members welcoming the guests. "Merci, akbelik (*I hope it will be your wedding next*)," she replied. Thanks to the numerous weddings I had been to, I was ready to master the entrance ritual, say the right words, do the proper handshake, and smile at each woman or man welcoming the guests. I did all that while at the same time I was looking at the camera to have my pictures taken. I was captured both by camera and on video.

One of the elegant hostesses led me to my table. There was no sign of the bride and the groom. Their appearance wasn't scheduled before another half hour or hour when most of the guests would have arrived and been seated. The camera crew was scattered all around the garden taking photos and videos of all the guests, making sure not to miss anyone.

"Leila is so tasteful!" I told myself as I read the name of my table: Tulips.

I was early for a change; most seats were still empty. I didn't notice any familiar faces, but three of my classmates were going to attend the wedding as well. Gluglugooops. I covered my stomach with my hand. This was not a good time for my tummy to make weird sounds.

"Good evening," a young man dressed smartly in a dark blue suit and light blue shirt smiled at me.

"Hi." My eyes twinkled. I smelled his strong perfume, which covered the roses' fragrance, as he took a seat beside me.

"My name is Moe," he introduced himself.

"I'm Noor."

A waiter holding a tray of crystal glasses filled with tomato and pineapple juice asked us what we wanted to drink. I asked him for tomato juice while Moe went for the pineapple option. There were a few minutes of silence, which he broke by asking me if I was a friend of the bride or the groom. "Both actually, we took French together in school."

"Of course! Dany keeps practicing his French whenever we're in Paris, but he's still struggling. I've heard Leila is more fluent." He laughed and took a sip from his glass.

"Oh yes! She takes classes very seriously. They're such an amazing couple. How do you know them?"

"I met Dany at the aviation school in Scotland, and we became good friends. Now we're colleagues, working for the same airline."

"What a stroke of luck," I thought. A pilot was sitting next to me. I took a quick glimpse at his hands and was relieved to see that he was not wearing a ring.

"I never understood how anyone would intentionally decide to be up in the sky. It's too stressful for me." I shrugged.

"Are you scared of flying?" He looked at me with piercing black eyes.

"I pray throughout the journey. I refuse to eat or drink to be aware of everything happening around me. I don't know if I would call it being scared. I would call it utter panic."

Glug glug. I had to cover my stomach with my hands to stop the growling. I hoped he wouldn't hear the sounds with all the wedding commotion going on around us. Like many other young men, I expected him to be ironic or make fun of my fear, but he didn't. On the contrary, he took the topic very seriously and explained how a plane functioned from a scientific point of view. His voice was deep and clear. He explained things to me in a simplified way, providing statistical data about aviation safety.

While he was talking, I looked at his eyes, which reflected his clear passion for flying. I also tried to listen to what he was saying. It was vital information, but I got distracted by the growling of my stomach, which was getting louder and more frequent. It must have been the lasagna I had had for lunch. Its strong taste still lingered on my taste buds. At first, I was nervous because I didn't want Moe to hear these sounds, but later it was not just about the sounds anymore. It was more catastrophic. I needed to rush to the toilet. The growling turned into an emergency.

"Moe, would you excuse me for a minute?" I stood up and walked away as elegantly as I could. The moment I was out of his sight, I rushed with wide-open eyes to the villa, asking guests right, left, and center for the nearest washroom.

The bride and the groom had a lovely washroom. I learned this firsthand as I spent some quality time there. Three hours to be precise.

I heard the Zaffe music, the dance music, then "Conquest of Paradise," and I was still in there when the music turned softer. That was when I was finally able to leave the washroom. Many guests had already left, and the venue was half empty. Others were queuing to congratulate the newlywed couple before leaving.

"Noor, have you just arrived now?" I bumped into one of my classmates. "What a pity! You missed the whole wedding. It was beautiful." My friend kissed me goodbye. I looked at my watch; it was almost midnight.

I walked straight to my table, hoping to find Moe waiting for me, but he was not there. I searched the whole garden, I even went back to the villa and looked for him there, but I couldn't find him. He had already gone. I felt like leaving too, but I had to take another picture with the bride and groom before heading home.

*****

"There's Noor." Ruba pointed at me as she escorted a delivery man holding the most beautiful red rose bouquet I had ever seen.

"Ms. Noor, this is for you. Can you sign here, please?" The young man gave me his notebook and a pen. I signed quickly and searched for the card. "Who sent them?" The delivery man explained that their customer had asked to stay anonymous.

Ruba smirked. "Come on! Surely, you must know who the sender is and want to keep it a secret."

"No, I promise I have no idea," I said.

Ruba smelled the beautiful roses. "Look at the name of the shop." They were from Exotica, one of Lebanon's most expensive flower shops.

I thought of Moe, the pilot, and wondered if he was the one who had sent the roses. Who else could they be from? True, our conversation had been short but pleasant, and I had looked amazing. It must have been him. I couldn't stop smiling as I got up and put the roses in a vase on my desk. What a gentleman! What a fabulous bouquet! Everyone at the company thought so too. They were a big hit among all my colleagues at DanielCo, including Toni.

"Who is it from?" he asked me curiously. "I didn't know you were in a relationship!"

I didn't comment.

Mr. Nader asked me to come to his office for an "important topic." He had lots of papers on his desk. "I've reviewed your sales figures for this year. You've done an amazing job. Your figures are above your target, and you single-handedly brought an impressive net revenue to our department."

I was proud.

Mr. Nader cleared his voice, "I've asked you for this meeting because … Look, the thing is that you're a girl, and you're quite young too. Your sales commission is more than that of any other salesman in the division."

I knew that.

Mr. Nader continued, "Someone your age should not be earning that amount, not yet, so I've decided to cut your commission by half starting next month."

I couldn't believe my ears. "Excuse me?! Are you serious? After all my hard work? I'm working overtime. I'm taking care of sales locally and in the Middle East, and I'm helping the company with the ISO system. Is this how you reward me? You can't do that!"

"I can, and I will," Mr. Nader replied.

I was shocked. I had expected positive reinforcement and encouragement, not a slap. I left his office disappointed and confused about how to react. Should I resign? But where could I find a new job? I considered talking to Mr. Daniel regarding my commission cut, but knowing him, he would applaud any way to increase his profit.

*****

After the conversation with Mr. Nader, I started fishing around for jobs. Having worked at DanielCo, one of the most important companies in my specialty line, it was almost impossible to find the same caliber position anywhere else. There was one interesting opportunity, though, a consultancy job at a small and young firm. My ISO degree and sales experience were well appreciated, so they offered me a job.

Despite all the turbulence in my life, there was one beautiful thing I looked forward to every week: my Tuesday rose bouquet. It became a constant pleasure. The sender was still officially anonymous, but I almost believed it was Moe. Who else could it be?

"Ms. Noor, can I talk to you for a second?" It was Joseph, Mr. Daniel's bodyguard.

"Sure, Joseph, is everything ok?" I stood up, barely reaching his shoulders.

"I don't know how to begin. My girlfriend is going to the hospital next week; she has to undergo surgery."

"I hope it's a minor issue?" I asked

"Yes, it is. How can I say this? I was wondering, are you getting a bouquet next Tuesday too? I'd like to bring my girlfriend some roses, but I can't afford such a beautiful bouquet. Do you think I could have yours?"

"Of course, Joseph, the bouquet is yours. If I get one, that is."

*****

I sat on our kitchen marble floor having dinner, fried eggs in olive oil. The only food I knew how to make. Dad was attending a lecture, and Naya was with one of her friends. It was a free evening for me at home. I had a lot to think about.

I could hear Granny Imm Hesni's voice in the background. She was our old neighbor living next door. She lived with her youngest son because her older son Hesni had passed away a few years ago. It is unacceptable in Lebanon to send an older person to an elderly home. Our tradition is that they live with their children where they are well taken care of. It was nice to hear her voice. She was on the phone with her son, a lawyer. "Our building's committee should do something about the acoustics," I murmured. Privacy was non-existent. We all knew that Granny was a determined woman. She would never take no for an answer. If she put her head into something, she was surely going to get it. It was only a matter of time before her son would give in to her request and promise to come home early. He was not the only one who followed her orders to the letter; many others did before him, including a fierce sniper.

In one of the battles our neighborhood witnessed, a sniper took position on the roof of the building facing us. We all took cover, closed our curtains, and made sure he or other militia members didn't see us. There were street fights between two neighboring militias, using weapons like missiles and tanks. Our building was right in the middle. Many people got killed, and many homes were destroyed. Granny Imm Hesni didn't bother about that at all. She had something more important to take care of her laundry. Her white bedlinen was known to be spotless, and nothing was going to change that, war or no war. She opened the curtains, carried her laundry basket outside, and started hanging the sheets on her laundry ropes, facing the sniper's rifle. The armed man couldn't believe his eyes. After all, civilians had to respect the rules of war.

The sniper stood up as if saying, "Hello, I'm here!" Then he waved with both hands, shouting, "Go back, Granny, go into your home, go back!" But she ignored him. Instead, she kept talking to herself, "There's no power cut. I have to do all my laundry before the next power cut." Granny continued hanging her laundry. After several attempts, the sniper gave up and went back to his job, whatever that was.

Still sitting on the marble floor of our kitchen, I thought of my job and relationship status. I needed inspiration from a powerful woman, someone like Granny, but I decided to call my sister in Kuwait instead. I told her that I was at a crossroads at work and hadn't found my other half yet. "I'm frustrated! What should I do?" I asked her.

"My sweetie, don't be afraid to leave your comfort zone and move to a new phase in your life. You could be positively surprised. So what if you're going to search for a new job or haven't found the man of your dreams yet? You're a strong girl. To me, you are like a Baalbek column (of Baalbek temple), as unique and resilient. Even when you're standing on your own, you stand tall and proud. Never doubt yourself."

I felt better. "I love you, sis."

*****

Chapter Thirty-One - Girls Just Want to Have Fun

Mood Music:
"Girls Just Want to Have Fun" by Cindi Lauper

"It's too cold today." Naya closed the buttons of her wool jacket. Rawad banged a heart of aces on the table, teasing her, "Don't blame the weather for your defeat." It was a hot summer day at Ocean Dew beach, but Naya had a different inner thermostat.

"Yaaayyy," I cheered, as once again Rawad and I won against Jana and Naya. The four of us were addicted to Tarneeb, a popular Lebanese card game that Jana had taught me when we were kids in the shelter during wartime.

Drops of water on my back and loud laughter interrupted our conversation. It was Joudi who came back from her jet-ski adventure super excited. "Noor, thanks to you, my jet-ski ride was for free!"

"Thanks to me? Why?" I asked.

"The lifeguard over there told me that he was your friend." Joudi pointed to the shore. I squinted my eyes, trying to block off the sun with my hand. "Who? Where?" She turned me to the side, pointing at a lifeguard with red shorts, waving. "There."

I waved back. "Ah, that's Jad. I once went surfing with him. He's such a nice guy ..."

Naya interrupted me, "Hold on! I didn't know you surf."

I laughed. "You're right. I don't."

Belle, our model-looking friend who looked way better than Pamela Anderson in her best days, came walking towards us with all eyes on her. She wore a blue swimsuit, covered by a matching see-through top and pants. "Hi, guys!" She sat on a chaise lounge and put aside her favorite pastime, a tarot book. It was her new thing that summer: She tried to reveal our destiny, and we were all single and willing.

Belle was the only one with a long-time boyfriend, a real one, although none of us had ever met him. He was a successful private banker who was supposedly too busy to meet us. Rumors had it that he was a wealthy young man but had a teeny-weeny bit of a problem: He was an asshole by all standards. We knew he was not imaginary because of the tremendous pain and suffering he caused Belle every day. Another proof of his existence was the Bulgari gifts she received after each fight.

"Who won in cards this time? Belle couldn't contain her laughter when she heard it was Rawad and me again.

"Guys, I need to share with you what has just happened," she whispered in a secretive tone. Her eyes were twinkling cheekily.

"Wait, don't start. I need to get chocolate ice cream from the beach bar first. Who also wants ice cream?" Naya, of course, wanted ice cream too, and the rest asked for water.

"Now, you can start." I sat comfortably and took my first ice cream bite.

"Ok," Belle leaned forward and, with a sneaky smile, said, "I crashed Ramez's Porsche today!" She clapped her hands a few times, fascinated by what she had done.

"You did what?!" At first, I didn't believe her. I looked at my friends, who were as shocked as I was.

"You know how Ramez keeps fighting with me, lying all the time, and lately, I haven't told you this, but I have a hunch that he's cheating on me ..."

Joudi interrupted, "No way! He can't be cheating on you. He's not blind. Where would he find another gorgeous and smart girl like you?"

Belle nodded. "True. Right? But anyway, I think he's cheating on me. He told me that he was going to his office for work. But I didn't believe it and decided to follow him."

"Where did he go?" Naya asked curiously.

"He went to Riviera Hotel at the beach, and I followed him from a distance. I waited for a while to give him the benefit of the doubt, but he didn't come out again. I was waiting for two hours. Can you imagine?! I parked my car outside the hotel and sneaked in, looking for him in the restaurants and the coffee shops by the pool, but I couldn't find him anywhere, so I concluded that he must have been in one of the rooms with a slut!"

Rawad tried to convince her that she had no proof and that it was just speculation but in vain. Belle emptied her glass of water without saying a word. "Rawad, she has a strong gut feeling about it, so I think she's right," I leaped to her defense.

Then Belle continued her story, "I went back to my car, roamed around until I found his beloved Porsche, headed straight towards it, and boom boom boom, I crashed it." She could barely continue because she was laughing too much. "And guess who came running towards me like crazy?"

"Ramez?" we all asked automatically. "No, the security guards." Belle was still laughing. "They came running towards me, yelling, "Stop, stop, what are you doing?" I didn't care. I did what I had to do, so I remained calm. In the end, I told them that the car belonged to Ramez Rihan, a guest at their hotel and that they should go and tell him Belle crashed his car."

"Oh my God, women are malicious." Rawad shivered.

Belle's phone didn't stop ringing as she spoke. "It's him." She smirked. "He's going crazy." She turned towards me. "By the way, Noor, can you please drop me at home? My mom drove me here because I destroyed my car too."

"But what are you going to do? About your car, I mean?" Jana asked.

"I know what will happen: He'll make sure both cars are fixed and buy me a Bulgari gift. Then he'll behave."

"Only for a while, you know that, Belle. He'll be his old self again in no time," Naya interfered. "You can't go on like this forever. It's been going on for three years. You have to stop this nonsense," she added.

Belle nodded. "I know, but this is his last chance. I gave myself a deadline for Christmas. If he's not a better person by then, he'll be out of my life for good."

I raised my eyebrows. "Belle, you know, you aren't going to do that. You're head over heels in love with him. You genuinely love him."

Uh oh! Naya had been waiting for such a remark. "Noor, haven't you noticed that you're stuck in the same situation?"

"Me? No, I'm not in love with anyone." I replied.

"Yes, you're in love with the Daniel Company. No matter what they do to you, you insist on working there!" Naya's comment caused me stomach cramps.

Rawad changed his voice, imitating me, "I love Mr. Daniel. He's my mentor."

I gave Rawad a nasty look, but he was right. They were both right: I couldn't leave DanielCo. I wouldn't know where else to go. It was like my second home.

Naya scowled at Belle and me. "You two have to make a decision right now! You, Belle, have to break up with your asshole boyfriend. He's not the one for you. You're a gorgeous, smart, decent girl who deserves to be with an amazing person like yourself." Belle looked sad as she gazed at the horizon.

Naya gave her the space she needed and continued her lecture, addressing me, "And as for you, Noor, you're intelligent and successful. You don't need the bullshit of DanielCo! Move your butt and find another job."

I had been half ready even before she had mentioned the topic. I was on edge. Working for DanielCo for many years with increasing tasks and decreasing income didn't make sense anymore.

"You know what?! You're right. Tomorrow morning, I'll submit my resignation."

"Exactly!" Naya hugged me.

"Wait, don't make such a critical decision right now. Sleep on it. You don't have another option yet. You don't know what you'll do next." Rawad, being the rational one among us, tried hard to persuade me not to resign, but it was too late. I had made up my mind.

*****

First thing in the morning, I called the consultancy firm and accepted their job offer. Then I submitted my resignation letter. Mr. Nader never thought that I was ready to take that giant leap. Well, I was.

"Noor, are you serious? You're one of our most valued team members." Interesting! He only realized how much I was worth when I decided to move on.

"Mr. Nader, thank you for all your support throughout my career here, but I've made up my mind, and there's nothing that can change it now."

"If it's because of your commission percentage, perhaps we can re-discuss that. We have big plans for you. We want to expand our food business even further."

I smirked. "Really? That sounds too tempting, but no, I can't. I need to move on."

*****

My resignation caused a commotion at DanielCo. No one had expected it. Many people tried to convince me to stay, including Mr. Daniel himself. The only one who kept himself out of the whole issue was Toni. He just wished me good luck.

I had to inform my clients. That was the hardest part. My clients were as precious to me as my colleagues at DanielCo. I exchanged personal email addresses with most of them and agreed to stay in touch.

Out of all my customers, telling Sunny Juice, I was leaving was the hardest. I always felt like a part of their family, and the thought that I would not visit them anymore was heartbreaking. Mrs. Maria and I had a long talk. Her eyes were watery, and so were mine. We hugged for a long time and promised not to lose contact.

Mr. Jean-Paul had a poker face when I told him. He barely looked at me and just asked me which company I was going to join. His only comment was, "Good luck."

Preparing to leave was a busy period. I worked hard to find a suitable replacement for me. When I found a fresh nutrition graduate, I made sure to inform her about the ins and outs of her new job.

That week, I got a quick call from Mr. Jean-Paul, who informed me that he was ready to see Mr. Daniel.

He confirmed the appointment for Friday afternoon at our office. Mr. Daniel came to our floor early and checked if we were ready. It was a special event that a businessman as important as Mr. Jean-Paul would visit us.

"You see, Mlle Beyrouti, Mr. Jean-Paul has finally asked to see me. He knows that we're the most important player in the market."

I nodded quickly. I was too busy preparing for the meeting.

Mr. Jean-Paul arrived on time, and I escorted him to our meeting room, where Mr. Daniel was waiting for him. After some formal greetings, I excused myself to go back to work, but Mr. Jean-Paul insisted I stay.

Mr. Daniel said, fixing his colorful tie, "Thank you for visiting us. It's a great pleasure to have you here. I'd like to discuss our mutual business relationship and how we can expand it."

Mr. Jean-Paul interrupted him with a wave of his hand. "I asked Noor for this appointment as I want to discuss her future with you."

I glanced at him. Was he serious? He had come because of me. Mr. Jean-Paul, half Mr. Daniel's age, spoke elegantly but also arrogantly, "How can you let someone as professional as Noor quit your company? Where can you find another girl with her qualifications, ethics, and work attitude? You should promote her and increase her pay, instead of letting her go! What kind of a company are you running here? Are you selling potatoes?"

Although I felt embarrassed, I was delighted with Mr. Jean-Paul's lecture. He went on and on while Mr. Daniel listened carefully. I was worried that an explosion was bound to happen. Finally, Mr. Daniel exhaled forcefully and said, "Merci, I thank you with all my heart. Everything you've said about Mlle Beyrouti is correct. She's a real asset to us, and we don't want to let her go. I'm glad to announce that Noor will continue working with us."

What? I didn't agree with that. Mr. Jean-Paul was happy about the decision, and so was Mr. Daniel. The meeting was over.

Shoot! Now I had to resign all over again. I wanted to cry.

*****

Chapter Thirty-Two - Wind of Change

Mood Music:
"Wind of Change" by Scorpions

"Bonjour, Ms. Noor." I saw a familiar face. The rose delivery man walked up to my desk, smiling, "Here's another bouquet for you."

I scowled. "But it's Monday, how come?! You normally deliver my bouquets on Tuesday."

He winked. "There's a card attached this time."

"Really?" I quickly opened the envelope and reached for the small white card inside.

"If you want to unfold the secret and know who I am, then tie your hair up in a ponytail tomorrow."

Ruba and the delivery man were standing in front of me, both curious to know who the sender was. I read the card out loud. "Do you believe me now? No name yet. Tomorrow we'll find out." I gave the delivery man his tip.

Ruba went back to her desk, rolling her eyes. "What is this? An extra-long Mexican movie? And why haven't you put them in a vase yet?"

"Not today. I'd rather take the bouquet home for a change." I didn't want the whole company to know I had plans to give them to Joseph.

I had to wait just one more night until Moe would reveal himself. I was hoping from the bottom of my heart it would be Moe. But I also started to have doubts. I couldn't imagine that a pilot would have that much spare time to plot such a time-consuming plan.

*****

In the morning, my hair was tied in a ponytail, as the note requested. I entered the building and rushed to my desk, searching for a letter or a note that would give me the answer. But there was none.

I had no interest in work that day. Meeting my secret admirer was far more interesting. I wasted time, chatted around, made myself several hot chocolates, checked my hair again and again in the mirror, and called everyone I could think of until finally, the rose delivery man arrived. He was carrying a glamourous wedding-style bouquet of twelve fresh red roses. Its design was a masterpiece. It was out of this world. There was a card which I read instantly.

I hope you like my rose bouquet.
Please accept my dinner invitation for tonight.
Chady

"Chady?! How shocking! It's been ages since we last talked. He didn't forget about me! Why isn't Moe my secret admirer? I want Moe." I threw the card on my desk. "How silly of me! All my daydreaming was for nothing!"

I covered my face with my hands and took a long breath. "God, please help me. I have to be strong. He's so kind to me, but please give me the strength to say no, and say it firmly."

When I finally came to my senses, the poor delivery man had already gone without his tip, and Ruba was at her desk working.

Later, when Chady called, I told him how I really felt. "Chady, you're one of the nicest people I've ever met. You're a gentleman, considerate and thoughtful, but I don't think it will work out between us. I truly wish you the best, and I hope that one day you'll meet a girl who will love you as much as you love her."

A few months later, I bumped into him on the seaside corniche, walking hand in hand with a young lady. He introduced her as his fiancé. I was truly happy for him.

*****

Soon after I left DanielCo, I started working as an ISO consultant. It didn't take much time to realize that consultancy was not for me.

When my former colleague at the German supplier contacted me to offer me a job, I accepted immediately. I was ready to give up anything to go back to sales.

Before I knew it, I was an area sales manager for an international company — great title, great job, and above all, great income with great benefits. Our MD invited me to attend an induction workshop during my first week on the job. The business trip included visiting the company's factories all over Germany, then going to Spain for technical training at their Spanish production facility.

I scrolled down to the list of the other participants: Silvina, who I had met before, George, an Egyptian guy who was married with children, one Japanese, and one German.

At that point in my life, I was ready to find my soulmate.

"Not again! I'm going to remain single all my life." I was disappointed. There were no eligible bachelors for me. I knew I was not going to marry either a German or a Japanese man. I needed a man who had an Arabic background like me.

Despite my disappointment, I loved the idea of going to Germany again. I liked everything about Germans. As a sign of appreciation, I supported their economy: My car was a BMW, my mobile was a Siemens, and for our bathroom renovation, I insisted on buying Hansgrohe. I thought German music was horrible until I discovered that both Modern Talking and Scorpions were German bands.

I had already visited the company's premises in Heidelberg many times, so being there again was easy. Too bad Jan (the Tom Hanks look-alike) had already left the company. I would have loved to see him again. After routine greetings with my colleagues, Samir, the R&D Director, took me around to introduce me to the other people who were going for the induction training. First, I saw Silvina, the area sales manager for Latin America, a lovely lady about my age. We clicked right away. Later, I was introduced to Takeo, the Japanese area manager. Samir then took me to an open-spaced, busy office, where people were walking around holding papers or speaking on the phone in foreign languages. I felt lost in all this turmoil. Samir tapped my shoulder, saying, "Noor, let me introduce you to our sales manager for Africa, Herr Alexander Klein. He's our star; he single-handedly opened up the African market. He's doing a fantastic job."

I stood there facing the young German version of James Bond. He was quite tall and looked a lot like Ben Affleck. I felt overwhelmed by his seriousness and shamelessly piercing hazel eyes.

"Nice meeting you," he said with an unnoticeable smile. His firm grip made me realize that his hand had been holding my hand for a few seconds. It felt warm, and I had no intention of removing my hand first.

"Too bad guys like him are never single," I told myself, wondering what his girlfriend would be like.

*****

The next day, our group was waiting in the hotel lobby for our airport pick-up. We were five people, Silvina, Takeo, George, Alexander, and me. The plan was to travel to Berlin first, visit our factory there, and then have a workshop at our Spanish branch in Valencia.

As we waited for our flight to Berlin, I chit-chatted with Silvina and got to know her better. We mainly talked about work and the differences in our cultures. I also joked with hilarious George, but I didn't speak much to Takeo or Alexander. Takeo didn't speak a word of English, so it was pointless to have any conversation with him, and Alexander seemed too arrogant. He didn't mingle with the group much. I already felt that he was distant when we were in Heidelberg. I noticed that he mainly spoke with Inken, a young German girl who always seemed around him. I observed them on several occasions, exchanging glances and having side talks. She had an angelic face with big, striking, honey eyes.

*****

It was a warm evening in Berlin. I freshened up and joined the group walking to Potsdamer Platz. Alexander led the way together with Takeo and George while Silvina and I followed them. Alexander checked the map now and then. It was fascinating how he could read maps easily – something I couldn't do.

After a lovely stroll around the streets of Berlin, we reached the city's renowned center, where Alexander explained its history to us. We were all quiet, mesmerized by his deep voice and knowledge.

"Potsdamer Platz, the rebuilt center of Berlin, is one of our main touristic attractions. After World War II, this area was almost completely destroyed. After Germany's reunification, Potsdamer Platz was rebuilt and is now considered a symbol of reunification. From here, please." Alexander led the way inside Sony Center, adding, "The conically designed roof above us was inspired by Mount Fuji in Japan." We looked up and saw a beautifully designed glass ceiling.

Takeo nodded.

Wandering through the streets of Berlin was a great experience. I tried to imagine the Germans' excitement when the wall was finally demolished in November 1989. I could visualize their joy and eyes filled with hope for a newly reunified Germany and a better world. We got to see what was left of the Berlin Wall. Once separating the eastern part from the western part of Germany, the wall became a symbol of freedom instead of suppression.

The wall was covered all over with graffiti and messages. It wasn't only Germans who made sure to leave their message on that piece of history, but many others who came from different parts of the world.

> "I painted over the wall of shame so that freedom is not ashamed no more. Inferno ruled too many years until the people chose the light. I put my faith in you Berlin and give to you my colors bright"– Fulvio Pinna, Italy.

> "Dancing to freedom, no more wars, no more walls, a united world"– Anonymous.

We asked Alexander tons of questions about life in Germany before and after reunification. From what Alexander told us, I figured out that Germans didn't like to discuss politics much. They were quite reserved and preferred to indicate facts rather than opinions. They didn't generalize or use phrases such as "all Germans" or "none of the Germans" but instead backed up their statements with numbers, such as 10,000 students or 60% of Germans.

At Sony Center, we all agreed to eat pizza. Takeo miraculously understood the pizza menu, except for the word "spinach," and insisted on knowing what it was. Silvina, Alexander, and George tried to explain what spinach looked like, where it was grown, and for which food it was used, but Takeo didn't understand. I tried a different approach. I spoke to the child within Takeo, "Do you know Popeye, the cartoon figure?" I pretended to gulp spinach can like Popeye and then showed him my biceps, "Spinach makes you strong." Alexander laughed at me, saying, "He won't understand that!" But Takeo did.

*****

At 9:00 am, our technical workshop started. The workshop's purpose was to give us, the international area sales managers, solid technical information on our company's products produced in Berlin. Being the only area sales manager who had studied food technology, I was interested in the information given and asked many specific questions. All the team was attentive, except for one: Takeo.

"What's going on?" I whispered to Silvina, who spoke fluent German. Takeo seemed to be bothered, and several team members tried to solve his problem.

"I have no idea." She shrugged.

It turned out that Takeo couldn't follow the explanations because he didn't understand English. The management suggested getting him an interpreter. We were told that we had to wait until the problem was solved, an excellent opportunity for me to mingle around and meet our technical team in Berlin.

Although an interpreter arrived rather quickly, Takeo was not pleased with all. For some strange miscommunication reason, the interpreter didn't speak a word of Japanese. She was an English-German interpreter. How was that supposed to help a Japanese?! Back to square one. Finally, we decided to continue with our workshop because it was impossible to find an English-Japanese interpreter on such short notice.

*****

For our second evening in Berlin, we were all invited by our senior managers to a "Varieté" show held at one of Berlin's old theatres. Our international group got split up: George and I sat next to each other at a table with a few colleagues from our Berlin office. Alexander, Silvina, and Takeo were at another table with a few colleagues. As Alexander's seat was opposite mine, it was a perfect opportunity for me to observe him well. The hall was dark, and the music was horrifically loud. People were drinking heavily, laughing, and having a great time. As for me, my share of fun was limited mainly because of the language barrier. I didn't always understand what the show was all about. The striking act of the evening was a ventriloquist who pretended to be clumsy while his dummy kept repeating the same phrase over and over again, "Macht nichts, macht nichts *(does not matter)*." Why was that supposed to be funny? I didn't get it.

Amazing how the human brain works in some strange ways. The "Varieté" show organizers must have worked so hard to make it an unforgettable evening for the audience, but out of the whole show, only two words stuck in my head: "macht" and "nichts." Strangely enough, the same thing happened to me when I took a botany course in my sophomore year at university. The only two words I remembered for years to come were "zea" and "mays," which − for the record − means "corn."

When duty called, and I needed to go to the washroom, I walked with my eyes entirely on Alexander. He was like a magnet to me. He was charming in whatever he did, whether he was talking, eating, or laughing. His frown was to die for! It was like having a prince in the audience. Let's be realistic. Wouldn't every single girl stare? Or at least risk a glimpse?

As I was passing by his table – still staring at him – my ankle twisted for some unknown reason. I stumbled and ended up on all fours. I was on the floor right next to his feet, but thankfully he didn't see me down there.

A waiter beside me helped me stand up while I muttered in French, "Ça va, pas de problème ici (*ok, no problem*)." My brain spoke French during catastrophes.

I rushed to the washroom, hoping no one had seen me stumbling. I closed the door, squeezed myself into a corner, and whispered, "God, oh God, please either stop me from embarrassing myself further or send me back home."

Chapter Thirty-Three - I lost my heart in Heidelberg

Mood Music:
"Ich hab' mein Herz in Heidelberg Verloren" or
"I lost my heart in Heidelberg" by Billy Mo

Hola España! Finally, my childhood dream came true, and I visited one of my dream countries, Spain. I fell in love with Spain a long time ago when my parents' friends spent their summer holiday in Barcelona and wouldn't stop talking about it for several months. They brought us tons of gifts and souvenirs, which were all unique. But out of all those gifts, my favorite was a Flamenco dancer doll dressed up in a traditional red ruffle dress with her hair tied up in a low bun. She was beautiful. My mom kept that doll on the dressing table in her bedroom. I used to sneak in whenever she was busy, holding a pair of castanets in each hand and dancing with my chin up, pretending I was a Spanish dancer too.

During the taxi ride to our hotel, I didn't take my eyes off the buildings, the Spanish people, and the scenery. I was swept away by Valencia. It was amazing how the atmosphere, homes, shops, and loud cafes reminded me of Beirut. Our coffee shops were as vivid, and the people were at least as loud. I smiled to myself when I saw two women having a conversation from one balcony to another. Yep! It was déjà vu.

Finally, we reached our hotel. It was about time. I needed a power nap terribly. But instead, I lay in bed thinking about my journey so far, the places I had been to, and the new friend I had made: Silvina, George, Takeo, and yes,

Alexander crossed my mind too. In the last few days, I noticed that he was not all bad. He had a few good qualities as well. The most obvious one was, of course, that he was drop-dead gorgeous. He was also an innate leader, intelligent, hardworking, polite, and kind to others. We hardly spoke with each other, though. Frankly, I tried to avoid him and pretended he didn't exist. First, he didn't seem to care about me at all, and second, I didn't want to embarrass myself further after my Berlin incident.

Our first Spanish morning was busy. It started off with a tour of the factory and ended up with intense business discussions. For lunch, the management invited our team to a beautiful seafood restaurant close to Malvarrosa beach, where a waiter convinced me to order a Paella dish.

"Señorita, did you know that Paella originated from here? From Valencia?" I had no idea.

When we were done with our meal, we couldn't resist taking a quick walk along the beach to enjoy the warm weather. We took off our shoes and walked on the golden sand facing a never-ending blue sea. It was simply breathtaking, and I loved it. A couple of middle-aged women took off their swimsuit tops for tanning right before our eyes. I pretended not to see their private parts, but the view traumatized me as I was not used to nudity.

Throughout our journey, our group was virtually divided into two teams: the girls' team consisting of Silvina and me, and the boys' team consisting of Alexander and George. They were also having a great time by themselves. George insisted on calling Alexander Ben the whole time, after Ben Affleck, while Alexander kept teasing George about various issues. I can't remember if Takeo was with us in Spain or if he had already returned to Japan.

Alexander and I didn't say a word to each other. I concluded that he was either racist towards Arabs or sexist. Both my theories proved to be wrong because Alexander seemed to get along pretty well with George, who was Arabic, and with at least two girls: Silvina and Inken. Finally, I concluded that he just didn't fancy me.

In the evening, the four of us, and perhaps Takeo as well, went to discover the nightlife of Valencia. Many loud men on the streets were laughing and annoying pedestrians, which kind of scared me. Of course, they might have been harmless, but I expected them to attack us with knives. Silvina assured me that I shouldn't be worried and that Alexander and George were ready to protect us if anything happened.

"I'm not so sure about that," I replied.

"I heard you, Noor. Do you think we aren't brave enough?!" Alexander shouted from behind us.

"Great! Now he dislikes me even more," I thought.

*****

I didn't want to say adios to Valencia, Germany, or Europe. I was having a great time and didn't want to go back to Beirut, not yet, in any case.

"I'm going to get myself a bottle of water. Does anyone need anything?" I asked my colleagues, who were all relaxed in Valencia's airport lounge, waiting for our flight back to

Germany. Alexander had a smirk on his face. "If we need something, we can get it ourselves. You're not our servant."

How rude! I looked at him full of rage. "Where I come from, people are friendly and warm. Of course, I'm not your servant. I was just being nice."

I didn't wait for his answer and headed directly to a small shop where I bought the biggest chocolate bar I could get.

At Frankfurt airport, a minivan had been organized to pick us up.

"I don't really like my hotel," I told Silvina, who was sitting right next to me. "I don't know why the company booked for me in Schwetzingen and not in Heidelberg. It's such a small town, and there's nothing there. Did I tell you that there's no restaurant in my hotel?"

Silvina shook her head.

"Imagine that! Whenever I need to eat something, I have to walk to the town center, but even there, no one speaks English, and they don't have any English menus. Argh! My weekend is going to be dreadful."

Alexander, sitting in front of me, turned his head, saying, "I live in Schwetzingen, and if you'd like, I can take you out for lunch tomorrow."

"Yeah, right! He doesn't like me, and he's rude. Why should I go out with him?" I thought. But I thanked him politely.

The taxi stopped at my hotel. While the driver was getting my bag, I turned to say goodbye to the team, "Have a lovely weekend and see you on Monday." Alexander put his hand on my shoulder. "Do call me tomorrow. I'll take you for lunch." I felt he meant it.

*****

Time passed quickly while shopping in the numerous shops of Heidelberg city center. By the time I was done, it was already 3:00 pm, and I was exhausted. I struggled to get through my room door with all my shopping bags. I also bought an additional suitcase because my bag would never fit all the presents I bought. After taking a shower, I wore my pajamas and munched on several chocolate bars from the minibar while watching a movie. I remembered that I had to call Alexander. I took a deep breath and called him on his mobile.

"Hello, Alexander? It's Noor."

"Hi Noor," he said, but nothing else.

"Well, you asked me to call you if I want to go have a bite."

"Yeah, right, so have you decided where you want to go?"

Seriously? He wanted me to choose a place. I was only a visitor in Germany, and my knowledge of restaurants was limited. Plus, he was the one who suggested that we should go out in the first place. He should have made a plan. Men behaved differently in Lebanon.

"You know what? I'm going to take a nap now. I'm too tired because I went shopping in the morning. If you decide on a place, then please call back. Otherwise, I'll see you on Monday. Ok?"

I felt relieved, and I was seriously hoping our outing would be canceled. Although Alexander was a charming man, he was also talented in getting on my nerves, and I preferred to stay as far from him as possible. He agreed and hung up. What nerve! He had managed to ruin all the positive feelings I got from my shopping.

I turned off the TV and fell asleep instantly. Alexander called half an hour later. He said he was waiting for me in the lobby. I put on my jeans, and a cute t-shirt I borrowed from Jana, and grabbed a jacket in case it got chilly.

Alexander suggested we go for coffee as it was not the time for lunch or dinner. He chose a cozy little German coffee shop in Heidelberg. It was more like a forest cottage. The whole place was made of wood – the chairs, tables, flooring, even the ceiling, and the windows. He took the stairs up to the first floor, and I followed him. We sat on two wooden benches facing each other. Despite the warm and cozy atmosphere, I was not relaxed at all.

The silence was annoying, and I needed an icebreaker. "So, where's Inken today?"

"Inken? I don't know, but she mentioned last week that she had a family event this weekend," he replied vaguely.

Hmmm. How strange!

"Did you enjoy your induction trip?" he asked me.

"I loved it. And you?"

"It was like a vacation for me. Next week I have to get back to my work routine. I'll be traveling in Africa for two weeks." He explained how his job was physically demanding and sometimes even dangerous.

I couldn't stop wondering why he went out with me, and his girlfriend was not there, so I asked him abruptly, "How long have you known Inken?"

"One year, more or less." It was impossible to get information out of him.

"And how long have you two been dating?" I added.

His eyes went round, and he choked on a piece of cake. "No, no, we're not dating. We're just colleagues. Inken has a boyfriend. He's our colleague from marketing."

"Ohhh! My mistake. It's just that you two seemed so close," I clarified.

It was the beginning of a long talk about Alexander and his love life. He said that he had no girlfriend. He couldn't be in a relationship because of his demanding job and constant business trips. I liked everything about him except that he was younger than me by two years. No way! He looked way older.

The loud voice of a man coming from the ground floor was too disturbing to proceed with our conversation. From the man's voice, we assumed he was an overly drunk tourist. He kept shouting in English, "Bullshit, bullshit!"

"Shall we leave?" Alexander winked and asked for the bill. We went for a stroll in the pedestrian area. It was brightly lit, and many people were passing by or standing in groups chit-chatting over a cigarette. Heidelberg was a city full of life around the clock.

With time, Alexander got more relaxed. He told me jokes and teased me about my love for chocolate and shopping. Before we knew it, we had dinner, and then we had a hot chocolate break. We spent several hours eating, talking, and laughing. He finally dropped me at my hotel a bit after midnight.

"Are you free tomorrow?" he asked. "I know a restaurant that offers amazing brunch on Sunday. Would you like to go?"

"Sure, on one condition, though; this time, it's on me!" I insisted.

*****

"Dad, I miss you." I felt it was ages since I had left Beirut.

"I miss you too, my sweetie. Only two more days, and you'll be back. By the way, what are you doing today? It's a Sunday, and everything must be closed in Germany, right?" His voice was as warm and loving as always.

"One of my colleagues is taking me out for the day. He's very nice. He resembles my cousins, the twins." Dad highly regarded my twin cousins, Dr. Nabil and Dr. Jamil. They were both successful doctors in their fields, a dentist and a cardiologist. They were kind, helpful, highly appreciated, and respected.

"If he's anything like your cousins, then bring him with you to Lebanon." I heard Dad's distinguished laughter.

"Dad," I replied sheepishly. "He's just my colleague."

Dad cleared his throat and changed the topic, "I'll pick you up from the airport tomorrow night. Take care of yourself and have a great time, my sweetheart."

I hung up, wondering what he meant. "Will he be fine if one day I end up marrying a non-Lebanese? Is he that desperate? Or is he genuinely open-minded?"

*****

Rüdesheim am Rhein was one of the most beautiful places I had ever been to. I could not stop saying "wow" the whole day. First, Alexander and I went to a restaurant by the Rhine River and had an open buffet brunch. I loved their potato salad, but mostly I went crazy about German bread and pastries. I had no idea why French croissants and éclairs were famous all over the world while German Berliner and Nussecken were hardly known outside of Germany. I had always thought that Black Forest cake, which was extremely popular in Lebanon, was originally French, but Alexander corrected me, explaining that it was German. It originated from the Black Forest area where Alexander came from. "You're kidding me, right? I can't believe that you ruin our traditional Black Forest cake in Lebanon! You swap cherries for canned fruit salad!" he protested.

Alexander wouldn't let me jaywalk. "Wait! We have to wait until the light is green, then you can go, but only on the white stripes."

I had seen that on TV, but we didn't have any light signals in Lebanon. "Why?" I asked.

"Because it's the law. Cars will wait for you to cross."

I thought that was ridiculous, considering that the street was empty. "Why do we have to wait?" I teased him.

Alexander pulled me by my hand, "It's green now. Honestly, sometimes I feel you're still a little girl."

In the afternoon, Alexander and I went for a stroll in the vineyards. I loved the grapes of Rüdesheim am Rhein, although Sawfar's grapes were much more delicious. I asked him if they grew figs in that area as well. "Not on a large scale, just for individual consumption," he answered. Then he gave me statistical data on plants harvested in Germany. I just wanted to taste their figs.

Walking through the vineyards was relaxing and stress-free. Alexander pushed me gently from bumping into a random plant, "Be careful! If you touch its leaves, it'll irritate. My sister once fell into a nettle bush, and I can't describe how itchy she was. She didn't stop crying for hours." I moved away.

"It's so beautiful here. It's like being in a postcard," I said.

"What's on German news normally? I mean, you don't have any wars, power cuts, or street fights. What do they say on the news?" I asked.

He laughed. "Easy! They update us on Lebanese politics."

The paths in the vineyards led us to an old stone church. He pointed towards it, saying, "St. Hildegard founded this abbey in the 12ᵗʰ century. She was an abbess, a writer, a composer, and a philosopher; let's have a look." I followed Alexander as he opened the big wooden gate and entered quietly.

The walls were beautifully decorated with golden paintings. The wooden ceiling was high, giving the hall a lot of space, and light entered through numerous windows. There was no one there to disturb the church's peace and quiet except our own footsteps. Luckily enough, I found a small kind of sink where I could wash my hands because they were sticky from picking grapes. As I was dipping my hands in the stone bowl, Alexander covered his mouth with his hands, his eyes widened, and he rushed toward me, "What are you doing?"

"Me? I'm just washing my hands. They're too sticky."

"No, no!" He shook his head in disbelief. "Stop right now. This water is not for washing your hands."

I looked at the bowl. "Why not? It looks clean to me. It must be for cleaning your hands after eating grapes."

"Excuse me!" He was utterly shocked. "This bowl contains holy water. Believers dip their fingers in it before drawing a cross on their foreheads."

*****

"Hi, Noor," I heard Alexander's voice from behind me as I was getting coffee. I turned to say hi. He was in a joyful mood, looking extremely elegant in his dark greyish suit with a striped tie and white shirt.

"You're leaving in less than an hour, right? Would you like to pass by my office?" he said.

I gladly grabbed my cup of coffee and followed him. It was a spacious and well-lit room. Alexander sat behind his desk, his eyes sparkling in the sun. I felt awkward but happy. I had nothing to say. He nervously tapped with his fingers on his desk and asked timidly, "I was wondering what you were doing for Christmas and New Year? Are you traveling somewhere?"

"No." I shrugged. "Normally, I spend it with my friends in Beirut downtown. We list our resolutions, which we never keep, take pictures, and just have a cozy, friendly time. It's a lot of fun. You should come."

He stood up and flipped through his wall calendar to the month of December. "I'll be off from the 18th to the 24th, after which I'll be with my family. Will that suit you?"

"You mean you want to come to Lebanon? Sure, I have nothing planned." Wow. My heart was beating fast.

"Shall I plan a few tours for you around Lebanon?" He smiled warmly. "Naturally, I'd like to see your country, but mainly Noor, I'd like to see you."

I didn't tell him I felt the same, but my red face exposed me.

Before I climbed into the cab, Alexander handed me a sealed water bottle. "This is for the road, in case you get thirsty." I held it with extreme care as if he had given me a golden treasure.

"See you in less than three months." His face lit up as he hugged me goodbye. I hugged him tightly too, and for the first time, I smelled his light perfume. I didn't know if I should cry out of happiness or just cry. I could barely say "Goodbye" back. I was too emotional.

In the taxi, I counted the months on my fingers: October, November, and December. Three months before we would meet again. I had to wait for three whole months, but if that was what it took to be with him again, then I would wait.

The words of Henry Van Dyke came to my mind:

> *Time is too slow for those who wait, too swift for those who fear, too long for those who grieve, too short for those who rejoice, but for those who love, time is eternity.*

----------To be continued----------

Have you enjoyed reading my book? I hope so.

It would be great if you would leave your review on Amazon or Goodreads.

Your opinion matters.

Reading reviews from happy readers just makes my day and would help other readers in their decision before grabbing their copies of this book.

Thank you in advance for your support.

Rana

About The Author – Rana Baydoun

www.ranabaydoun.com

Rana Baydoun was born in the buzzing city of Beirut and brought up in a typical Lebanese family amid lots of love and drama. Since she was a little girl, Rana loved telling stories to her schoolteachers, friends, and hundreds of cousins, aunties, and uncles.

Her love for storytelling grew stronger with her when she moved abroad. Even though she lived in amazing cities such as Hamburg, Athens, and Lausanne, Rana always had a strong feeling of nostalgia for her hometown of Beirut. She felt there was so much more to tell than just the usual cliché news of bombs and power cuts.

In her first novel, The Elephant Tooth of 1995, she takes her readers on a compelling rollercoaster journey portraying a typical Lebanese life through the eyes of a young girl called Noor.

Rana lives with her husband, three kids, and their on & off cat in Dubai.